THEIR SECOND FIRST DATE

TIF MARCELO

Harlequin
SPECIAL EDITION

If you purchased this book without a cover you should be aware that this book is stolen property. It was reported as "unsold and destroyed" to the publisher, and neither the author nor the publisher has received any payment for this "stripped book."

Recycling programs for this product may not exist in your area.

ISBN-13: 978-1-335-18031-5

Their Second First Date

For questions and comments about the quality of this book, please contact us at CustomerService@Harlequin.com.

Harlequin Enterprises ULC
22 Adelaide St. West, 41st Floor
Toronto, Ontario M5H 4E3, Canada
www.Harlequin.com

HarperCollins Publishers
Macken House, 39/40 Mayor Street Upper,
Dublin 1, D01 C9W8, Ireland
www.HarperCollins.com

Printed in Lithuania

"Ah, Francesca, I feel like we have so much to get to know about one another."

"Precisely. And maybe I also don't want you to think that I'm cynical."

His eyes shut for a beat. "I did say that, didn't I?"

"You did."

"I'm sorry."

"Yeah, well me, too."

He nodded. "I guess it's good we had this talk. With our kids being friends and all."

"And with you building the library shelves."

"That, too."

"And me helping you open your business."

"That's not necessary."

She shrugged. "It'll make me feel less guilty about the shelves."

"I'll think about It. But for now...truce?"

"Truce. And, you can call me Frankie."

He held out a hand, eyes meeting hers. "Nice to meet you, Frankie."

She laid her hand in his, and attempted to ignore the warmth that enveloped her when he squeezed it. But she was failing, caught in his stare, and how honest his expression was. "Nice to meet you."

Until the door slammed open and two pairs of feet galloped indoors. Frankie stepped away from the countertop, and tended to the children, hoping that Ty hadn't noticed.

Dear Reader,

What do you get when you mix a PTA president who can't seem to get past the first date, a veterinarian with a heart of gold who has a fear of commitment and their mischievous kids? *Their Second First Date*, that's what!

We're back in Peak, Virginia, but embarking on a new series with *Their Second First Date*, and I promise that it's going to be so much fun. The series name, The Single Hearts Club, is the unofficial name of the Peak Elementary School PTA, because of the sheer amount of single parents who participate in the organization. Along with the love for their children and service to their community, these single parents find their own romantic love among one another.

Frankie Espiritu and Ty Golden are no exception, though it takes a little bit of effort from their children, Liam and Aria, to make it all happen. Frankie and Ty had experienced their share of heartbreak and challenges in the past with their previous marriages. And though their personalities seem too opposite to meet in the middle, their kids become the bridge. Headstrong Frankie soon softens to new-to-town Ty. But will the fear of commitment residing inside each of them win out?

My years of serving on the PTA/PTO inspired this book. They were fun-filled, busy days of volunteerism, of getting to know wonderful people along the way. Though I witnessed no couplings in the groups I belonged to, I imagine The Single Hearts Club existed somewhere!

Happy reading!

xo, *tif*

Tif Marcelo is a veteran US Army nurse and holds a BS in nursing and a master's in public administration. She believes and writes about the strength of families, the endurance of friendship and heartfelt romances, and is inspired daily by her own military hero husband and four children. She hosts the *Stories to Love* podcast and is the *USA TODAY* bestselling author of adult and young adult novels. Learn more about her at tifmarcelo.com.

Books by Tif Marcelo

Harlequin Special Edition

The Single Hearts Club

Their Second First Date

Spirit of the Shenandoah

It Started with a Secret
Love Letters from the Trail
The Forever Wedding Date

Visit the Author Profile page at Harlequin.com.

To Carol and Sandy, two PTA/O queens
who were such great mentors and friends.

Chapter One

This had to be the worst date in Francesca Espiritu's life, and she had to find a way out of it. Fast.

Which was a shame, because the man in front of her was gorgeous and respectably polished, down to his perfectly tailored blazer and refined table manners.

"Francesca?" Across from her, Tyler Golden raised a groomed eyebrow. His fingers—with clean, trimmed fingernails, because these things mattered—grazed the tumbler of whiskey, which was wet with condensation. "Are you listening?"

She rolled her eyes. An immature move, but she was done, with a capital *D*. "Of course, I am."

He sighed. "I feel like we got off on the wrong foot."

"Do you mean when you insinuated that your ex-wife and I are similar? Right after you told me that she gave up custody of your daughter so that she could pursue her career?"

"When you say it that way... That's not what I meant." His face reddened, making his blue eyes take on a cerulean quality. It was stunning, she admitted to herself. Not that she would ever say that out loud. "What I meant was you and she are similar, in that you're passionate about your careers. Are you not?"

"I am. But I would *never* leave Liam for my career. That's neglectful and—"

“Hold up a sec. Harper and I might be divorced, but she’s still the mother of my child. You can’t judge her and her dreams. She and I had our differences, but she supported me through veterinary school, and it’s her turn now. Surely that’s something you can get behind.” He smiled, though it didn’t make it to his eyes.

Frankie growled. This conversation was circling the drain. Into the dark abyss.

There was something in the way they were communicating that wasn’t jiving. They’d jumped into talking about their families straight away, which in hindsight wasn’t the best move, because they were now wading in sensitive territory.

Nothing like exposing why their marriages failed on the first date to bring out their personalities. And though defending his ex should have been a green flag for Frankie, the fact that he thought she was like his ex was a red flag in itself.

This whole date was such a shame. She’d had high hopes.

Frankie’d met Dr. Ty at her appointment at Valley Pets Veterinary for her boxer pup, Snowball, last week. He was the new vet on staff. Snowball’s regular vet was Dr. Kyle Peters, but Frankie had gotten wind of Ty’s single-guy status well before he’d stepped foot in town in the New Year—Valley Pets’s front desk receptionist was a PTA mom like Frankie—and she’d made a concerted effort to run into him. Literally. With Snowball in her arms while the handsome doctor was coming out of a room, Frankie had stepped right in front of him.

Look, in a small town, a woman did what she had to do.

No one had ever accused Frankie of bashfulness. Especially with regard to her love life, which was, to her pleasure, on the up-and-up. Not in an it’s-time-to-settle-down-again kind of way, but in *it’s time to have some fun*. Too many years had passed with her focus on others—her mother and the family business, the Spirit of the Shenandoah B & B; her younger sister, who needed her as an emotional wing-woman; and her son, who had finally crossed over to an age where he took his own showers, could make something for himself in the microwave, and used a cell phone like no one's business.

And since the arrival of her newly discovered half-brother into the family, the pressure on Frankie's shoulders had lifted. The spotlight was no longer on her, the poor woman who'd been left by her husband four years ago because he no longer felt like being a husband.

Frankie was free.

So these days, she reveled in first dates, when things were exciting, and everyone was on their best behavior, and things didn't get serious.

Except for this date, it seemed.

It served her right, asking out a man who lived in Peak, rather than her usual, out-of-town encounters. Now, not only would she have her ex to face while grocery shopping, but there would also be Dr. Ty, too.

Speaking of, she leveled Ty with a glare, because she wouldn't be made to feel like she was insecure. "Oh, okay, let's get this straight. I can't comment about your ex, but you had plenty to say about mine." Frankie pressed the napkin against her lap. "You said that Reece felt trapped in our family. Which, he didn't." *He felt trapped around* me, she wanted to say.

"I was agreeing with you, validating your experience. You said that he asked for a divorce out of the blue, after a weekend away from you and your son, and I agreed that maybe he felt some of that freedom and wanted more of it."

"And that, quote, 'Sometimes it takes stepping away from a situation to realize how trapped you are.' As if I'd locked him in a closet and threw away the key. The man was and is grown. He left because he wanted to leave."

Rehashing it sent a pain through Frankie's heart. She wasn't newly divorced, but the breakup had been traumatic. To have it laid out so casually—it made her relationship to her ex feel like an afterthought. It also insinuated she was the cause of the marriage's failure.

He winced. "I swear I didn't mean it that way."

"Then what *do* you mean? Seems to me you change your tune when it's not convenient."

He down his glass. "I was trying to empathize."

"More like placate."

He half laughed, then raised a hand to their server, who headed their way. He lifted up his tumbler. "Could I get a refill? Francesca, are you sure you don't want some wine? What red wine would you suggest?" he asked the server.

"I prefer white wine to red. Always. And, I can order for myself." She smiled at the server. "But no wine for me. I'm driving."

The server excused himself.

Ty cleared his throat. "I don't mean to make you angry."

She peered at him. "You're assuming I'm angry."

"Are you not?"

"I'm annoyed, to be honest."

"I think that all we need to do is calm down."

"I know you're not talking about me." Frankie's annoyance? It bubbled up and spilled over, and was now all over the white tablecloth at Rothenburg Haus. The German restaurant was one of two fancier ones in town, and it was another strike against him that she wouldn't get a chance to finish her meal. As it was, her appetite was destroyed.

"If you say so," he said with a smile.

And with that, with the way he dismissed her statement with another flippant comment, was the last straw.

Tonight was a bust. There was no point in extending this date. "It's probably best that I go."

He frowned. "If you want."

"I sure do."

How did this happen? Ty's social résumé had been so impressive.

Served her right for raising her expectations because he was a doctor and a Chris Pine look-alike. She dug through her bucket purse for her wallet, thankful that she'd thought to put cash in it earlier. She fished out some money—it took her too long to find her wallet since her entire life was in the purse—and set three twenty-dollar bills on the table.

Across from her, Ty sighed. "Please. You don't have to—"

"Believe me, I'm happy to. There's even a little extra to cover your drink."

"What? Look… Francesca." He reached out, stopping an inch short of touching her. "Before you go, I fully apologize for everything I said. I don't mean to offend you."

It was commendable that he was willing to own up to his side of the argument. But it didn't fix this date, not in the slightest. How much time had passed? A half hour at most?

Frankie had a strong personality; this, she knew. It went beyond being type A. She was independent and wasn't afraid of conflict.

But she'd never been this contentious on a first date. Whatever Ty was made of was fuel to her spark. Something, somewhere, contained in that handsome exterior was triggering Frankie's defensiveness.

But as she looked around at the curiosity of the other restaurant guests, she eased herself back into her seat. She took a deep breath. In for two. Out for two. Then she tuned the volume of her voice down to four from seven, and said, "I appreciate that, but it's clear that we should cut this date short. I'll see you around town, Dr. Ty."

Then she stood, all the while exuding serenity, and without a look back, crossed the dim room, with her heels thudding against the carpeted floor. She inhaled the cool, late-February air when she walked out of the restaurant's glass doors.

It was only then that she allowed herself to soften. *Damn.* That was bad. The worst of the worst. And inside, she felt her heart feel the weight of disappointment.

She jumped into the driver's seat of her car, dug her phone out of her bag, and dialed her best friend, Vivian Lim.

"So?" Vivian answered, without preamble, on the first ring, her voice teeming with anticipation. Frankie could envision her sitting on her couch with a bowl of popcorn, ready for a detailed breakdown of her date.

"I'm in the car."

"Wait. What? You texted me twenty minutes ago."

Frankie glanced at her car clock. "Twenty-two."

Her voice lowered. "Oh, no. What happened?"

"Besides the fact that he compared me to his ex? And then said that I should calm down?"

"I mean, that's definitely not the thing to say to a woman. But were you not calm?"

Frankie shifted in her seat at her best friend's knowing tone. Vivian had a way of calling Frankie out when her temper got the best of her. And she was usually right, not that Frankie would admit it to her. "No, but he still shouldn't have said it." Silence met her on the other end, but Frankie continued. "It doesn't matter, because I left."

"Whew. Another one bites the dust."

"I would rather be single than unhappy," Frankie said.

"I support you there…" Vivian's voice trailed off. "Are you okay?"

Frankie shut her eyes as she leaned back against the headrest. "Yeah. I just wish that this could all be easier. I thought for sure that he would be second-date material."

"What's that I hear in your voice? You keep telling me that first dates are all you're open to. Are you looking for something more?"

Was she? Frankie had made a pact to herself that she would

focus on one thing: to have fun. Life had been stressful since becoming a mom. The dates she went on were to blow off some steam, to laugh with someone attractive, to flirt with them, and maybe more. But lately… "I don't know."

"That, my friend, is something you and I are going to have to discuss. Except not now." Her voice dipped. "My mother's here, and she's on a decluttering rampage."

"Oh, auntie's in a mood."

"Yes, and you know how that is." She sighed. "And Ryan's on the way here to grab Ian for his weekend, and Mom's intent on making him a good meal."

Vivian co-parented Ian with her ex-boyfriend, Ryan, and what they had was an aspirational relationship, something Frankie had tried to emulate with her ex, Reece.

Though if anyone asked Frankie, she thought that Viv and Ryan still had it bad for one another.

Envy sparked within Frankie. How did it feel to have it bad for someone? And would she ever feel it again?

"I have to get home, anyway," Frankie said. "There's a fifth-grade graduation to plan." At the thought of the event coming up in about three months, Francesca's mood flipped to excitement. Nothing brought her more joy than doing something for her kid and his school. Every dollar she helped raise benefited the community directly.

Vivian cackled. "Boo. You're such a PTA nerd."

"Says the treasurer."

She sighed. "Only because I'm deeply loyal to the president herself. Please, promise me that you won't work too hard on a Friday night. Wait. I take that back. Promise me that the to do list won't be a mile long. Our kids are only in the fifth grade."

"It's my last event before Liam moves up to middle school. But… I'll try."

After Frankie hung up, she buckled her seat belt, and as she pushed her ignition on, the door of the restaurant opened. Ty walked out, shoulders slumped. He meandered to a car idling at the corner, and it drove off seconds later.

She felt a tinge of regret. Maybe she'd been too hard on him. She would likely run into him around town, and she didn't know him well enough to anticipate if he would avoid her, or try and forget this bad date and be cordial.

Then again, while Frankie had her flaws, one thing was for sure: she would not lower her standards for anyone.

The next day at Valley Pets Veterinary Clinic, Tyler felt the aftereffects of his date with Francesca like a hangover. Which was inconvenient, because he was on duty. As the newest vet on a staff of three doctors, he'd understood that he would be pulling more of the weight for weekend calls. But while getting ready this morning, he'd fought tooth and nail against his own conscience to call in sick.

He approved a refill prescription on the computer then pressed his fingers against his eyes. Tonight, after he got his daughter, Aria, into bed, he was going to have an ice-cold beer, sit outside on his newly purchased Adirondack chair, and stare at the sky.

Ty had never been walked out on so blatantly as he had been last night.

He took it back. His ex, Harper, had walked out on him in the same manner, though not so publicly. And while Harper had left him in a molasses-slow way that he hadn't even realized she was gone until she'd served him divorce paperwork, Francesca's departure had been swift and decisive, without a single bit of remorse on her face. She'd blown out of that restaurant like a gust of wind, which had rendered him unsteady and breathless. Her stepping away had decimated his pride, and even bruised his heart.

Not that he had fallen for her, but good heavens, he'd had high hopes when she'd asked him out. Francesca was like a celebrity around Peak, if how she'd interacted with the staff and the waiting room full of pet owners in his office had been an indication. His initial impression was that she was outgoing and fun, exactly what he was looking for.

To be honest, Ty was lonely. He hadn't known a soul in town when he'd accepted the opportunity to work at Dr. Kyle Peters's practice. But Peak had been named "one of the best small towns to live in" and boasted a stellar school district. On one online school-rating website, Peak Elementary had five out of five stars, citing caring teachers and close parental involvement.

It had also been time for change—he and Aria had both needed it.

Now, though, what he yearned for was a couple of days to lick his wounds.

Thank goodness, his patient load this morning had been light. A couple of physicals for vaccines and follow-up appointments for pet injuries. The clinic was closing early, as per usual on Saturdays.

He looked up at the clock. One more hour to go.

"Dr. Ty?" Maddie Su knocked against the doorframe. A woman in her thirties, and wearing the practice's mauve scrubs, she was his veterinary tech for the day. Worry laced her features.

He'd only been on staff a few weeks, but he'd learned some of the staff's tells. If Maddie was concerned, then it was something to pay attention to. "What is it?"

"We have a puppy who's consumed some chocolate. They're on their way to exam room one."

Ty's brain fog and hurt pride left him in one fell swoop. "I'll be right in. In the meantime, could you get the activated charcoal ready?"

"On it." She smiled and turned around. He stood as a text buzzed his pocket. From Aria: Dad, when are you coming home? I don't like this one. She's so annoying. Even Bubba doesn't like her.

This one, meaning the babysitter. A high-school senior named Phoebe.

Ty sighed. First of all, their goldendoodle, Bubba, loved everyone, so he knew that Aria was exaggerating.

Second, everyone was annoying to Aria these days. Every*thing* was annoying. Everything was awful, and it was all his fault, apparently, because he'd moved them to Small Town, USA, after her mother had decided to follow her career to London.

Ty's friends with children had told him that this was normal for her age. That in the fifth grade, their kids had started to "feel themselves," which came with tapping into their freedom of expression.

Still, Ty didn't know what to do about it. How could he explain that taking this new job would help secure her future if she was always angry at him?

Then again, at least Aria was speaking to him. It was lightyears better than when he had her every other weekend, and she'd given him the silent treatment the whole time.

He texted back: PSP

It stood for *patient, so patience.* His standard response when he was caught up with a patient and would call her back soon.

Though if he was being honest, sometimes it was he whose patience was running thin.

Being a parent is hard.

He shoved that thought away as he marched down the bright, narrow hallway of the clinic to exam room one. He opened the door to a white boxer puppy lying down on the raised exam table, steadied by his owner's hands.

"Hi there, I'm Dr. Ty," he said, eyes straight to the puppy

for an immediate assessment. The dog was alert and friendly. As he neared, she stood, and her nub of a tail shook.

His heart rate slowed; the dog was okay at the onset, a good sign. “So tell me what happened.”

Then his eyes scanned upward to the puppy’s owner, someone whom Ty had considered pretty, beautiful even, until they got to talking. Francesca Espiritu. The date who’d ditched him last night. Next to her was a young boy, her son, Liam, if he remembered correctly.

Ty had known he would run into Francesca again. But he hadn’t anticipated it being this soon.

“Hello,” he said, stunned.

Today, though, her expression was markedly different. Gone was the anger, and what replaced it was fear. She didn’t have any makeup on, and her dark wavy hair was rolled into a messy bun. Her lips trembled. “Hi, Dr. Ty. This is Snowball. Um…she ate some chocolate, probably an hour ago.”

Despite the situation, relief flooded him that they weren’t going for round two of their verbal sparring here at work. Nodding, he held his hand for Snowball to sniff. “Hi, sweet girl. How are you today? Can I take a look at you?” He scratched Snowball behind her short, floppy ears, then palpated her belly. He listened to her heart, her lungs, and her stomach.

Through the process, the sweet puppy leaned into his touch, a reassuring sign that she wasn’t in crisis. Then again, symptoms could still arise.

“It was my fault,” Liam said, eyes rounded in fear. Tears filled them. “I left my lunch box open on the ground in my room. Mom told me to bring it to the kitchen when I got home yesterday, and I forgot about it.” His voice cracked.

He looked to be Aria’s age, and Ty’s heart went out to him. To lecture him wouldn’t have helped an iota—the kid understood the repercussions. Ty gestured him forward and offered him a smile. “I know you didn’t mean it, bud. Accidents happen. Here, why don't you pet Snowball to keep her more comfortable, and we can figure out how we can help her, okay?"

"Okay." Liam did as he was told, and his breathing steadied as he pet his dog.

It was like magic, the effect a pet had on a person's anxiety.

Ty asked gently, "Do you know what kind of chocolate she ate, how much of it, and when?"

Liam looked back at his mother.

Francesca offered him a plastic baggie, which had a wrapper sealed inside. "This was what we found. It was torn open."

"It was a good idea, to bring this in." Ty opened the bag, and fished out a mint-chocolate granola bar, about three quarters of the way finished. He exhaled in relief. From his experience, some granola bars weren't made with real chocolate. Some were made with very little chocolate, with a flour-and-oat blend. And depending on the brand, it might only cause a puppy mild discomfort. "Why don't I let her off this table and you can play with her while I head back to the office to do some research on the ingredients in this bar. As of right now, though, she's acting appropriately, which is a good sign."

Both Francesca and Liam nodded. As Ty set Snowball onto the ground, he caught Francesca's eyes. She looked away, which sparked unease inside of him.

What about their interaction last night had deserved a walkout? He'd been himself at that date, so what did that say about him?

He schooled his features and left the room, and looked up the ingredients of the granola bar. Then he measured the approximate amount ingested against Snowball's weight.

He breathed a sigh. There wasn't enough chocolate to be considered dangerous, though as he'd suspected, it could cause mild gastrointestinal discomfort.

When he informed Francesca and Liam of the news, their

bodies slumped in relief. Liam wrapped Snowball in a hug. Francesca pressed a hand against her heart.

"Thank you, Dr. Ty," she said. The wrinkles between her eyebrows deepened.

"I'm happy to help. Now, this doesn't mean that she's completely in the clear. She may have tummy troubles and might not want to eat her dinner tonight. She might even vomit, so keep an eye on that. If she becomes lethargic, or acts unlike how she usually is, don't hesitate to bring her back. Our clinic closes in an hour, but here's the number for the twenty-four-hour animal hospital in Lynchburg." He handed Francesca the card, then bent down and rubbed a gentle hand against Snowball's forehead. The puppy panted a smile. "She's a sweetheart, alright, but resourceful."

"I promise I'm going to keep my food off the ground from now on," said Liam.

"I know you will," Ty said. "But like I said, everybody makes mistakes, you know? You did the best thing by bringing her here. So good job."

Liam nodded.

Ty looked at Francesca, who had an unreadable expression. "Maddie'll take care of you at the front desk whenever you're ready. Have a good day. See you around, Snowball."

Then Ty left the room, nodding at Maddie at the front desk before turning into his office.

Before he approached his desk, a knock sounded behind him, and he turned, expecting Maddie…

Only to find Francesca. Her arms were wrapped around her waist, and her eyes darted from the room she came from to him. "Dr. Ty?"

"Yes?" He tried to ignore how much he was attracted to her, still. A wavy tendril had escaped her bun and brushed her face, and he had the urge to push it aside.

Instead, he braced himself for whatever else she had in her arsenal.

"Thank you, for helping us," she said.

Stunned, he shook his head. "It's why I'm here."

"But how you were with Liam… He blamed himself on the whole drive here and he wouldn't listen to me. The way you spoke to him…it helped."

He smiled. "I have a daughter just around his age. I tried to talk to him the way I do her."

"Aria, right? Liam said they're in the same class. He's eaten lunch with her a couple of times."

"Yes, that's her." Discomfort tumbled inside of him. Dropping Aria off that first day had been a gut-wrenching experience. It was the look she had given him. That he was causing her all kinds of pain.

"Welcome, then, to Peak Elementary." She cleared her throat. "And thank you." Then, with a haphazard wave of a hand, she turned back down the hallway.

Ty sat and took stock of his body. Still intact and not riddled by insults. And the welcome? It had been like a small Band-Aid to the oversize bruises he'd endured the last few months.

That was a switch. Maybe today was going to be a good day after all.

Another buzz in his pocket. Aria: So annoyinggggggggggg.

Well, maybe not so much.

Chapter Two

It was Sunday night, and Ty had been looking forward to a quiet dinner at Staircase Diner with Aria, but it was becoming annoying seeing his daughter's face aglow with the light of her phone from across the dining table.

He set the menu down, though he withheld the sigh that threatened to escape.

His daughter knew the rules: no phones at the dinner table. While the diner was far from fancy, with patrons around him similarly on their devices, she continued to push the boundaries.

"Aria."

She didn't look up, and answered with a "hmm?"

"Put the phone away."

"I'm texting Mom." She flipped her phone around and showed Ty the screen, as per phone rules. Sure enough, it was Harper. It was close to midnight in London.

Well, crap. There went Ty's attempt at parenting tonight. Aria was only allowed to text a handful of people: him, her mother, Harper's sister Tilly in Arizona. Of all, *Mom* was like a get-out-of-jail-free card.

Get off the phone.

But I'm talking to Mom.

Who mailed you this package?

Mom did.

Are you wearing lipstick?

Dad, it's lip gloss and Mom said it's fine.

For the eighteen months that he and Harper had been divorced, Ty had tried to balance discipline and lenience, because he only had Aria every other weekend. But now that he had full custody, it felt like he was hired for a job well above his pay grade. A fine line existed between putting his foot down and him not being sympathetic to Aria's needs. It was also the same line that made him look like the bad cop in this situation.

And since he was already a default jerk by being the only parent around, he waited for her to quit texting. And waited. They ordered, and he waited. He stared at the customers crowding the bar. He looked at his own phone for any notifications, and decided to fire off a couple of texts to his friends back in Devon.

Man, did he miss them. Had he still lived in Pennsylvania, after his flub of a date the other night, Vince and Jeremiah would've been at his door with a couple of beers to help him lick his wounds. They'd never minded playing the cool uncles to Aria, and they could have served as backup to tonight's dinner.

Though, he didn't miss the Philly traffic, or the sheer number of people around. He also didn't miss the stress of his previous job at the twenty-four-hour county animal clinic.

The thought of the hours, the crises he had to deal with, and the sadness of his patients' families had been enough for him to find a practice that was relatively low-key.

Finally, Aria put the phone down, then stood up to look above the walls of their booth.

Ty turned halfway around. “Everything okay?”

“Uh-huh.”

“How’s your mom?”

“Fine.” Her eyes scanned the restaurant guests as they passed their booth. Her butt was barely on the seat, and she was biting her lip. “She says she’s sending me a box of stuff.”

“That’s good. Um, why don’t you stay seated, sweetheart.”

“Just wanted to see who was here.”

“You expecting someone?”

“Sort of.” She settled into the leather seat and sipped her water. Ty waited for more, but Aria was looking off into the distance, almost unseeing.

“Do you want to elaborate?” Dang, this was like pulling teeth. It was as if when Harper left, she took all of their daughter’s communication skills with her. Except, it seemed to only affect him. Aria spent hours on FaceTime with her mother and friends from Devon.

“About what?”

“Never mind.” He sighed, then decided to change course. “So, how was school this week?”

She shrugged.

He frowned, concern rushing through him. Aria always had a story to tell. He remembered what Frankie mentioned, about her son, Liam, having lunch with her.

“I met someone from your class today,” Ty said.

“I know.”

Eyebrows raised, he asked, “You do? How?”

“How what?”

But their food arrived, served in front of them, breaking whatever stalemate they had. She was all smiles for the server, then busied herself by setting her napkin on her lap.

He would need to follow up later.

Aria hummed as she ate, a good sign that she was enjoying her food. Since arriving to town, Ty had made it a point to sample a different restaurant every time they went out, and so far, none had been a bust. The diner was Aria's pick.

They were still in the midst of unpacking, and the last thing he wanted to do was fire up the stove on the weekend.

The momentary peace allowed Ty to settle into the booth and sink his teeth into the burger he ordered. It was greasy and heavenly, and would probably give him heartburn by bedtime, but he savored it. The slice of bliss was punctuated by the sound of distant laughter.

It was going to be okay. He and Aria were just in a rough spot. He would find the way to bridge the gap between them, but right now, they were both…okay.

A gaggle of people entered the dining room and the noise level ticked up.

Then, a low voice said, "Dr. Ty, is that you?"

Ty looked up to Chip Lowry. Lucky, Chip's four-year-old boxer, was one of Ty's patients. Chip was also the previous owner of the house Ty had just purchased.

Ty set his food down and wiped his mouth. "Hey, Chip."

"Great to see you here." His grin was wide, spanning his face.

Ty made introductions.

Aria had shoved fries into her mouth, and she spoke around them. "Hello."

Chip laughed and briefly looked over his shoulder. "I'm just here with my girlfriend and her family." He pointed out a dark-haired woman talking to a server. "That's Gabby. Next to her is her mother, Eva. She owns the Spirit of the Shenandoah B and B."

He nodded, though everything Chip had said was scrambled in his head. He was still getting to know the names of his animal patients and local businesses—it was a miracle he connected Chip to Lucky.

When Ty had joined the practice, patients had been split up among him, Dr. Peters, and Dr. Peters, Jr., his son, and it had been the luck of the draw that Chip's dog made its way to his pile.

"The B and B on top of the hill?" Ty asked. Its flat roofline could be seen from the town square, just above the height of the trees.

"That's the one. Gabby's puppy goes to your clinic, too, though she sees Dr. Peters. Her dog's name is Six."

He sorted through the file folders in his head now, for the names of patients and their pets. "Ah, Six is the puppy of your Lucky, then?"

"That's right. Lucky is Six's mom, also Snowball's mom. Gabby's sister, Frankie, owns Snowball."

All of the information righted itself, and what came with it was this odd feeling of hesitancy. Did Chip know that he and Frankie had gone on a failed date? Forget six degrees of separation. In Peak, it was more like two. "Wow."

"Small towns, right? Even down to the pets." He grinned. "Well, I'll leave you to your dinner. Just wanted to say hi. See you around town."

"See you." Ty watched Chip walk to the other side of the dining room, where he sat next to his girlfriend, who, if she had darker skin and wavy hair, would be a spitting image of Francesca.

Frankie.

Somehow, knowing her nickname softened her image a touch. It was only for a moment however, because the universe picked that instance for Francesca to walk into the diner with her son trailing after her. She was wearing a dress tonight, and her hair was down.

He had the inkling to hide, though his curiosity kept her in his sights.

He watched her round the table with Liam to greet everyone. His heart squeezed at the sight of such a big support system. His life, previous and current, consisted of very few people. He was an only child of deceased parents, and now he had an only child.

He wondered how it felt to have such a safety net, where one's mistakes could be mitigated, where one's needs could be filled by a simple family group chat.

Ty managed his life understanding that the buck stopped with him, that every risk he took not only affected him but ultimately Aria. It was why he kept his friendships close and why it was of utmost importance that he and Harper remained amicable despite her decision to up and leave the country.

What he did know was that the Espiritus were a whirlwind of noise, which Ty would need a break from occasionally. But it must have been fun to experience.

It would have lessened the pressure, that's for sure, of being the only one, which he felt quite acutely now. Was he enough for his daughter?

"Do you see them?" Aria said just loud enough for him to hear.

"Who?"

"Liam and his mom." Her eyes darted to the left. "You should say hi."

He lowered his voice. "Why?"

"His mom does everything. She plans *ev-e-ry-thing*." Aria pronounced that last word phonetically.

"And?"

"Forget it," she whispered. "Never mind."

Ty ate swiftly, but it wasn't just because of his daughter's vagueness. While he and Francesca had ended their last interaction civilly, every second that he was within her vicinity spiked his heart rate.

Ty asked for his check, paid, and left the restaurant. After less than eight minutes in the car, they were in their driveway.

"Dad, you have to join the PTA."

These were the first words Aria had spoken to him since leaving the restaurant, and they were so comical that he snorted. Walking up the driveway, he took note of the things he had to improve. Adding driveway lights was one thing—with the tall oak trees, they shaded any light from the moon. Before the fall, perhaps he'd commission an arborist to survey what branches he would need to cut down to protect his home.

That would mean extra wood for him to work with for his projects.

Not projects, but work.

Ty smiled to himself.

"I mean it," Aria said from behind him, while he unlocked the front door.

Inside, he was greeted by a large, furry body that wrestled him to the ground.

"Bubba." Laughing, Ty gently pushed aside his doodle's face, which had dug itself into Ty's neck. Bubba thought he was lap-sized, and he had the energy of a two-year-old dog even though he was pushing eight. "Okay, buddy. Yes, I love you. It's like I've been gone a year."

"Dad, are you listening?" Aria said. She was in the kitchen now; she'd opened the pantry door and retrieved a bully stick. "Here, Bubba, wanna treat?"

The dog all but forgot Ty and bounded toward Aria.

Ty stood, though at the sight of his L-shaped couch, he threw himself at it and slung a hand across his face.

He exhaled.

Home sweet home.

Then, his arm was lifted off his face. Aria peered at him with bright hazel eyes. “Dad.”

“Hmm?”

“There’s a meeting next week. You should go.”

“What meeting?”

“PTA.”

“No, sweetie.”

She stuck out her bottom lip. Then he watched her walk backward to the *L* part of the couch and flop down into the cushion. Dramatically, she slung her arms across her chest.

“Oh, don’t do that,” he said. Aria was eleven, but this attempt at a silent tantrum harkened to when she was two.

She knew exactly how to get to him.

“Dad. It’s the only way I’ll make friends.”

“That can’t be true.”

“It’s true. That’s where all the parents hang out, and if they like you they’ll like me, too.”

He sat up to take in Aria’s seriousness. His memories of himself at eleven were foggy, but what stood out was that he’d fended for himself. Elementary-school Ty hadn’t been a popular kid. He hadn’t been a kid that did sports.

His parents had never attended a PTA meeting. Nor had they been involved with school functions.

Were those the reasons he grew up with few friends?

Perhaps not. But he needed to score a few points with Aria. And if one meeting would put him in his daughter’s good graces, then he would do it.

“Okay, fine. I’ll go.”

She planted a kiss on cheek. “Yay! Oh, can I go play video games?”

He couldn’t win tonight, so he said, “Half-hour, tops.”

A half hour after returning to her cabin from Staircase Diner, Frankie’s phone buzzed in her pocket. It was the family's security camera that was trained on the private parking lot of the Spirit of the Shenandoah B & B, the Espiritu family business.

Only those who lived on property—Frankie, her sister Gabby, brother Jared and his wife Matilda and their mother, Eva and her fiancé Cruz—and their guests were allowed to park in that lot.

On the screen was a dark pick-up truck, which slipped into a space next to Frankie's car.

She frowned. He was early.

"Liam. Your dad's here," she called out. Liam had rushed in ahead of her after dinner at Staircase Diner, and she predicted he was already elbows-deep into his video game, with his headphones on, and Snowball at his feet.

She padded to the living room, where, sure enough she'd guessed correctly. At her entrance, Snowball bounded to her, a ball of energy, and rubbed up against her leg.

Frankie leaned down and patted Snowball on the head, her body relaxing.

This weekend had been too eventful, from her date with Ty, to finding out that Snowball had ingested Liam's granola bar, and then their visit to the vet to come face-to face with Ty again. The swing of emotions had been vast, from disappointment, to sheer panic, to pure gratitude that everything was going to be okay. Not to mention, the awkwardness when she'd seen Ty again at Staircase Diner, though she'd pretended that she hadn't. She'd been ashamed of their date, and the thought that perhaps she'd acted rashly against a person who seemed to be good at the core.

Thinking back to their fight now made her wince. Sometimes her mouth did get the best of her.

She pushed all that down, though. It was no use to dwell on things she couldn't change. Instead she approached Liam who was mumbling into the headphone microphone.

She slowed, peering at the screen to read the person who he was chatting with. She'd been strict with Liam's participation on online multiplayer games, setting his profile to private and only allowing family members and his friends from school to play with him.

The name on the upper right hand corner was unfamiliar.

She tapped her son gently on the top of his head.

His eyes darted to her for a beat; he swiped the headphones off his head, though he continued to play. "Yes, Mom?"

"Your dad's here."

His face lit up. "Already?"

"Yep, but first. Who's MelodyMoo?"

"Aria."

"Aria…who?"

"Aria from my class."

"Oh." Stunned, she was unsure of what to say.

She was glad that Liam had reached out to Aria. Proud that he extended his welcome. But she hadn't told him about her date with Aria's father—Liam knew she dated but she hadn't shared details of the men she'd met—and she wasn't sure how he would feel knowing so.

Liam tossed the controller to the side and was on his feet before she could gather her thoughts. He took off for his backpack, and wedged his shoes on.

Just as the knock on the door came.

She screwed on a smile in time for Liam to throw the door open and wrap his arms around his waist.

He ruffled Liam's hair though he nodded at her. "Frankie."

"Reece."

Oh, she hated these handovers. Four years of cold but cordial hellos over a threshold, and yet every single time felt like it was the first. Reece was wearing his usual Carhartt overalls over a shirt, adorned with random smears of grease from his body-shop business. He was growing a beard, and among the tufts of red hair were strands of white.

They were doing things differently these days when it came to their custody agreement. They'd been going with the flow, in accordance with what Liam wanted and their schedules.

Lately, Liam had wanted more time with his father, and he was spending the full week with him.

Was she grateful that Reece was accessible, that he lived in town, and was a great father? Yes.

Was she thankful that they'd been able to co-parent in a way that actually worked? Absolutely.

But she wished she was never divorced in the first place. Not necessarily for herself, but for Liam, who juggled two households.

Because she had to share her son.

Okay, so maybe it *was* for herself.

She shook her head as she watched Reece walk right into the kitchen, tramping in dirt from his shoes.

He never liked to take off his shoes upon entering her home, or *their* home when they'd been living together.

A cardinal sin.

One of his many cardinal sins, including deciding over one long weekend that he no longer wanted to be married.

Never mind.

She *was* glad to be divorced.

He looked down at Liam who slung his backpack over his shoulder. "Ready?"

"Yep." He spun to Frankie and clutched her around the belly. "'Bye, Mom."

Then, after hugging Snowball, he bounded out the door, leaving Frankie alone with Reece.

Yep, she hated that, too. How easy it was for Liam to leave her. Parents always spoke in foreboding tones about the time their kid leaves after high school, when they're off to college or their next adventure. But every week there was a little bit of that in Frankie's home.

Now, without Liam, Snowball sat at Reece's feet, and looked at him with soulful brown eyes, begging for a pet. Unsurprisingly, Reece didn't acquiesce.

"I still can't believe you have that," he said.

She slung her arms around her chest. "You mean the sweetest dog on the planet?"

"Yeah, basically." As usual, he wasn't giving her anything. Not a bit of emotion, not a single reaction. It still stung, that she'd missed the moment when their love had turned to an emotionless partnership.

She would never let that happen again. She'd made that mistake twice with Reece.

"Her name is Snowball, and you can pet her."

"It's okay." He fixed his green eyes on Frankie. Eyes that had contributed to Liam's hazel ones. "I wanted to tell you something real quick."

"Oh?" She stood straighter. Ninety percent of their communication was through texting, unless it was important, and then it would be by phone call.

"I'm with someone."

She raised her eyebrows. "Meaning…it's serious?"

He nodded.

Frankie felt no ill will, or jealousy, or FOMO for the other woman, for Reece finding love. They were past all that. He knew about her dating life, she knew about his. They were part of the active Peak rumor mill. And sure, they'd had a bitty bounce back about a year ago. It had been a mistake, the kind she wouldn't repeat. She was done with Reece; another person could take crack at his grumpy and cold nature.

But this—this sounded like it was something else.

"It's serious. And I wanted to tell you because I'm going to introduce her to Liam tomorrow night."

Frankie had to brace herself against the kitchen countertop. From below came a whining noise. Snowball lifted on his hind legs and pawed her shins. She bent down and picked her up, and the hug quieted the puppy and settled her own nerves.

"Who is it?" she asked, while focusing on Snowball's soft fur.

"Bianca."

Her hands stilled. "Bianca Lorton?"

"Yep," he examined her face.

Frankie steeled herself before she exposed all of her cards. Bianca was beautiful and had the reputation of being cheerful and optimistic. Unmarried and without kids, she owned Mon Amour Bakery, a French pastry shop, which touted handmade croissants and other delicacies, all from her grandmother's recipes.

And that was the problem. Bianca was perfect. People were sure to compare *her* to Bianca. Frankie was known for getting things done, but her style tended to gravitate toward straightforward assertiveness. Or, as some people thought of her, tough. Okay, aggressive. She wasn't ashamed of it, but next to Bianca, Frankie was a monster.

"Wow," was all she could say.

"I just wanted to give you a heads-up that she'll probably be spending more time with us."

"Do you mean sleepovers?"

He looked puzzled. "We're having sleepovers now, if you must know."

"I'm talking about sleepovers while Liam is there."

"Oh, no, not when Liam's with me. We're not there yet. But maybe soon. I'll let you know."

Frankie took a deep breath. This journey as a divorcée continued to push her emotional boundaries. She figured she would be in her eighties with Liam married with his own kids, and she would still feel the trauma of their breakup.

Especially if you don't have someone by your side, her subconscious said.

The words were a sucker punch and she grimaced. As if hearing her thoughts, Snowball whimpered. "Thanks, for letting me know," Frankie said.

Reece headed for the door. "Thanks for understanding. That went better than expected."

He was already walking down the path, but she asked, "What do you mean?"

His shoulders lifted in a shrug. "Listen, you're not always easy to deal with."

"Why, because I'm honest?"

"There is a downside to honesty, too, you know."

"And what is that supposed to mean?"

"It's hard for people to be honest with you, because you don't cut them any slack at all."

This was bait, and she wasn't going to fall for it. But in the next second, she changed her mind. She said, "What I've learned is that the people who are afraid of being honest are the ones that have the most to hide."

He raised a hand in goodbye and then continued down the path.

She growled, unsatisfied with him pretending to be the bigger person.

Good riddance. Sometimes she wondered how she'd actually been married to the guy. What had she not seen?

Just because he had Bianca, now he had more gumption to needle her?

Two could play at that game.

Frankie shut the door with care—no need to take it out on her beautiful cabin—and marched her way to her living room. She sat on her plush leather sofa, where beyond the television, windows overlooked the view of the Shenandoah Valley. The sun had set, though the last bit of light in the sky cast a bluish hue that solidified her decision.

From her phone, she clicked on the One Date dating app. A notification on her dashboard showed she'd been matched. One by one, she scrolled through faces.

No one piqued her interest.

To be honest, One Date didn't sound appealing at all.

Frustrated, she tossed her phone to the side and buried her face in her hands.

She couldn't dwell on Reece and Bianca and this feeling of unease she'd been contending with. There were more things to deal with, things that she knew would yield fruit with the effort she put in.

Something that wouldn't give her heartburn in the way men had the last few years.

And that was the PTA.

Chapter Three

The Peak Elementary School PTA met every first Friday of the month at 5:00 p.m. And for the four years that Frankie had been president, starting when Liam was in the first grade—she'd taken his kindergarten year to orient herself to the school—she'd had a library full of parent attendees.

Except for this year.

She looked out onto the sparse group of parents sitting in tiny chairs that even Vivian, who was five foot two, looked too big for. Fifteen people, if she did a quick count. Last year, there were easily twice as many volunteers, but those parents either had children who graduated from the school, or had lost interest. There was a natural attrition to these organizations, phases of life with families that kept them from coming.

Fifteen, however, was dismal, and she could tell that those who were here were exhausted. This was the same crew that put together the Boohoo Breakfast—the first day of school breakfast for kindergarten parents—the Fall Festival, the holiday fundraiser, and the yearbook, which was coming out next month. Now, on the steady march to the fifth-grade graduation and party, she was losing soldiers left and right.

But, by golly, she wasn't going out without a fight.

"Thank you, everyone, for coming today. I hope you all had a good week. Can you believe it's March?" She displayed the biggest smile she could muster and glanced down at her notes. She intuited she had a half hour, max, before the group fell apart. "I'm going to stay real focused today, since we've got a lot on our list. We will be discussing the fundraising for the new bookshelves the library requested. I'm sure you all know that the entire nonfiction area collapsed during President's Day weekend."

Nods came from the group, though no one spoke. She charged forward.

"There's PTA elections in May, which I don't have a hand in, but something to keep in mind. And then there's the fifth-grade graduation, and we're in charge of the party. It's the whole shebang, much like the Fall Festival, with vendors and games. This will be the final fundraising opportunity for the year, and a great way for us to leave a little bit of money in our account for future parents to use." She gestured to a few current fourth-grade parents.

Pride shot through her, for Liam. That he'd made it through elementary school.

It wasn't about the schooling but more the transition he'd endured when she and Reece had broken up. His second-grade year had been a tumultuous one, and for a couple of months, Liam dreaded going to school. He hadn't wanted to be the kid who had divorced parents. Little did he know that most of the parents here in the PTA had been divorced or were single.

Frankie had secretly called the PTA the Single Hearts Club. A book could be written for every one of the folks seated here today.

Speaking of, Frankie had to keep their attention.

"Before we dive into all of that, I'm going to pass the floor to Viv to present the budget."

She looked to her best friend sitting across the room from her. She was Filipino American, like Frankie, with pixie-cut dark hair. With three piercings in one ear, and two in another, she was the opposite of Frankie, who couldn't bear to have a needle near her. But like Frankie, she was meticulous, which was ideal for the school PTA treasurer.

As Viv was talking, the classroom door squeaked open.

Yes, another parent, was Frankie's first thought. Perhaps it was Dante Sison, who'd promised that he would be more involved now that his mother was helping out with the twins. After all, if there was a persona that attracted the mamas to the yard, it was a firefighter.

But the person who walked in the door was someone she didn't expect.

What is he doing here?

Ty halted at the doorway as if hearing her thoughts. His eyes locked on hers.

For a moment, hesitation flashed in his expression. She could swear he took a step backward, one hand on the library door handle.

He was nervous; she liked keeping people on their toes. The last thing Frankie wanted to be was predictable.

In the silence, the other parents turned. Vivian snapped her head around like a doll, her face lighting up with mischief.

Oh, no. Frankie knew what her best friend was thinking.

And unlike Frankie, Vivian *was* predictable, and she pulled out the chair next to her and hailed Ty over, as if they were BFFs.

Ty all but tiptoed to the seat. "Hi. Sorry I'm late. I'm, um… I'll just sit. Thanks, I'm Ty." He nodded at everyone.

It was cute how he was so nervous.

Then again, he was cute in so many ways. But his attractiveness was not the issue. It was the way they mixed like oil and water.

She cleared her throat. Time to focus. Ignore him. "Go on, Viv."

With that, Vivian explained each line item of the budget

and answered questions. To Frankie's surprise, Ty took notes and engaged in what she could tell was active listening.

Then, the group voted on their currently healthy budget.

Frankie took the floor again. "I'd like to hear your ideas on how to raise money for the new bookshelves. We could very well cover the cost of having new ones built, but that will leave us with very little for the graduation party and beyond."

"The yearbook's going to turn a little bit of a profit and we can use that," someone said.

"Letty's Café mentioned that they're willing to host a dinner night and contribute a percentage of the profits to the school," another person said.

A voice piped up. "Just, please, no selling chocolate."

"But a wreath—a wreath I would buy. Maybe from Cloud Orchards?" someone said.

Frankie took down notes from those who spoke up, glad to hear enthusiasm in their voices. Then she assigned folks to follow up to see if any fundraisers could be arranged.

"Fantastic. Now, we still need to do the usual canvassing of donations with the businesses in town. Does anyone want to spearhead that?"

Again, crickets. By god, was she was going to have to drag the whole group across the finish line of the graduation? "How about I send out a sign-up list, and everyone can volunteer to handle a street?" She gritted her teeth into a smile and pushed on, understanding she only had a few minutes left of their attention. "I'll also send out an email to solicit volunteers for the graduation party, and that group can get together another time. Alright, we'd like to get this shelving project done before the end of the school year. Does anyone want to take this research on? We'll need to nail down pricing and what kind of shelves are appropriate."

Not to her surprise, no one raised a hand. She pleaded with her eyes. While she could coordinate like a boss and build a website from scratch, anything about home improvement was beyond her ability.

Then Ty raised his hand.

She turned her gaze away. What was he doing?

He wiggled his fingers.

Vivian cleared her throat. “Ty has something to say.”

Darn. “What’s your question?” Frankie asked.

He looked around, befuddled. He lowered his hand. “You asked for a volunteer.”

“Um.” Oh, the innocence of this man. He had no idea what he was volunteering for.

She had to word her next sentence carefully. No one needed to know that they had history, and that him just being in her presence unnerved her. “Spearheading this project is time-intensive and can be challenging.”

Deadpan, he said, “I know what it entails.”

“Oh? Do you have experience in, um…”

“Asking questions and sourcing materials? Yeah.” He grinned. “And, anyway, I can build them myself.”

She thought she was hearing things. It was hard to focus since he was sporting a smug expression. “Build them? I mean, all of us can build them. Instructions are usually included with bookshelves, right?”

She looked to the confused faces around her. To Olivia, her friend and elementary-school librarian who was listening from her desk, and wore a befuddled look that said, *Why are you being so weird?*

Frankie considered Peak Elementary her second home. From the moment she stepped foot into the school, she took it upon herself to be involved. Over the years, she’d had her hand in everything, and though she wasn’t an expert, and there were tasks she hated, she had a good idea what needed to get done.

Who could blame her for double-checking Ty’s intentions?

She didn't know the man, after all. And the bookshelves project was a big one.

Speaking of, Ty laughed under his breath and shook his head. "Actually, I can build them from scratch. I do it on the side. I don't mind taking a look at the space to see if I can have it done before the end of the school year. I would need to be compensated for the materials, but I can give you that quote, too, before I start."

The table erupted with newfound energy. Someone offered to help as one of his volunteers. Another person suggested that he be compensated for more than the materials. Another parent asked him about his favorite tools. Another dad offered his own tools.

The conversation took another path, with Ty explaining how he was a self-taught woodworker. As interesting as it was, this was Frankie's meeting, and it was losing its way.

Why was Ty so insistent on being involved? Didn't he have other things to do? Though he might be a good veterinarian, out of the office, Ty was the man she'd sparred with. He was a man who continued to surprise her, and surprises were not her thing.

But Ty was this project's only volunteer.

The question was: Would she be able to work closely with him?

What had Ty gotten himself into? Because he wasn't sure if he could work under Frankie's supervision.

After the meeting, Ty slunk away and to the elementary-school cafeteria to pick up Aria, where she and the other kids of PTA members were being watched by another parent and high-school volunteers. It was a brilliant idea—Frankie's, he was sure—so that parents could be involved with the school.

But when he got there, Aria was sitting with one kid at a

round table, while others hovered at other round tables together.

The sight was heartbreaking. At her previous school, Aria had been surrounded by friends, sometimes unabashedly the center of attention. Her social card had been full, and she was always invited to birthday parties and after-school playdates.

He took a deep breath. They'd been in town for only three months. Surely, as the days passed, Aria would settle in.

But now, he understood that attending the PTA meeting was for the greater good. He'd volunteer away all of his free time so that his daughter would be accepted.

It was worth the attention that Frankie gave him at the meeting, as painful as it was. The way she'd grilled him was almost too much to bear.

What was worse was how Francesca simply glowed. She was in a room full of parents, but she stood out. Her confidence and passion resonated with him and with others, and it showed in the way those parents trusted her with leading them.

It was criminal, really, how much he was attracted to her. That despite their continued tense interactions, he wanted more.

Ty waited until Aria looked up and raised a hand. He knew better than to approach her. She nodded and began stuffing her things into her backpack. It was only then that he recognized the kid she was with. Liam.

Interesting.

His phone chimed in an email, drawing him to check his inbox: few emails from work, one for tomorrow's schedule, and another from Dr. Peters:

Ty,

I was just looking ahead to next spring, because it will be here soon enough, especially since we're planning on some office expansion. Let's schedule a time to sit down to discuss

your extending your one-year contract with us. How about a drink in a couple of days?
Kyle

Ty inhaled a deep breath as uncertainty clawed through him. An email like this should have made him want to pump his fists in triumph. Financially, extending his contract was a win.

But it also meant another year of the rigmarole of the veterinarian life. Which he wasn't sure was what he wanted. The last couple of years of nonstop work dealing with the ups and the tragic downs of animal care, along with Harper charging forward toward her own dream, had given him clarity.

That life was too short. That, maybe, he shouldn't stay in a career he didn't love.

Guilt superseded uncertainty and soured his belly. He'd spent almost a decade of study to be where he was today. He had a long runaway of a career—he could very well own his own practice one day. And Aria was so young, with years of education and extracurricular activities yet to experience. He wanted to give her more than he'd been given.

And yet, wasn't this why he'd opted to move to Peak? So he could start anew in a place where he could explore more of himself, and give Aria a slower-paced life? To find his own happiness, too?

A text flew in from Harper: I made it to the next round!

All of his thoughts of work faded away, and he audibly gasped. Harper had been gone since December, and this current "work opportunity," as he'd described to others, was a chance at an amateur cooking reality show. Entering this contest required an NDA from Harper, and he'd been sworn to secrecy, too. He texted back: Are you supposed to be telling me this?

No. But I have to tell someone or I'm going to explode.

In that case, CONGRATULATIONS!

Aria bounded toward him so he put the phone away, and opened his arms to her. She wrapped her arms around his belly and squeezed.

"So how was it?" she asked, with an expectant expression.

"All I've got to say is that you owe me, kid."

Her eyes rounded. "You actually volunteered?"

In turn, he rolled his eyes. This last week, Aria had been incessant in her nagging. She'd made him promise that not only would he attend, but that he would also volunteer for something.

A grin spanned her face, from ear to ear.

"Though you're not out of the woods. Guess who's going to be my sidekick in all of this. You."

"Don't you worry, we're all going to help," said someone from behind him.

His body fizzled at that familiar voice, then he turned.

Francesca.

Her gaze slid past him and then down to his daughter.

"Hi there. You must be Aria." She offered her hand. Around her wrists were a stack of gold bracelets, matching her necklace. With the top of her button-down shirt undone, the charm of her necklace dipped into her cleavage, sparking his imagination.

And this close, he could smell her perfume.

As if hearing his thoughts, she looked up at him.

He stood back, giving her and Aria room.

Aria shook Francesca's hand. Her cheeks were pink. "Hi."

"Welcome to our school. If you need anything at all, or have any questions, you can ask me." She raised a hand and waved. "Though I'm glad you and Liam have met already."

As if summoned, Liam jogged up, out of breath. His gaze was at the cafeteria door, where a man was waiting. Liam waved to him.

It could only be Liam's dad, whom Ty had insinuated felt trapped in his marriage.

Ty grimaced at the replay of that conversation. It certainly wasn't just Francesca who'd said some disparaging things, but him, too.

"Hi, Dr. Ty," Liam said.

"Dr. Ty volunteered to build the bookshelves for the library," Francesca said.

"Whoa," Liam said. "You can build stuff?"

"Yep. My dad taught me how to put things together when I was little. And I kept learning along the way."

"I wanna watch, for sure." His eyes lit up.

"We're gonna do more than that. We're going to help," Francesca said.

"Cool!" Liam added.

And as the two kids began to chat, Francesca said, just loud enough for Ty to hear, "*Someone's* got to keep an eye on things."

He grinned to himself. While she'd put her dog's life in his hands, she didn't trust her precious bookshelves to him.

That was fine. She could continue to spit daggers, but he was going to counter with candy hearts. "You sure that's the only reason you want to be around me?"

It was straight-up flirtation, but he couldn't resist. She was so tense, and yet, underneath it all, there had to be something soft there. She couldn't be such an avid volunteer without a big heart, full stop. And Liam had shown nothing but his polite countenance.

And that softness she had hidden? Ty wanted to see it, even if his curiosity rang warning bells. It was another reason why he'd volunteered, despite his hesitancy. Something about her confidence had turned him on the moment they met, and these days, he wanted to be around people with strong convictions.

"Yeah, I'm sure," she retorted, though her eyes gleamed with something. Was it excitement?

He sought to test it, because what did he have to lose? "Okay then. I've got the day off next Thursday. We should meet with the librarians or the powers that be. Take measurements, come up with a budget. Buy the materials, and all that jazz."

"Let me see." She scrolled through her phone. Ty couldn't help but look down at the color-coded calendar that seemed to be full of things. Curiosity sparked at how she spent her spare time, what her hobbies were, seeing that they never got to that part of their date. He didn't even know what she did for a living. "I'm free early afternoon. I can drop our school librarian and the principal a note to let them know about our meeting, in case they want to join us."

"The more, the merrier." He grinned.

He was jostled to the side. Aria had hooked an arm around his. It was such a sudden show of affection that he gave her his entire attention for the moment. "Yes, sweetie?"

"Can I go?"

"Can you go…where?"

"Our dog trainer is coming over tomorrow and Aria wants to see," Liam explained. "Our dog needs help, in everything."

"Oh, don't say that. Snowball is perfect," Francesca said.

"Sure, Mom. She barks at nothing and doesn't know how to come when we call her. We've been trying for months."

"Every dog has their quirks," Ty said. "Like people, some folks learn differently. Some take a little longer than others. You never know what she ends up surprising you with."

"Our dog? She used to pee every time someone came to the door!" Aria laughed. "Not anymore, though. Thank God she grew out of that." She looked up at Ty. "Please? I want to see how the dog trainer teaches Snowball. And I can meet her, too."

"Um…" he hedged. Admittedly, this was a first for him, and he didn't know how to handle these playdates. When he and Harper shared custody, he took weekends, and she coordinated most of Aria's get-togethers.

Did he stay during the playdate? Or did he just drop off?

"Mom?" Liam queried.

"Oh, sure." Except her expression said otherwise, and he didn't blame her. It was one thing to see each other at school, but this comingling felt…too close for comfort. "Long as it's okay with you, Dr. Ty."

Gah, she lobbed that ball in his court. "Y-yeah, sure," he stuttered. "Why not."

Why not indeed?

Somehow, despite the cheers around him, he still wasn't sure it was a good idea.

Someone cleared their throat, and everyone looked to the man still standing at the doorway.

"That's Liam's dad." Francesca held up a finger to the guy, to ask him to wait. "Liam, time to go."

"Okay. See you tomorrow, Aria." Liam grinned at the two of them, then scurried to his dad. At the same time, one of the high schoolers called Aria back to their table—she'd forgotten her lunch bag.

Now alone, Francesca said, by way of explanation, "It's changeover time. And it's my turn, thank goodness, but Reece and I usually chat and touch base during our handoffs. Why don't I text you about tomorrow? I don't know, in case you can't come?"

She took out her phone and went to her contacts. Then she handed the phone to him.

"The kids'll be disappointed if we can't get them together," he said. He typed in his number, empathy coursing through him. Changeover time had always sparked a feeling of anxiety within him, whether or not Aria was coming or going. It was change, in and of itself.

He handed the phone back to her, and she rolled her eyes ever so coolly. "I think they'll be okay. But, yeah, let's play it by ear."

"Sounds good," he said nonchalantly, but as he watched Francesca walk out the cafeteria door to catch up with her ex-husband, none of what he felt was easy and relaxing.

And he couldn't wait to be around her again.

Chapter Four

Francesca: Hi, checking in about tomorrow. Liam hasn't stopped asking about Aria.

Ty: Aria's looking forward to it, too.

Dog trainer will be here at 11.

Okay. Question?

?

Do I stay? This is my first playdate. Obv not my playdate, but Aria's. On my watch, I mean.

LOL, you're fine. You're welcome to stay or leave her here for a bit.

Great!

"You're only staying a couple of hours." Ty glanced at Aria through the rearview mirror. She was sitting in the back seat, still too petite for the passenger seat.

She was grinning. "Yep."

"Say 'I promise.'"

"I promise." Though her eyes were focused out the window, her sarcasm was dialed up.

It was the next day, and as promised, Ty was on his way to drop off Aria at Francesca and Liam's house. He was exhausted after a few hours of unpacking. His body sagged from moving furniture around and his brain was fried from thinking about where to put the unpacked items. But his day wasn't over yet. Now that he knew that he could leave Aria for a bit, it was the perfect time to deal with the largest elephant in his own room.

He was meeting with Dr. Peters today, even if he hadn't yet decided how to respond. Was he ready to sign another contract? Was it wiser, safer, to remain where he was, when his heart was telling him otherwise? After his last text to Harper, from which he'd deduced that she wasn't coming home anytime soon, he couldn't take a contract for granted, could he?

Aria gasped, and Ty awoke to the view unfolding in front of him. They'd been on a slow climb up a winding path, and a stone sign greeted them, etched with the name *Spirit of the Shenandoah B & B*. He slowed, then, rounding the corner, they approached a modern building with a circular driveway.

The architecture stunned him. The facade was out of a magazine, in which the dichotomy of the building's straight lines and the natural features of the mountains and trees gave it an ethereal feel.

He navigated the car into the small parking lot, as instructed by Francesca in her text, and passed the sign that said Private Residences. After parking, he pulled up Francesca's directions. He was to follow that sign down the path, which would lead to her house.

He scrolled up to their previous texts over the last twenty-four hours. It had started with him asking a simple question about playdate etiquette, but it continued on about the bookshelves project and then about Snowball's separation anxiety. Their last text had been late last night.

He'd secretly hoped that there would be a text from her this morning.

"Dad, let's go." Aria had unbuckled her seat belt, interrupting his thoughts. "I'm ready."

But was he? He took a deep breath. What was he getting himself into, entering the woman's lair? He was going to regret this. Their texts weren't personal; they were transactional. "Alright, let's go."

She opened her door and hopped out.

A text flew in from Francesca: Saw you on my camera. I'm the first cabin on the left.

Nervous energy rushed through him. It was ridiculous, he knew, but Francesca kept him on his toes. He'd meant it when he'd accidentally insulted Francesca on their first and only date, when he had compared her to his ex. They were both passionate, they were both full of life, energy, and personality. With his ex, it was what had lured him and attracted him. For someone who had steady energy, who craved days of relaxation, being around his ex gave him a newfound gusto for things.

But it was the very thing that brought the two of them into conflict, too. After a while, a guy got tired and needed to relax. Admittedly, he couldn't keep up. And it wasn't Harper's fault.

And though it had taken them a while to be amicable, he realized it had nothing to do with who either one of them were, but who they were when they were together.

Ty felt that kind of vortex around Francesca, though in a different way. To voluntarily walk into it, even in this friendly manner—there was a great chance he would regret it.

He was feeling it now; he was being pulled in by that energy. She had a life force that he hadn't felt in a long while.

A knock on the passenger-side window startled him from

his thoughts. Aria frowned impatiently. And though he couldn't hear her, he could imagine the sigh escaping from her lips.

Nodding, he stepped out of the car.

Finding the house was easy. Aesthetically, the B & B and the surrounding nature was perfection. A stone path led them to a two-story cabin with a wraparound porch on the left. Beyond it was a massive yard, and in the distance a chain-link fence with tufts of green—a garden, if he surmised correctly. If they had continued down the path, it looked to lead to other cabins. To the right was the B & B's side property.

And beyond was a skyline that belonged on postcards and coffee-table books. Big sky.

Barking came from his left, and Snowball bounded down, her nub of a tail wiggling. Aria met up with the dog and laughed as she tried to pin her down with a hug. Then Snowball came up to him.

He knew that Puppy Training 101 meant that he should have the dog sit or calm down before he acknowledged her. But impatience won out and he got on one knee. He had a soft spot for puppies. If he had more room, or had more free time in his schedule, he would have adopted another dog, another puppy, if possible. Maybe two more.

Dogs loved unconditionally. They aimed to please. Humans didn't deserve them.

Snowball nuzzled his cheek. Ty looked into her eyes while scratching her head. "No granola bars today, eh, bud?"

"Nope, we have learned our lesson."

Legs came into view—shapely legs ensconced in leggings, with shapely thighs and curvy hips.

Ty looked away and stood up to reset his sights.

Except that her face was just as captivating. Today, her hair was up in a bun, though curly tendrils escaped from the style.

No makeup, and he wondered if this was what she looked like in the morning.

Stop it. He couldn't think of her that way. He was already thinking too much about this playdate, beguiled by how open she was on texts.

And her expression—it was back to how it was at the vet office: softer, relaxed. It took him aback, but also, he was suspicious.

He decided to tread lightly at first. He didn't know which Francesca he was getting.

"Snowball's looking good," he said.

"Right? Thank goodness." Her gaze bounced to the left, where Aria and Liam were chasing the dog in the side yard. She sighed. "I love seeing Liam so happy. If I knew that getting him a dog would make him smile like that I would have done it sooner."

"It means that Snowball's a good match for your family. Because that's important, too."

"Do you have pets?"

"Are you asking a vet if they love animals enough to have one?" He playfully side-eyed her. "We have a goldendoodle named Bubba."

"Bubba? That's cute."

"Aria named him. But I've had dogs all my life."

"Snowball is our first." She shrugged. "Hence, the dog trainer. Because apparently I'm the problem."

"Oh, you don't say?" He grinned.

"Ha ha." She sighed. "It seems that I'm not firm enough. I am—" she made quotations with her fingers "'—a softie.'"

"Wow." He bit his cheek.

"Please, don't act too surprised."

"I've seen how you are at the PTA." Then, he added lightly. "Not to mention the first time we met."

"I lead with strength with everyone except my puppy."

Strength and stubbornness, was what he added in his head, though he didn't dare say it aloud.

"Speaking of," she continued. "About our date."

He shook his head as a surge of guilt and relief flooded through him, that she'd addressed this hurdle between them. "No, me first."

"Okay." Then, she grinned, eyes fluttering up to meet his.

A full-bodied laugh burst out of him. *This woman.* "I shouldn't have suggested that your ex felt trapped. I can see how it insinuated that he had no fault in it, when it was his choice to leave."

She nodded. "Well, I shouldn't have said that your ex was negligent. It wasn't my place. I think it's great that you support her dreams."

"And maybe I shouldn't have asked you to calm down." He inhaled. "Not my best moment."

"Me walking out wasn't mine, either."

Beats of silence passed in which they both looked at one another. Ty's tongue tied at what to say next, not wanting to ruin this reconciliation.

"So…" she said finally, with a smile. "We should be done here at three, and Aria's welcome to stay for a snack, if you'd like."

"Oh, no, I don't want her to impose. She already pushed her way in to hang out with you all."

"No, she didn't at all. I like having other kids at our house. It's just me and Liam, and the B and B's like a compound for our family, and he's the only kid here, with us not living in one of the neighborhoods. Anyway, Liam asked, and I don't mind at all. I do have a date tonight, but that's not until six."

"A date." He raised his eyebrows. "Kind of hurt you've moved on from me so quickly."

"Oh, please. No one will beat your record of the shortest date." She glanced at him with a smirk.

Ty had the errant thought of kissing that expression off her face. "Okay, then. I'll give Aria a text in a bit to see how she feels."

"Great. But like I said, you're more than welcome to stay for the lesson."

He rested a hand behind his head. "I actually made an appointment to meet up with Dr. Peters for coffee. Work stuff."

"Ah. Well, good luck with that."

I'm gonna need it. "Thanks," he said as Francesca did a double take to something over his shoulder.

Her hand shot up. "Hey, Griffen."

A young man wearing a *Pawrific Training* shirt strode up to the kids.

It was Ty's cue. "Aria?"

Aria turned.

Ty held up his phone, to signal that they would text. She blew him a kiss, which he pretended to catch.

He extracted himself from the group and pointed his car down the hill. As he rounded the town square, his thoughts flipped from his conversation with Francesca to his career.

He found parking next to Tin Cup Café and only exhaled after he shut the car door. It was time to be an adult, to do a hard thing, to take chances.

Dr. Peters could be seen sitting at a round table through the glass front doors. With a steaming cup of coffee in front of him, he appeared relaxed, wearing a casual polo and jeans. His phone was in his hand and he was scrolling.

Ty entered the coffee shop, shook the doctor's hand, and sat in front of him.

"Glad you could meet me." Dr. Peters raised a hand to a server, who came to their table. "Coffee?"

"Yeah, sure." Unlike the older, gray-haired man in front of him, Ty was the epitome of anxious energy. He was ready to take the leap. He'd made his plans prior to coming to Peak. All he needed to do was say them aloud.

"I have to say, Ty, Junior and I, we've enjoyed having you at our practice. The way you've handled yourself with our patients' families. How you've settled in with our staff. We've been impressed."

"That means a lot," he said, with sincerity. "It's been a good transition."

Better than he could have wished for, work-wise, if he was being honest. There wasn't a mean person in the practice, and all had the same mindset of taking care of the community. It wasn't that way everywhere. Even veterinarians could be cutthroat.

"As I mentioned in my email, I'm hoping you'll consider staying on staff after next year," Dr. Peters said. "I know it's early. You've only been here a few months, but gosh, son, we really think you're a good fit."

At the word *son*, Ty softened to goo. He hadn't been called *son* in years. Since his father passed away.

With it, all of his convictions to negotiate his contract melted away, too.

"I ain't getting any younger, and I can tell that you and Junior would make a great team."

"You know it this early?" Ty linked his fingers together on the table. At that moment, the server came and set down his cup of coffee.

"They don't call me an animal whisperer for nothing. But I'm pretty good at people, too." He smiled then, taking a sip of his coffee. "The moment you walked in, all I saw was the future of Valley Pets."

"The future?"

Dr. Peters drew a scene with his hands. "A future where we can continue to be a part of the community. With retirement on the horizon, I doubted that Junior could take it all on. But with you there, you both can. Would you like to take part in that?"

Ty felt himself getting swept into Dr. Peter's vision. He thought of himself in the older man's office space. Of wearing the white coat, of watching the puppies he'd met so far, like Snowball, grow older.

Uncertainty twisted and turned in his gut. Because the other side, his other dream, involved *things*, not animals. It involved getting dirty for a totally different reason.

But that future wasn't clear. And what he had in front of him—this offer—was.

And who was he to turn that down?

"I do."

The creak of the back gate shifted Frankie's focus from her task of slicing apples at the kitchen counter to her backyard window. Outside, Liam was returning from beyond the gate. He held up a tennis ball and chucked it to Aria.

Aria missed the catch, and when the ball fell to the ground, Snowball tumbled for it and flipped upside down. Both kids laughed. Liam clutched his belly.

At the sight, Frankie's chest expanded. Liam had had playdates, but he didn't show his full self to many of his peers. He got along with others, there wasn't a doubt about that, but he had the introvert's social battery.

But Liam and Aria had been at it for three hours now. The trainer left an hour ago, and Liam had yet to suggest that they come inside.

It was all due to Aria. She was mature, and she didn't crowd him. Though she had opinions, she allowed Liam to express his. They'd spent a good half hour rocking on her back porch swing, just talking and laughing.

It dawned on Frankie then that Aria was much like her father in this regard. Watching him interact both at the PTA meeting and with Aria showed that he was an invested and kind father.

On the counter, her phone buzzed with a notification from the One Date app.

She set the apples down and washed her hands; she took her time to wipe them on the kitchen towel.

Frankie picked up her phone, pressed on the app. While she leaned against her kitchen counter, her messages loaded on the screen. She clicked on the most recent one.

Hi,
Sorry, can't make it tonight. Something came up.

"What do you mean something came up?" She glared at the phone. She paced, biting a fingernail while staring at the empty response box. "You mean someone *better* came up."

Frankie had been doing this dating scene, and especially this app, long enough to discern what these rejections meant. She knew she shouldn't take it personally.

But at the moment, she was. At the moment, she had the desire to chuck this phone out the window for Snowball to fetch.

What was going on with her love life? And how did she end up here, when her ex had locked down one of the most eligible bachelorettes in town?

Her phone buzzed with a notification from her security camera. Someone was driving into their parking lot. A minute later, the grainy image revealed Ty getting out of his SUV.

Her heart, the traitor, beat loudly.

Their follow-up conversations had been more than civil, their apologies to one another sincere. They'd been friendly, flirtatious even.

But that was all they could be. Now that he was in the PTA and working on the bookshelves, she surely *couldn't* explore where this friendship could lead.

A knock sounded and Frankie answered it, unwilling to give her attraction another thought.

But when she opened the door, she found a man who looked like he'd aged a decade.

"Hey," Ty said. "Thanks for having Aria over. I swear I had to remind her that she had a home."

It would have been easy enough to grab Aria and to say goodbye. But Frankie was nothing if not curious and straightforward. "Wanna come in? You look like someone delivered you some bad news."

He stalled for a beat and looked at the floor as if he was physically rooted to the spot.

"C'mon," she said. "I might have a loud bark, but I don't bite. And I've got dessert, better than drinks, and safer since you're driving."

"I can't really say no to dessert," he said after a second, with a tired smile. He stepped in, eyes landing on the shoes next to the door.

"You don't..." She'd begun to excuse him from taking off his shoes, but he stepped out of them, anyway. "Thanks." Then she led the way deeper into her cabin, biting the smile off her face. "The kids are in the yard playing. Time with the trainer was productive."

She gestured to the bar chairs at the kitchen island, where he could sit, but he stalled by the back door, which overlooked the yard. His cheeks pinched into a smile. Then, he stuffed his hands in his pockets and looked as if he'd descended into a deep thought.

Now, Frankie's curiosity was piqued. From the cake stand on her kitchen counter, she sliced a piece of ube cake and slid it onto a plate. She set in on the bar countertop.

"Ty?"

He did a double take as if he was startled from sleep. His

face brightened a smidge, and he slid onto the chair. "Wow. What's this?"

"Ube cake with vanilla frosting."

"Looks delicious. I've only had ube in halo-halo."

She schooled her shock that he'd had the iced dessert. "You've tried halo-halo… That's…great."

"Pretty big Filipino population in our neighborhood just outside of Philly. To be honest, though, I only know the basic foods. Adobo, pancit, lumpia. And oh, there was a sisig truck near where I worked."

The fact that he was apologetic for not knowing enough Filipino food? Who was this guy? He continued to fly green flags, though she was less suspicious today and more curious as to what made him tick. "My brother, Jared, baked that cake. He's the chef here at the B and B."

"Must be nice to have a baker in the family." His eyes darted up to meet hers, his fork at the ready. "You having some?"

"Listen, he gave me half the cake and I've already eaten a quarter of it. So I can also stand to share some, even if I don't really want to."

"Then I'm honored that you cared to give me a piece." He forked up the bite of cake and ate it.

As she'd suspected, with that first bite, color returned to his cheeks. "It's good, right?"

He moaned and shut his eyes. "Damn good. The best thing about today, actually."

Her chest fluttered at his reaction, at the way he moaned. A picture of the two of them, deep in throes of lovemaking, flashed in her imagination, and she blew out a breath to rid herself of it.

She really needed to have another first date.

And maybe a sip of cold water.

She filled up two glasses of ice water and slipped one to Ty. "I'm sorry, did you want coffee? Or tea?"

"I would love some, but it's already after noon, and it'll keep me up."

"Ah, same here. Coffee does something weird to my body. Earl Grey tea with milk's more my style."

"Same-o, sort of. Coffee with milk is my hot bev of choice."

She smiled and waited for more. After a few seconds, she prompted, "So what's up?"

He shook his head and had another forkful of cake. "It's nothing. Just…work."

She crossed her arms. "Nah…you're not just going to come and eat my cake and not even talk to me."

Her cheeks heated. Had she really said *eat my cake*? She cleared her throat. "You're here already, and you look like you need to vent."

"It's complicated."

"Life is complicated. I'm a single mom. I know complicated."

He set the fork down and peered up at her. "Even if I did say something, how do I know you're not going to tell someone?"

"Are you saying I'm a gossip?" Stunned by the thought, she pressed a hand against her chest. "Though, it's fair to assume that I'm vocal."

"It's not that I think you're a gossip…but it's work related, and I wouldn't want for it to get back to Dr. Peters."

"And you think I'll tell him?"

"No, but you'll tell one of your friends, who might tell him inadvertently. I didn't realize how small this town was until…" His voice trailed off.

"Until what?"

He looked at her squarely, then placed his fork down. "You want the truth?"

"Yeah. Always."

"Until I saw you everywhere."

That made her laugh again, and it elicited an eye roll from him. "It can't be that bad."

He clutched his chest. "Hurts my pride even more that our date didn't have an iota of an effect on you."

She schooled her face. No way was she going to let him know that it was the other way around. That she hadn't stopped thinking of him. That while he was gone today, she was on pins and needles for when he returned.

"What can I say?" She shrugged, to deflect the heat rising to her cheeks. "But truly, if I say I'm not going to say something, then I won't."

"Alright then." He heaved a breath. "I think I want to leave the practice."

"Whoa." She sipped her water and absorbed the implication of this decision. "But Dr. Peters… You've only been there, what…"

He winced. "Three months."

"Does he know?"

He shook his head. "I met with him this afternoon. My contract is for a year, and it's a perfectly good job, you know? At this meeting, he asked me to stay beyond the year."

"If it's a perfectly good job, then what's wrong?"

"I want to have a little more control over my schedule. With Aria, and with my ex. I don't want to feel hemmed in. I like the staff. Love the clients, obviously—it's why I came into the field. The health care benefits…that alone is priceless." He straightened, then, as if he was hit with a rush of energy. "But I want to do something else. I thought I would pursue it when we moved and after my initial contract was up. I've been preparing for the jump a while now, though I took the contract so that I could kind of get to know the town a bit and save more money. Settle in." He ran his hand through his hair. "I don't know, a part of me thought that maybe moving to a new clinic might change my mind. It's scary, you know?"

"No, I get it." Frankie thought of Reece. He, like Ty, had been great on paper, too. Perfect, actually. Would she have stayed with Reece forever had he not left her? Yes, she would have, because she would have convinced herself that she had nothing to complain about, even if it had become perfectly clear that they were drifting apart. "It's a life-changing decision."

"And what kind of person leaves a stable job when they have a child for a passion? I can't risk that. Even if I want to."

"I hear you." Her brain went into puzzle-solving mode. "What's your passion?"

"Woodworking, if you must know." His face lit up.

"No way." She pressed her hands against the countertop, pleasantly surprised. "So the good doctor *did* know what he was volunteering for."

"I do. I've had, what someone could say, steady clients for years now. I've built every kind of furniture you can think of, from bookshelves to kitchen tables, to bedframes. I worked these projects on my days off, and I had big plans to reinvent myself here. But three months have passed and I still haven't unpacked. The business plan I made up months ago feels overwhelming now. There's so much to do, website, social media. Researching self-employed health insurance plans." He shook his head. "This would be my first try at starting a business, except for dog walking when I was in middle school."

A younger Ty flashed in her head. "I bet you made a killing."

"I did. Paid for my eighth-grade trip to New York City. Otherwise I wouldn't have gone. My parents really didn't have much."

"Aw," she couldn't help but say. She imagined Ty putting

all of his dollars away for this trip. "Can I help you with anything? I've got business experience."

She bit the inside of her cheek. What was she doing? Ty wasn't a friend.

As if she had the extra time to spare.

"You and all of your extra time?" He echoed. "You were good enough to have Aria over, and for listening to me. I didn't realize that I needed to talk all of that out. Definitely better than our first date."

"Light years."

"Agreed." He looked up from his plate and crossed his arms over the countertop. "I still don't know how our conversation imploded so quickly."

She thought about it. "I did think that you were too nonchalant."

"Nonchalant?" He rested a fist against his chin. "Interesting."

"You were so calm, almost cheerful. It felt like you were sweeping things under the rug. You answered everything with a smile, even the hard questions. Even while you sit there, you have this aura."

He looked around him in jest. "Sure it's not my Great-Aunt Martha?"

"Nope, and you shouldn't kid around about stuff like that."

He peered at her. "Ah, Francesca, I feel like we have so much to get to know about one another."

"Oh we will, with you building the library shelves."

"I look forward to it." He smiled sincerely, which sent tingles through her.

"And," she remembered, "with me helping you open your business."

"That's not necessary."

She shrugged. "It'll make me feel less guilty about the shelves."

“I’ll think about it, Francesca. But for real…truce?”

“Truce. And you can call me Frankie.”

He held out a hand, eyes meeting hers. “Nice to meet you, Frankie.”

She laid her hand in his and attempted to ignore the warmth that enveloped her when he squeezed it. But she was failing, caught in his stare, and how honest his expression was. “Nice to meet you.”

The door slammed open and two pairs of feet galloped indoors. Frankie stepped away from the countertop and tended to the children, hoping that Ty hadn’t noticed.

Chapter Five

Entering Peak Elementary School library on Thursday, Frankie's phone buzzed with a notification. It was the One Date app once more, with a message from a different guy, named Gerald: Can't wait to see you tonight.

She smiled. She had a good feeling about this one. Gerald had answered her messages immediately. He lived in Charlottesville—thank goodness, because she wasn't going to date anyone from Peak ever again—and his texts were casual, not creepy, or presumptuous.

"Here she is," Olivia Fullerton, the school librarian said in a singsong voice. She loaded books onto another woman's arms. "Always five minutes early."

"But, of course." Frankie grinned. "I'm excited about today."

Today was the day Ty began the bookshelves project, and Frankie wanted to be present for every step of it.

"We are, too." Olivia's face lit.

Olivia was a soft-spoken person, though strong and focused. One could read the emotions on her face well before she could express how she felt. While she might appear buttoned up, with her blond hair parted in the middle and pulled back into a ponytail every day, a select few folks, Frankie and Vivian included, knew that Olivia possessed a fun streak.

And the kids sure loved her.

Frankie bet that Olivia'd read each and every book in their library.

"Wait, have you two met?" Olivia asked. "Frankie, meet Christine Casalme, our newest assistant librarian."

"Nice to meet you, Christine," Frankie said. "I didn't realize we were getting a new librarian."

"I convinced Principal Murray that we had more work than I could handle. The listing was up for less than a day."

"And we moved into town just last week. Perfect timing," Christine said.

Olivia gestured at the boxes of books piled against the wall. "Definitely in time to help clean things up and organize the books when the new shelves go up. You're going to be such a help at next fall's book fair."

Footsteps sounded from the doorway, and Ty entered the library, cheeks pink, his hair windswept. In each hand was a to-go cup.

Oh, hello. Ty was wearing a grey crew-neck sweater over khakis. He exuded a relaxed vibe; it screamed *let's snuggle.*

"Morning. I don't think we've met," Olivia said.

The nudge brought Frankie back to present. "Olivia Fullerton, Christine Casalme, this is Ty Golden. Ty, these are our school librarians."

"Nice to meet you both." He nodded, then pushed a cup into Frankie's hand.

She almost fumbled it, confused. "This is for me?"

She sniffed the Earl Grey, and her cheeks warmed with the scent. He remembered.

"With a splash of milk," he said as a matter of fact, then turned to Olivia and Christine. "I'm sorry, I can head back out and get you both something."

"No, it's good. I've had my caffeine for the day. Thank you, though," Olivia said, eyeing Frankie conspiratorially.

Which Frankie tried to ignore, yet felt in every part of her.

After all, this was Ty's personality. He was friendly to all, down to four-legged creatures.

"Should we take a look at the space?" Frankie said so she didn't get sucked into the spiral of her thoughts.

"Yep. Good idea. Christine, I'll be right back." She led the way to the back of the library, darkened by the drawn curtains. She pulled back the shades, and they all stared at the wall dotted with drill holes and small damaged areas.

"This is a nice sized wall."

"We had eight shelves." Olivia walked to the farthest part. "And they extended all the way down here."

Ty sipped his coffee. "Do you have a photo of what the shelves looked like before?"

"Oh, I think I do." Frankie pulled out her phone and scrolled. "I took a bunch at the last book fair, and we had a cashier set up here. Hold on."

"Ms. Fullerton?" a soft voice said from the front of the library. A student.

"Excuse me," Olivia said, before stepping away.

Leaving the two of them alone.

Frankie shifted in the awkward silence as she continued to scroll through her photos. Golly, she had thousands of them. Dozens of the same scenes, even. "I swear I'm getting close," she lied, because her focus was shot. It alternated between furtive glances at Ty, who appeared so serious in his evaluation of the wall, finding the right photo, and reexamining their last interaction.

The last time they were together was less than a week ago, when they'd both agreed to be friends, and that she would be available to help him with his fledgling business. But since then, he hadn't reached out.

People usually jumped for joy for the help she could provide. She considered herself a knowledgeable person. And she never hesitated in reaching out to others when she needed help.

After not hearing from him for a couple of days, she'd assumed that he truly wasn't interested.

But now, this tea felt like an olive branch and maybe something more. Was this just a simple, friendly gesture?

Was she reading into it?

History would say yes.

A set of familiar photos snapped her out of her thoughts. "Aha. I found it."

"Sweet. May I?" he asked, fingers above the screen. He was asking permission to zoom into the photo.

"Oh, yeah. Sure." Ty sidled up to her, and their shoulders brushed. He smelled good—spicy and woodsy—and she leaned in even closer.

"Ah, the old shelving was pretty basic." His voice was a rumble in her ear. "I can do better."

"Okay, confidence." She looked at him, their faces close. The proximity took her breath away.

"I do know what I'm doing sometimes." He grinned.

Then, in the next second, he stepped to one side of the wall, his departure a shock. A tape measure appeared in his hand, and he extended it for her to take. "Frankie?"

"Yep." She took the end and pulled it to the opposite side of the wall, discombobulated. Was she the only one feeling this way?

He mumbled something into his phone—he was voice-noting. "Okay, you can let go now."

She did so, and the tape measure recoiled back with Ty's coaxing. "We'll have to see what Principal Murray wants for the type of wood, and what budget the PTA has for this project. I can make them as simple as shelves on brackets, or basic built-ins. Built-ins can transform this space, though. Individual shelves will take less time, though we do have spring break coming up where I can devote some more hours..." he mused.

Frankie was half-listening, her thoughts in a loop. Then, she blurted out, "You didn't text or call me this week."

His eyebrows raised. "Was I supposed to?"

"I offered my help."

He smiled then. "I know, and I really appreciate it."

"You said you would think about accepting it. It's been five days."

"Well." He took a breath. "I guess I didn't want to presume… We only hung out once, and I thought…I thought you were just being nice. I wasn't going to push my luck."

"Oh." She hadn't thought of it that way.

"Were you waiting for my text?"

"Yes, I was." Then, at the sound of that, she retracted. "I mean, it's your loss if you don't want my help."

He grinned.

"What's that look for?" she asked.

"Because…you know, you could have texted *me* if you wanted to hang out."

Her cheeks burned and she felt like a high schooler with a first crush. She shuffled through her retorts like a deck of cards. "It wasn't to hang out."

"In that case, are you free tonight?"

"No, not tonight. I've got a date," she said proudly, though belatedly realized that maybe she shouldn't have said so.

"A date, huh? Who's the unlucky guy?"

She rolled her eyes. "Just…someone." She took out her phone and thumbed to her calendar. "How about Sunday?"

"I can do Sunday. My place?"

"Okay." She proceeded to add the event into her calendar. "What's your address?"

"Here, let me." He took her phone and entered in his address. Then he pressed another button and lifted her phone. He turned it and in a split second had taken a selfie.

"What the…"

"Just to make sure you have my face in your phone."

"How do you know that I want to see your face in my contacts?"

"It'll give you a smile when you need it. You'll see."

He was too smug for his own good, but there was no time to think about how their banter gave her butterflies, because Olivia walked in with Principal Murray.

Principal Murray was a former professional NFL football player, and the man took up space. Broad-shouldered and tall, he commanded the room, but at Peak he was the biggest teddy bear of them all. "Morning, friends," he boomed with a smile. "This must be the man of the hour."

Ty shook his hand, hearts in his eyes. No doubt, he was a football fan. "Just did some measurements. Now, it's time for your wish list. What would your ideal bookshelves look like?"

Principal Murray rubbed his hands together, then launched into his wishes. Frankie watched and half listened as Ty took notes and asked questions. These two were the same kind of people: They spoke freely and their conversation meandered from wood types to Principal Murray's last NFL game, to how Aria was adjusting to the school and then back to Ty's experience in woodworking. They laughed without reservation, with ease.

Frankie was never ashamed of who she was but she was keenly aware that she was capable of putting up barriers against people, especially folks first-introduced.

Not that she wanted to change. She'd gotten to where she was because of *who* she was. But to approach people and situations with a certain level of trust? She wanted that for just a moment. She wanted to enjoy the moment more. She wanted to believe people at face value.

She awoke from her thoughts only to realize that both Principal Murray and Ty were looking at her expectantly. "All good, then?" she asked.

"All good on my end," Principal Murray said. "Thank you again."

"You don't understand how this is going to change everything in our library," Olivia added.

"I'll follow up with Frankie with all the details. It'll be a mess for a bit. If there's a room where I can put my tools..." Ty said.

"That's easy. The classroom next door is used for storage, but we can clear it out."

"Perfect. That's it for me."

The bell rang, and a chorus of voices preceded the stomping of feet. Kids filled the hallway.

"Here they come." Olivia beamed.

"We'll leave you all to it," Frankie said. To Ty, she added, "I'll walk out with you."

After a quick hug from Olivia, she and Ty left the school, halting at the parking lot, in between their two cars. "Thanks for meeting up," Frankie said.

"Easy enough. And I'll see you Sunday?"

"Great." She clicked her key fob, thinking of her Sunday plans. "Oh, how about I bring Liam? I have him this week."

He grinned brighter. "Even better. Aria would like that. Why not bring Snowball, too? It'll be a good time to introduce her to Bubba. Great for socialization."

"Okay, see you then." Her spirits lightened. And there went those butterflies again. But she told them to calm down. She and Ty were friends, and for the sake of peace, that was all they would be.

"Can I help you, sweetheart?"

Ty tore his eyes from one of the TV screens hanging from the ceiling of Nuggets Bar and Grill—it was March Madness and each of the four was streaming games—and set his eyes on the bartender.

He cleared his throat and spoke above the noise. “Pick up for Golden.”

“Give me a sec.” She smiled, ducking to the back of the bar.

Oh, how his life had changed. Here he was, at a bar and grill a good five miles down the highway to pick up dinner on a Thursday night, not for a date, but for his daughter, who insisted on trying their fried wings, which she’d sworn had gone viral online.

Then again, he didn’t miss this type of nightlife. First, it was loud. The games on the screens, the music that piped through the surround sound, the people talking. It was sensory overload, even for an extrovert. Second, he was exhausted. Aria had a take-home social-studies project this week that took every last bit of Ty’s emotional bandwidth. Bubba was finally showing transition stress and had an accident at least once a day this week. And his patient schedule was full to the brim.

What he did miss was having people to spend time with. Grown-ups one could watch R-rated films with. People who he could speak and debate with. People he could vent to.

He also wouldn’t mind a person he could take home afterward, could share a quiet cup of coffee with after a night together.

Or tea.

He laughed to himself, remembering his and Frankie’s conversation this morning. And while he knew they were romantically incompatible, it was nice to know that it wasn’t just he who felt that there was something there between them.

What he was most touched by was that she *cared.* That she wanted to support him and help get a dream off the ground even if he wasn’t sure if it would really happen.

As if the universe read his mind, Frankie came into view among the faces in the busy dining room. She was seated in a booth, across from a guy with short brown hair. She was smiling, though not sincerely; her eyes were flat and uninterested.

Frankie was on her date.

The idea of her being here with a man did something to his belly. When she'd mentioned the date this morning, he'd had to keep himself from asking more questions about the guy.

Like, what about this guy made him special enough to take any of her time?

And how different was he to Ty?

Not your business.

Still, curiosity had him moving in their direction before he thought twice.

Coming up from her side, Ty marveled at her profile, now on full display with Frankie's hair pulled back. Her jawline and cheekbones stunned him, and her red lips were a beacon. But before he stepped out of the crowd, he examined her date. He was objectively handsome, bearded, with short hair. He was obviously taken by her, with the way he couldn't keep a goofy smile off his lips. He spoke animatedly, with his hands. In the middle of the table was an appetizer.

The guy had obviously made it past the twenty-some minutes Ty had with her.

What roared up next was something unexpected: jealousy. He felt it in his throat. Because they looked like they were having a nice enough time, even if she wasn't adding to the conversation. It was infinitely better than the argument that they'd had.

Someone from behind shoved Ty forward. "Oof…sorry, dude," the person said.

Ty recovered just as Frankie turned his way. Her gorgeous lips parted in surprise.

Now that he was here, he didn't have a choice, did he? So he fully committed to the moment and schooled his features. "Hey, Frankie."

He stepped up to the table.

"Ty." Her gaze bobbed between him and her date. Her eyes searched his. "Ty, this is Gerald. Gerald, Ty."

He didn't bother to offer his hand and tipped his chin up. "Hey."

"Evening," Gerald said.

"Ty's in the PTA with me. His daughter and Liam are friends." She smiled with all of her teeth, baring them, as if to say *please go.*

But what caught his eye was the drink in front of her.

I prefer white wine to red, always. Her words from their first date came back to him.

"Red wine, huh?" he asked her with a smirk.

"Yep," she said defiantly.

"The best on the list," Gerald said. "Though that doesn't mean much with this place, am I right?" he said, as if he knew Ty at all. "But beggars can't be choosers."

Ty gave Frankie the side-eye. Was she watching this and staying silent? He opened his mouth to defend small towns, even if he was a new resident himself. But a server interrupted, and said, "Ready to order, folks?"

"High time," Gerald mumbled under his breath. He cleared his throat. "We're both having the short rib."

Ty raised his eyebrows at Frankie. "Oh, so you're ordering for her?"

"Gerald, will you excuse me, please? I have to, um…" She raised a hand as if someone was calling her from afar. "I'll be right back. Ty, walk with me?"

"My pleasure. Later, Gerald. Enjoy the short rib."

He was tugged by the elbow away through the crowd, and by the time they both made it to the dark hallway that led to the kitchen, Ty was laughing.

She spun to him. "What are you doing here?"

"Picking up dinner."

"Where's Aria?"

"Our neighbor, Mrs. Grayson, offered to watch her while I grabbed food. But my turn—what was *that*?"

"What was what?" She crossed her arms.

He took in Frankie in all of her date-night glory. A fitted, black long-sleeve top and black slacks with a flare. Heels, a gold belt. She looked good. More than good. Beautiful. Stunning. "The red wine. Him ordering for you. You hate that."

"Who said?" She lifted her chin.

"The red wine? *You* said. And the ordering for you? Come on. That's not like you." Frustration coursed through him, though he knew he didn't have the right.

Then, he realized. It had been *her* choice that he didn't have a right.

He hung his head and laughed. "I don't get you. You gave me so much shit that night. You made sure I understood that it was your way or the highway. And with him, you just let him order for you?"

"It's because I want him to like me, okay?" she blurted.

It was as if the world quieted around him, and he wondered if what he'd heard was correct. "I don't understand."

She heaved a breath. "I didn't want a repeat of our date."

The thud was quick against his chest, like a double tap of rejection. But the words quickly sorted themselves. "You wanted to have a good time."

"At the very least, to make it through dinner without having a fight. Look, I'm trying, okay? I want to be a strong person. I don't want to be taken advantage of. I want to be the kind of mother that my son can rely on." She swallowed, and a beat passed. "But I don't want to be disliked so much that I end up alone."

He let out a breath and took a step forward. His first inclination was to take her into his arms. The idea of being alone affected him to the core, too. He supposed every divorced person had had to grapple with the idea that perhaps the love they'd lost was the only one they would experience. When he and Harper broke up, it had jolted him so much that he'd lived in a stupor for weeks. He'd thought that they were okay, that they'd been in a lull in their relationship.

"I know how that feels, to be lonely," he said softly, gently. "But shouldn't a person like you for you? Shouldn't a person see you for who you are?"

"Someone who thinks it's their way or the highway?" She parroted his words.

"Someone who has high standards and values the truth." He spoke with as much sincerity as he could muster. His words mixed with the smell of her perfume, which he wished he could dive into.

She looked up at him with her serious dark eyes. He noted that her eyelids had a little bit of glitter, and her cheeks shimmered. Little glints of whimsy that intrigued him. She contained multitudes, and Ty wanted to explore each and every facet.

"Frankie," he said, more to stop himself from thinking too deeply about this woman who had clearly moved on from him. "You shouldn't have to change who you are to make people like you. At the very least, you need to give these guys a hard time on the first date. What if you had given me all the chances? What could have happened?"

"I don't know. What *could* have happened?"

He allowed himself to consider the idea, drawn into her spell. Instead of discussing their failed date, he would be kissing her every chance he got, given the way he was so tuned into her. He, at the very least, would strive to put a smile on her face.

The bartender interrupted, with a bag in her hand. "Sorry about the wait. Your food?"

Frankie stepped back, and Ty exhaled, accepting the bag, lifting it. "Thanks."

The bartender left, and finally alone again, whatever spell she had had him under was broken. Frankie was looking over his shoulder; he remembered that Gerald was still out there.

"What would have happened," Ty said, "is that I would have at least taken some of that German food home."

"Right, ha." She stood taller and avoided his eyes. It pained him, but it was a reminder of where he stood.

"I'd better head back home. Aria's probably counting the minutes until she gets her hands on these wings."

"Buffalo?"

"Sweet and spicy."

"Ah. Your girl's got good taste." She smiled, and he noticed that it did make it to her eyes. "And they're much better piping hot."

"I'll see you on Sunday?" He wasn't sure now whether they were still good. If he'd crossed boundaries by challenging her.

Or by allowing in thoughts of what could have been.

She nodded. "I told Liam and he's looking forward to it." And with a final goodbye, she walked away.

Leaving him with a bag full of dinner, though he lost his appetite.

The woman he hungered for was heading to someone else.

Chapter Six

Ty typed *Date with Sadie* into his phone calendar for next weekend as he heard Aria run through the hallway and then out the back door.

He groaned and popped the back kitchen window open. Aria cradled a basketball under her arm, and she was jogging to the cement half court. “Aria.”

She didn’t bother to turn and instead launched the ball toward the net. It clanged against the rim, and missed. “Yeah?”

“Phoebe’s coming to babysit next week. I have a date.”

“N-o-o-o-o,” she whined before flailing her arms.

Maybe basketball wasn’t her thing, and theater should be her focus with how dramatic she was.

He didn’t bother to answer when he closed the window.

It had to be done; he’d joined a dating app called One Date and asked out the first person he matched with. It was time to get out and about. His last date had been Frankie, and seeing her the other night with her own date was a reminder that he was heading into a rut. He deserved to have a good time, too, exhaustion aside.

Speaking of exhaustion, he dug around the freezer to see what he could make for dinner. Something that required minimal effort.

Chicken nuggets and french fries it is.

The back door slammed open just as he shut the freezer door.

"Aria, I'm not arguing right now. Phoebe's babysitting and that's that."

"But, *Da-a-ad.*"

His kid was so good at getting under his skin. But he had to stay strong. "Nope."

She appeared from around the corner. "Why can't I just go to someone's house while you're on a date?"

He peered at her. Something was different. "Why do your eyes look different?"

"Clear mascara."

"Since when?"

"Since forever. Mom says it's okay."

He shook his head; he couldn't seem to keep up. "But where would you go? Which friend?"

Her shoulders slumped. "I don't know. But Liam gets his aunt to come over, which is so much better than a stupid babysitter."

"Phoebe isn't stupid."

"I didn't say she was. I said babysitters are stupid."

He shrugged. He couldn't win. Though something she'd said sparked his interest. "Liam's aunt comes over, you say? How do you know this?"

"He told me. We FaceTimed the other night while we were playing *Minecraft* while his aunt was watching him. I even got to talk to Ms. Frankie when she got home."

"Huh. What time?"

"I don't know. Before bedtime. Why?"

"No reason," he said while biting back a smile. Aria's bedtime was 9:00 p.m. on school nights. Which meant that while Gerald made it through the entire dinner, they didn't make it an overnight.

Stop it. He was being a Neanderthal. It shouldn't matter what time she came home.

Then again, it did.

But, no, it shouldn't.

In the distance, Bubba barked, then bounded through the back door, and leapt on the couch. He perched his front paws on the windowsill.

Aria laughed. "They're here!"

Ty resisted leaping up himself and hung out in the kitchen until the doorbell rang. Aria threw open the door and kept a hand on Bubba's collar. The dog had the sense not to jump on strangers, but a hand on his collar reminded him to keep all his paws on the floor.

On the threshold, Liam and Frankie held Snowball like a football. Frankie wore leggings and a long-sleeved top under a puffy vest. Her cheeks were pink from the cold, her curly hair halfway up.

Man, she's so cute.

"Hey," he said, thinking of the other night at Nuggets, alone with her in that hallway.

"Hey." Her smile was tentative, but with the way her eyes volleyed between both dogs, it had nothing to do with their interaction. Snowball wiggled in her arms, a good sign that she was interested in being social.

"Let's have them meet. May I?" He opened his arms to Snowball, who was amenable. Ty bent forward and placed a free hand on Bubba. "Wanna meet someone new, Bubba? This is Snowball. Gentle now."

Ty was confident that Bubba would be fine during this interaction. Bubba was the gentlest dog he'd ever owned, much less come across, but the introduction needed to be done correctly nonetheless. The two dogs sniffed one another, and he didn't feel an inkling of anxiety from Snowball. So he set Snowball down.

"Aw, Snowball's tiny compared to Bubba," Liam said, sitting down on the wooden floor.

"Bubba likes puppies. He won't hurt Snowball," Aria said.

They spent a couple of minutes right there in the foyer, with the two dogs circling and sniffing one another. Then Bubba trotted toward the kitchen.

When Bubba retrieved a ball, and laid it at Snowball's feet, Ty knew that all would be well.

"Oh, thank goodness," Frankie said, smiling now. Her body took a more relaxed posture.

"Dad, can we go out back?" Aria said.

"Yep. But let's keep the dogs in here for a bit, just to make sure they get used to one another."

"Okay!"

The kids left them both in the living room, and the dogs loped through the first floor. Frankie meandered in. "Your place is…nice, and unexpected."

He laughed. "Unexpected how?"

She gestured to the framed canvas hanging on the largest wall in the living room. "You've got art."

"You don't think I'm an art kind of guy?"

"I didn't say that." She walked up to the piece and inspected it closely. "I guess I didn't know what to expect. We *are* still getting to know one another."

Ty couldn't decipher her tone. "Well, that one is called *Peaches*."

"It's very pretty."

"My mother painted it."

She looked over her shoulder at him. "No way. How awesome."

"This is one of my favorites. It didn't sell, so I begged for it."

"Must have been neat to have grown up with a painter. I imagine you had works-in-progress everywhere."

"Not just that. But paint and brushes. She had easels set up in all areas of the house." He smiled at the memory of his mom's paint-stained fingers. "But it made for a childhood that was financially unstable at times."

"Ah, the artist's wage."

"An artist and a guy who got bored easily. My dad hopped from job to job. My parents were good together, just not rich." He thought about those moments when his dad was in between jobs, when there wasn't much in the pantry.

He didn't want that for Aria, who deserved a stable lifestyle, especially without Harper around.

At the thought, he swallowed against the guilt of wanting to switch careers. That perhaps this meeting with Frankie was a waste of time after all.

He cleared his throat to move the moment forward. "But yeah, thanks for coming over to give me some advice."

She rubbed her hands together. "Lead me to where the magic happens."

"Well, the magic happens out in the work shed. The paperwork though…" He took her down the hallway and then to the formal dining room which he'd made into his office. "Voilà."

His cheeks heated at the piles of papers, old taxes, and medical records that had taken residence on the floor, stacked against the walls. Boxes were piled on the far side. A couple of plastic tubes sat here and there.

"Your desk is immaculate."

He laughed, seeing now how it stuck out like a sore thumb from the mess.

She skirted around the room. She fingered the curtains hanging from the window that overlooked the backyard. Beyond, the kids were practicing a handshake. "About the other night."

He groaned. "I feel like this is a déjà vu of the conversation we had last week."

"I think it's warranted. Don't you?"

"Okay then…" Arms outstretched, he made a come-hither signal with his hands. "Tell me what I did wrong."

She faux gasped. "I take offense to that."

"When do you *not* take offense."

"Maybe people offend me all the time, and it's their issue and not mine."

"That's fair," he said. "And I'm sure ninety-nine percent of the time, it's warranted. But there's that one percent when maybe taking offense is a bridge too far."

She frowned and crossed her arms. The fact that she didn't answer was a big enough win to him. Then she said, "I wasn't going to berate you just now. I was going to say thank you."

He shoved his hands in his pockets, properly taken aback. "This isn't a trick?"

"No. It's not. You were right. That date was…not going well."

Frowning, he scoured her face. "Nothing bad happened?"

"No!" She stood straighter. "Nothing like that. But I was giving him a lot of leeway. I was…pretending."

"Why?"

"I don't know. I guess I wanted to feel what it was like to be able to advance to a second date."

He snorted. He couldn't believe what he was hearing.

"Seriously. I've been on a lot of first dates, all by my choice. I didn't think I was ready for a second date, and none felt good enough to do that with."

"Oh, I know. I still have scars from ours."

"Ha."

"You laugh as if I'm joking, but…" He sat in his office chair. "Go on."

"That night, I took on a different persona, I guess. As an experiment. And the date was going well. I think it would have progressed to a second date. But then you interrupted." She shrugged. "It's fine, though. I got home in time to watch some reality TV and eat actual good food from my own kitchen. And I slept in my big, comfortable bed, diagonally."

The idea of Frankie not returning to her own bed, of her sleeping diagonally on someone else's bed, soured Ty's belly.

"I don't want to talk about it anymore, but to say thanks," she said.

"You're welcome."

Frankie rounded his desk and took his side. "Let's get to work. Can you show me your business plan?"

"Yep." He forced his mind to turn the page. "Wait, let me get a chair for you."

She was already moving toward the door. "I'll grab it."

"Nope. You sit here." He hustled out of the office, into the kitchen, and snatched a chair. He slowed as he entered the office, watching Frankie as she looked at the frames lined up against the walls, waiting for their turn to be hung. She lingered at one he knew like the back of his hand—his family photo with Harper and Aria.

She did a double take as she saw him. "Oh, sorry! I couldn't help but look."

"It's fine." He cleared away the things in his path and set the chairs together.

"Aria was such a cute baby."

"She fussed that entire time during the sitting. We were lucky to have that one shot out of dozens. I felt bad for that poor photographer."

Frankie sat down as he did, and her eyes widened. "Wow, what a difference three screens make."

He grinned. "Right? When you're reading and comparing notes to labs or radiology, it's so much easier to track with three screens." He clicked on a file. "Here's my business plan."

"Do you mind?" Frankie leaned in for the mouse, and her fingers brushed against his, sending a jolt of electricity through him. She started saying something about articles of incorporation, but all he could think of was how close she was, closer than they had ever been.

He showed her the bare bones of his website, and she jumped right in and discussed her first impressions. She was professional but kind, critiqued in a way that was nonjudgmental. All the while though, his heart thumped against his chest.

Did she notice what he was feeling for her, whatever this was? Attraction, sure, but a connection that went against all logic. His mother always said to believe people when they showed you who they were. Because he'd been an overly trusting kid, he'd gotten himself into too much drama growing up, caught up in people's webs.

If he went by that advice, then Frankie was as endearing as she was frustrating.

And here she was helping him with his business and website…

"You look lost," she said, half-laughing, snapping him out of his thoughts.

"I am." *In every way, actually*, was what he wanted to add.

"Well, then, I'm glad I'm here. It looks like you're truly in the beginnings of starting up. But I can draw up a step-by-step plan for you, and we can start there. Probably much faster than it will take for you to build those bookcases."

"Right, but I'm actually going to enjoy building them."

"Then it's a good trade-off, because this is my forte. All I'm going to need is your credentials for logging in to your website, and I'll send a survey to see what kind of colors you're looking for, and we can go from there."

He felt himself sag a little from the burden that was lifted off his shoulders. He was really going to get this done. "That's it?"

She laughed. "Not entirely. There's a lot of work ahead, but you'll get there."

He leaned back and rested his linked hands behind his head. "Wow."

"Is that a good 'wow' or a bad 'wow.'"

"Good 'wow.' You don't understand. The list of things to do for this house is a mile long. And then there's work, and Aria. I was starting to think that maybe I shouldn't even try."

She sat back. "It's up to you to figure out if you *should* do it. But you definitely *can*. This is a good start."

He nodded reflexively.

"Ty, you mentioned the other day that you were scared, and it's okay to be. This is a new thing you're doing. But if this is something you love..."

"It is," he jumped in, because that was something he knew to be true. "I can't explain it, except that when I'm building something, it feels...good. It's unlike how I feel now, walking into the office, as awful as that sounds."

"I'm not judging your motivation." She smiled. "Though I *will* judge you if you don't follow through with this." She gestured to the computer screen.

"All right, then." He heaved a breath, steeling himself.

"So start here." She highlighted a couple of the bullet points. "Got it?"

"Got it." He nodded, and though still processing, what he felt was hope. "Thank you."

"You're welcome." After holding his gaze for a moment, she looked out to the living room, where the two kids had migrated. She glanced at her phone, face up on the desk. "It's probably time for us to head out. Liam, hon, start getting your things together."

A chorus of no's answered back.

If Ty was being honest, he kind of agreed with them. But he had to side with Frankie. "Aria..."

"But Dad, I just turned on a movie. Can they stay and watch with us? The dogs are sleeping."

Frankie walked toward the couch. “Oh, my gosh. How cute.”

Bubba was curled up in his extra large fluffy bed with Snowball, tucked against him, snoring.

Ty looked at Frankie, and a silent agreement passed between them.

“I’m good if you’re good with it,” he said.

And to his relief, she nodded.

Frankie felt like she was on her very first date, keenly aware of Ty’s hand, all by its lonesome, resting in between them. Ensconced in darkness except for *The Parent Trap*, the Lindsay Lohan version, playing on the television in front of them, she felt tempted to reach for it. If her hand happened to migrate next to his, would he hold it?

Then the dark blob in front of them moved, and a giggle arose, snatching her bravado away.

Liam and Aria.

Right.

She shouldn’t have been thinking about trying to make out with this guy with children in the room. She shouldn’t even have been thinking about him in a romantic manner, seeing that he was the father of one of Aria’s friends. A local father, to boot. And a father who was managing a big project for the PTA.

Where was her brain?

In the gutter, that was where, swirling in the ocean of her giddy feelings, ever since her flubbed date with Gerald. When Ty had appeared at the restaurant, it felt like a sign of some sort, and she didn’t even believe in any of that. But he’d been there, and had talked sense into her.

He’d been right. She shouldn’t have settled. She shouldn’t have to pretend.

Frankie loved living in Peak because didn’t have to make

excuses for herself. People knew what she was made of, and she didn't have to hide.

But to be reminded of her self-worth, to be validated, was a turn-on, if she was being honest.

"Want a soda?" he said now, turning toward her. He ran his hand through his hair, which had gotten floppier throughout the evening. He had that look of someone who'd just gotten out of bed, with the trace of sleepiness. And in his grey sweats and black hoodie, she felt the urge to snuggle into him.

"Frankie?"

"Oh…sure." She shook her head. "I mean, no. I can't drink caffeine this late. I won't be able to sleep."

"I've got sparkling water."

"That would be great."

"Shh…" said one of the kids in front of them.

She rolled his eyes at the same time he did, and a giggle escaped her lips.

"Mo-o-om," Liam pleaded. "This is the best part. She's about to sabotage her dad and his girlfriend."

"Okay, okay," she whispered.

Ty gestured for her to follow him, and she did so, picking up the paper plates and napkins from their dinner of chicken nuggets and french fries. His living room looked like a blanket explosion, reminding Frankie of the blanket forts Liam used to make when he was younger.

"They really made themselves comfortable," she noted, tossing the trash in the can.

"Yeah, they get along well." Ty was rummaging through the refrigerator; bottles clinked like wind chimes. As he continued, she spied the magnets on the refrigerator, where a few photos were posted. Aria as a baby, Ty holding Aria when she was a toddler. Aria with Harper.

Harper and Aria had the same heart-shaped face, though

Aria had her father's blond hair. Aria's big smile was definitely from her father.

And Harper was beautiful.

During Frankie and Ty's first date, he had alluded that she and Harper were similar, in that they were passionate and self-assured. And here the two of them were, single.

"Okay, so here's what I got for drinks. And dessert." Ty emerged from the refrigerator carrying all two sparkling water flavors, a can of whipped cream, and ice cream. His foot caught in the kitchen rug, and he tripped. "Whoa!"

"Oh, no." Frankie lunged forward, laughing, as the cans threatened to spill. She caught them before they hit the ground, but stumbled into Ty. He wrapped his arms around it all—the stuff and her.

Her laugh died in her throat, replaced by anticipation. Time stopped in his arms.

"You okay?" His cheek was against hers, his voice a rumble, breathless.

"Yeah." It was all she could conjure now, with how her body hummed at his closeness. But… "The kids."

"Right." The grip he had around her loosened. And so did the things in between them, which they both righted and set down on the counter.

Then she looked over to the TV. What once were two blobs under blankets were flat clumps of fleece.

"They're gone." She half laughed.

"Who?" Ty had turned to wash his hands.

"Our kids." But when she said "our," it took her aback. No. Not *our*. "Liam and Aria."

He wiped his hands on the kitchen towel, and he looked over. "Where'd they go? Ari—" he began, but Frankie yanked him back.

"No, wait." He settled back by her side, and it took every bit of her to take her hand off his arm. She heaved a breath, unsure what more to say, though remembering how the kids were the other day on the swing, how Liam had endeared himself to Aria. "Let's give them a few minutes to talk. They've become good friends."

"I noticed that, too," Ty said.

"And with the changes in our family. See, Reece—Liam's dad—has a serious girlfriend, and he told Liam about her. But Liam hasn't really opened up to me about it. I'm wondering if he needs a friend right now."

He smiled. "To be honest, I'm glad that Liam's around for Aria, too. Makes me feel good that she has someone to talk to, because it's certainly not me."

She heaved a breath. "One day I think this is all going to get easier. Parenting, I mean."

"You let me know when that happens so I can mark it on my calendar. In any case, I'm glad that Aria will have at least Liam to talk to at the class field trip—"

"Ah, shoot. I almost forgot about that." She pressed a palm against her forehead. It was an overnight trip to see the cherry blossoms and a few landmarks in Washington, DC. With a small class and the overabundance of volunteers, it was a mellow school trip as far as those were concerned, especially compared to the average high school DC trip.

"How can that be? Didn't you volunteer?" he asked.

"I did, of course. But with everything going on…"

Like thinking about the opposite sex.

She grinned sheepishly. "Since Aria's going, I'll make sure she's in my group."

"Thanks, but I'm volunteering, too."

"Aw, that's sweet."

"I would have said yes, anyway, but Aria insisted. Demanded, really."

"Sounds like we're going to be hanging out even more." She spotted shadows pass by the doorway and raised her eyebrows to signal Ty. "We should get going, soon. I've got an early morning."

"Dessert before you go?"

Aria stuck her head in. "Did you say dessert?"

"Yes, please!" Liam appeared from behind her.

Ty laughed.

"I guess I'm outnumbered, so yes," Frankie said.

And as she helped serve up bowls of their sweet treat, she felt what she could only describe as giddiness and comfort, despite not having a taste of ice cream.

Chapter Seven

At her office at the Spirit of the Shenandoah B & B that Tuesday, Frankie was sneaking in PTA work among fielding guest reservations and website inquiries. There was no rest for the weary, since her work at the B & B spanned both overall operations and back-end processes.

As it was, she couldn't focus on her current task of planning out summer vacation employee schedules. Her mind was caught up in the email she'd sent the day before to her PTA parents soliciting fundraising help that had gone unanswered.

She texted Vivian: People are ghosting me.

Vivian responded: ?

No one wants to take charge of the fundraising.

You only sent the email yesterday.

That was twenty-four hours ago.

No comment.

Frankie set her phone down and sighed. She had a sneaky suspicion that she was going to end up doing all the fundraising herself.

She stood, frustrated, and went to the window overlooking

the side yard, out toward the cabins that belonged to her sister, Gabby, and her mother, Eva. She shimmied the window up, and the spring air wafted in, along with the distinct smell of the Shenandoah Valley: nature, trees, wildflowers, and wet grass.

Her body relaxed. This was probably the biggest reason why she'd never thought of moving away from Peak or from the Spirit of the Shenandoah property. Nature grounded her and reminded her that she was a minuscule speck in this big world. That so many things made up the sights and the scents of her surroundings, and she was simply an observer.

From her mother's cabin came voices. Eva's front door opened and she walked out with Cruz, her fiancé. They were both in their fifties, and they'd met and gotten engaged in the last year. Witnessing them falling in love and growing together gave Frankie hope that she might find connection with another person again. Frankie's father had died in Iraq during a deployment over twenty years ago, and Eva had remained largely single ever since. Until Cruz.

Their love story could have been a movie; they'd been pen pals, but unbeknownst to one another. And they were getting married this Christmas.

"Wait. Did I turn off the oven?" Eva asked.

"Yes, and you took your curling iron with you," Cruz said.

"Wait. My blood-pressure pills—"

"I packed them. Sunscreen, too."

Cruz dragged two carry-ons while Eva slung a bag over her shoulder. They were escaping to Vegas to check out Sphere. It had taken a lot of handholding by Frankie and Gabby to convince their mother that she could take the next few days off. Weekdays weren't as hectic as the weekends, and late March brought fewer reservations.

"'Bye, you two," Frankie yelled.

Eva halted and turned her way. "Oh, my God, that startled me. Now, you know to call me if you need anything."

"Yes, Mother."

"And you *will* call me, right?"

"*If* we need to."

"Cruz," Eva pleaded. "Maybe this wasn't a good idea—"

"Nope. We're going. C'mon, we don't want to miss our flight." He gestured for Eva to follow. "Frankie, help?"

"Mom, I promise to call if anything happens. But there's me and Gabby, and, of course, Jared and Matilda," Frankie said of her half brother and his wife. "Among the four of us, we'll figure it out. Promise. Love you. Now, go!"

"Love you." Reluctantly, Eva trailed after Cruz. Soon, what was left was silence.

That is, except for the sound of her email notification, and specifically her PTA inbox. Heart leaping with hope, she charged back to her seat.

It was a response to her call for fundraising help.

Yes.

The sender: Ty.

Frankie,
Though I've never solicited for donations before, I'm happy to help.
Ty

Frankie bit the inside of her cheek, thinking of the last time they saw each other, on Sunday night. By the time she and Liam had returned home, it was almost nine in the evening. Ty'd continued to bring out desserts and snacks, and the kids would go off and play or find something to watch. They'd discussed the budget for the library bookcases, and he'd drawn up a sketch of the project. Then somehow, she and Ty made it to the backyard, where he'd shown her the additional dwelling unit that he planned to use for guests.

Coming home had been anticlimactic. Her cabin was too

quiet. So much so, that she listened to podcasts the rest of the night, and she'd fallen asleep with the TV on.

Was more time with Ty wise? She didn't know, except that she needed help and he was willing to give it. She pressed Reply and wrote:

Ty,
Don't you worry, I'll show you the ropes.
Frankie

Seconds after she sent the email, her phone rang. She smiled at the caller ID and answered. "Mr. Golden?"

"I thought it would be easier to call instead." Enthusiasm laced his tone, and she found herself warm from it.

"You're not busy with the town's dearest four-legged friends?"

"Oh, the clinic's packed. But I can always make time for our PTA president."

"Ha-ha."

He laughed and the sound of it heightened her mood. "Seriously, though, are you really down to help?"

"Yes, Frankie, I am." She could hear his smile through the phone. "Text when you're planning to head out to canvas, and if I'm free I'll come with."

"Thank you. Do you know that you're the only person who wrote me back?"

"Really? Sorry about that."

"Not your fault. It's nobody's fault, really. We're all volunteers," she said.

"Yeah, well, you might not like what I'm about to admit."

"What's that?"

"I had a few people contact me about working on the bookcases."

She sighed.

"Are you mad?" he asked.

"Nope." She leaned back against her office chair, which tipped slightly. Eyes to the ceiling, she visually traced the outline of the ceiling fan. "Your project is way more fun."

"I don't disagree. We're picking up the wood tomorrow after work."

"That's awesome. Now, speaking of projects," she said, thinking of the past Sunday. "My inbox has yet to receive your website wish list."

"I'll get to it." His voice faded.

"Uh-huh," she teased. "And you should set up your social media and use this project to promote your work."

"You know this phone call wasn't supposed to be about me," he retorted.

"This is what you get for asking for my help. Because I *will* follow through."

"Yeah, yeah…" His voice trailed off and there was silence for a beat. "I've got to run."

"Okay. And hey, Ty. Thanks again."

"Anytime."

The call ended, leaving Frankie to look off into space, feeling just as calm as she did when she looked out her office window.

Then a knock sounded at her door, and Jared stepped in. Her brother was in a B & B-branded apron. "We've got someone here who's trying to check in, but it looks like they were double-booked. Matilda needs backup."

"Got it." Frankie stood and gathered herself, straightening her shoulders. No rest for the weary indeed.

"You should just come with me." Ty looked down at his watch as he stepped into his sneakers. He was supposed to be at Skyline Drive Superstore already to meet Desmond, one of the PTA dads, to pick up the lumber. But the clinic had been packed for the second day in a row, and his last patient, a sweet Ragdoll kitten in for his first exam, had run long. He'd arrived seconds early before Aria got off the bus, and she was picking today to put her foot down about staying at home.

"But I have homework. And I'm eleven."

"Right, still too young to stay at home by yourself. Mrs. Grayson's not home to peek in on you and—"

"I looked it up, and in Virginia there's no rule about who's too young. You said that you stayed home by yourself when you were in the third grade."

"That was in the late nineties and we did things differently then."

"Dad. You'll be gone an hour. And Bubba's with me. Please." She pressed her hands together in prayer. "Ple-e-as-s-s-se."

Time was of the essence, and it seemed that Aria knew this. He huffed. "Fine. Keep your phone with you. If I call or text, you answer, got it?"

"Got it." She all but pushed him out the door. Ty staggered over the threshold and the door closed behind him followed by the clunk of the deadbolt.

He turned to face the door and opened his mouth to say something.

"I'll be fine!" she screamed from the other side.

Finally, Ty forced himself off the porch and in a few minutes drove into the parking lot of Skyline Drive Superstore towing a small trailer at ten past five.

As he pulled up the emergency brake on his SUV, a call came through the Bluetooth. He checked the caller ID and answered. "Hey, Desmond."

"Dr. Ty, hey. Shoot, I'm sorry to have to do this at the last minute, but I can't make it. Sully's sick," he said of his son, with remorse in his voice.

"Oh, crap. I'm sorry. Don't you worry. This is just stuff."

Ty meant every word, but he leaned back against the headrest. He was looking forward to checking this off his list. The school remained open until six thirty every day after school, and this would have been the perfect day to transport the lumber there. As it was, he could only use his portable woodcutter from two thirty in the afternoon onward, so as not to disrupt the students.

Logistically, this project was starting to get more complicated.

"Thanks," Desmond said.

"Hope Sully feels better soon."

After they hung up, Ty scrolled through his emails to track down the parents who expressed interest in working on the bookshelves. The lumber wasn't so much heavy as it was cumbersome, and he needed another pair of hands.

He went down the list of four names and send them a group text: Anyone free before six tonight to load lumber into my trailer and take it to the school?

His phone pinged as he received responses.

Aw, dang, I'm still at work.

Sorry, baseball practice.

I can do 7:30.

We're playing hooky, out of town!

He inhaled and wished for patience and scoured his brain for someone who could help him last-minute.

Or someone who knew everyone in town.

Frankie.

It was always Frankie on his mind these days. It was as if their worlds had been intrinsically intertwined. Spending

Sunday with her had felt so natural that he'd missed her when she and Liam had walked out the door.

"Wow." Frankie answered on the first ring and without preamble. "That's two phone calls in two days."

"I didn't want you to miss me."

"You don't give me a chance to."

"Ha." He could hear Snowball barking in the background. "I don't want to take too much of your time, but I was wondering if you could help me out."

"What's up? Is it Aria?"

"No. Though she did convince me to leave her at home by herself for a couple of hours."

"Ah, no way. I'm not ready for that yet."

"Same. It's like she's the one pushing me out of the nest. Anyway." A car turned into the space in front of him, the lights blinding him for a beat. "I'm here at Skyline Drive Superstore to pick up lumber. Desmond was supposed to meet me, but he can't make it. I texted the other parents who volunteered to help, but no one's available. Do you know anyone who—"

"Yep, I know just the person. And he just so happens to be in my house."

"Who?" Curiosity piqued. She'd said *he*.

Not your business.

"Chip. My sister's boyfriend."

"I know Chip!"

"He brought over Lucky, Snowball's mom. I'll send him by."

"Oh, wow. Thanks. I'm parked in the right-side parking lot, next to the pick-up dock."

"I'll let him know, and hang tight."

He hung up. That was…painless, and impressive. He heaved a sigh of relief that he would get this done tonight. He texted Aria: Doing okay at home?

The response dots appeared quickly. Yep

It was a dry response, but good enough. No notifications from his security camera, so everything should be fine.

Ty scrolled on his phone until a dark-blue 4x4 truck rolled up next to him, but to his surprise, it wasn't Chip that hopped out of the driver's seat, but Frankie. He met her at the hood of his car. "What are you doing here?"

"Chip and Gabby had something they needed to get done, so they're watching Liam and the dogs. I took Chip's truck."

"But it's lumber."

"And I have gloves." She whipped them out from her back pocket.

"Are you sure? This stuff is heavy."

She slapped the gloves gently against his chest. "You're not going to get all 'you can't do it because you're a girl,' are you?"

"No. But…" He wasn't sure how to say it. Frankie seemed…

"Blurt it out."

"You don't seem the type to get your hands dirty."

She shook her head dramatically. "Yet another thing to learn about me. I started and maintain the B and B garden. I get plenty dirty."

"Okay then, I'll drive the trailer to the dock and load up. Then we'll head to the school, and move it all into the classroom."

"Easy peasy." She smiled.

The process was indeed just that. In under an hour, Ty was securing his trailer at the elementary school parking lot, the classroom now stocked with lumber and equipment for the project. Next to him, Frankie patted her jeans of dust and debris.

"Thanks for helping out," Ty said.

Her face was damp and flushed. Her hair, which had started out in a high bun, was lower now, and wisps of hair stuck to her cheeks.

"As Liam would say 'light work, light work.'"

"Aria says that, too."

They both laughed, and she wiped a hand against her forehead, leaving behind a trail of dust.

Ty, without thinking, reached up and ran a thumb over it, only to halt after realizing his faux pas. He pulled his hand back. "Sorry. There was dust."

Her eyes were on him. "It's fine. I… I'm jumping in the shower when I get home, anyway."

An image of Frankie in the shower flashed in his head. Of slick skin, suds, and his hands on her. "That's nice." He shook his head, wondering where those thoughts came from. "I should go."

Frowning, she said, "Keep me posted about the project."

"Absolutely. Thanks, Frankie." Then, he hopped into his SUV and blew out a breath.

It was he who needed a cold shower.

Chapter Eight

By Friday, Ty's schedule hadn't let up, and his shower before his date with Sadie was lukewarm.

"Damn." He rinsed off quickly and turned the water off. He was going to have to get that looked at.

He threw on his clothes, then headed back to the bathroom to put gel in his hair, when his darling daughter knocked on his door. "Dad?"

"Come in," he said, already bracing himself for the next onslaught of demands. Honestly, if Aria didn't go to law school he would be surprised. Everything was a negotiation.

Then again, it was better than how their relationship had been when they'd first moved. So he smiled when Aria appeared in the reflection of his bathroom mirror.

"What's up?" He slathered gel in his hands and ran it through his hair.

"Who are you going out with again?"

She was playing coy.

"I've said so already. Her name is Sadie Brown. She's a teacher in Luray, and she seems very nice."

"Where are you going?"

"Sweetheart, I already told you. Mountain Rush, in town. I left you the number of the bar on the kitchen counter, just as you requested."

She smiled. "Okay."

"Why's that?" He peered at her through the mirror, and turned, leaning against the sink.

"No reason," she said.

"Aria." He raised his eyebrows for effect.

"Ugh. Fine. It's so if I get sick and tired of Phoebe I can just have you come home, since you're so close."

"It's just dinner, so I think you can stand having Phoebe around for a couple of hours."

"Maybe."

He turned her by the shoulders. "Definitely. Now, go watch TV so I can finish up."

He wasn't keen on meeting Sadie at Mountain Rush, the karaoke bar in town, for their dinner. But he'd left it up to her to pick the location, and he didn't have a good reason to say no, except that Mountain Rush was the biggest hangout on Friday nights for Peak millennials. He might run into some locals, or his patients' owners.

And Frankie.

Why did he care? He shouldn't, end of story. Had he brushed some dust off her face like some guy in a corny movie? Yes. But it had been an automatic gesture, nothing more.

His phone rang as he was sliding on his belt. A group video-chat from his friends Vince and Jeremiah. He took it, and set the phone against the dresser. Vince, originally from Ohio, was in real estate, and Jeremiah, who was a native Pennsylvanian, worked in software. They'd all lived in Ty's former apartment building and had become fast friends.

They were both grinning. Cheesing, more like it.

"Talk fast." He'd texted them earlier about his date tonight, and they blew up the group chat with emojis.

It was embarrassing.

Vince was single and had no thoughts of settling down. He was a magnet for women and was rarely alone on weekends.

Jeremiah had a long-distance boyfriend of two years and was a homebody, to boot.

That made Ty their special project.

"You know we had to call to give you some pointers," Jeremiah began. "Seeing that you messed up that last date."

"Ha. It can only go up from here," he said, though he thought about it for a moment. He and Frankie were still hanging out with one another, though for PTA and kid reasons. And it wasn't bad.

Vince laughed. "This time, don't give opinions."

"No comments about exes," Jeremiah said. "Don't even talk about the past. Keep it light."

"Talk about the weather," Vince said.

"Movies, books." Jeremiah pointed at the screen.

"Uh-huh." Ty rolled his eyes.

"Just saying." Vince grinned. "You need a win."

"The last one wasn't really a lose," Ty finally said. "Frankie and I are friends."

His friends groaned. Ty'd sent them a few texts about him and Frankie. All of which they'd dismissed.

"You're just another PTA parent. Of course, she's being nice now. You're doing grunt work." Vince shook his head. "No offense, but if you hadn't gotten involved there, she would've avoided you."

Jeremiah nodded. "Yep. PTA is not real life, man."

Ty laughed, and they followed suit. "This conversation is ridiculous. I'm gonna go. I'll update you later."

After their goodbyes, the screen went black, and when Phoebe arrived, Ty extricated himself from his home. He drove the five minutes to Mountain Rush.

The parking lot was buzzing, and the sound of someone singing clearly out of tune permeated the air. Just before he went in, he took a breath and prepared himself for the noise.

Sadie had mentioned that she would be at the bar, and would

be wearing a pink top. After being stopped three times by people he knew from the clinic, he spotted a woman wearing pink sitting on a barstool with her back to him.

With a tap on her shoulder, she turned. Blue eyes met his, along with a friendly smile. She looked just like her picture, but better.

The breath left his lungs in relief.

One never really knew how these meetups would turn out. While it had never happened to him, he knew folks who were catfished by people who fibbed on some of their physical characteristics, or lied about their whole identity.

"I'm Ty." He offered his hand.

"Sadie." Her handshake was strong. She tapped on the bar top. "Want to sit?"

"Sure. I hope you weren't waiting long?"

"What?" She craned her ear toward him.

"Hope you weren't waiting long!" he repeated.

Except that was the moment the current karaoke singer tried to hit Whitney's high note in the *The Bodyguard* soundtrack song, "I Will Always Love You."

"Yeah, I know. I love this song, too!" she yelled back.

He laughed and so did she. She hiked a thumb over her shoulder, motioning to a corner table in the back. Nodding, he got up and followed her, and sank into the leather booth.

Though it was like being on the nonsmoking part of a sidewalk: they hadn't really escaped the noise.

"This is sort of better," Sadie half laughed. "Though I'm impressed by her bravado. And with that song?"

His back was to the stage, and he was thankful that he wasn't watching the singer for fear of secondhand embarrassment. "She's a brave soul. I'd need a couple of drinks in me to get up on stage." He raised his hand as a server passed. "Speaking of. Hungry?"

"Starving," she said.

"Well, hey there." Chip appeared by their table, wearing a black apron and carrying a round tray.

"Chip. You work here?"

"Yep. Part-time." He glanced at Sadie.

"Oh, Chip, this is Sadie."

"Nice to meet you," Chip said. "What do you both feel like having?"

They both picked a couple of things to share from the menu. Sadie asked for a cocktail, and Ty opted for a beer.

"Great. I'll get those drinks to you shortly."

They were left alone, and during the brief interlude when no one was singing, Ty asked Sadie some questions and she did the same of him. She was friendly enough. Polite, too. She'd lived for two decades in southern Virginia, though she was originally from West Virginia. Their drinks came and they chatted about his move to the area, and how it compared to Philly.

Then came food and more conversation, but as the minutes passed, it became perfectly clear that there was nothing happening between them. They could have been talking about photosynthesis, the lunar landing, the congested traffic on I-95, and he wouldn't have been able to tell the difference.

The sound of the same woman from earlier screeching her next song, this time "I Will Survive," was a relief from the awkwardness of the date. At least they could laugh in between stuffing their faces.

"Oh, my God, I know her." Sadie's face lit up. She jutted a chin. "The singer. Took me forever to figure out."

He turned, though a group of people passed by, hindering his view. "Oh?"

"I'm the PTA advisor for my school. And she's in the PTA at Peak and—"

Ty didn't need to hear more because the bodies parted, revealing that the singer was indeed Francesca Espiritu.

* * *

Frankie bowed after "I Will Survive," a deep one where she imagined that the crowd was full of royals. Clapping rose from the audience and she stepped off the stage and away from the white lights.

She stumbled into someone's strong arms. Not Gabby's, that was for sure.

"I had no idea you had such a set of lungs on you," the voice connected to the arms holding her said. Her body tingled with desire.

There was only one person who did that to her these days, even if it was highly inconvenient. She looked up to see Ty, who was sporting a grin. He wore black on black and he looked good enough to eat.

Then, she groaned. She hadn't expected him to be here. Why had she agreed to come out with Gabby? "N-o-o-o-o! Did you hear that?"

"I sure did. Watch out, *The Voice*. Or maybe *The Masked Singer*?"

"Shut up." She settled on her feet and jokingly pushed him away, though she kept one hand on him. Partly because she was a little woozy, but mostly because she wanted to keep touching him. "What are you doing here?"

"I'm here on a date."

"You are?" Her eyes widened, then they narrowed down to slits. "Who is it?"

"A woman who knows you, apparently."

"Interesting." Frankie straightened herself and her clothing. She had to meet this woman. And then, she realized. "She heard me, too?"

"Don't know how to break it to you, Frankie, but this whole place heard you. And probably half of Peak."

The idea that her voice projected through Mountain Rush's walls made her bust out in laughter. "Oh, no."

"Oh, yes." He was laughing now, too.

"You better tell me that I sang like an angel."

"You sang like an angel."

"You're lying!" She was tearing up. Next time she was going to stop at two drinks. How many had she had?

"You okay? Want some water?" Ty guided her gently by the elbow.

"There's my table! There's Gabby. Gabby!" She raised a hand toward her sister, who was talking to a woman. Frankie couldn't recall her name, but knew she was PTA-related.

The two women walked toward them.

"That's the person who knows you," Ty said.

"That's your date?" She eyed the woman. "She's pretty."

"I think so, too," Ty said.

Those felt like fighting words, but Frankie kept it cool. She was just being her protective self, as she was around her entire family.

Frankie wasn't jealous.

Nope.

"Dr. Ty, do you remember me?" Gabby said. "I'm Six's mom."

Ty nodded. "I'm starting to figure out how everyone connects together, and that the whole town's here on Friday nights."

"And you are?" Frankie asked the woman next to Gabby. The woman on a date with Ty.

Ty, who'd brushed the dirt off her face a couple of days ago.

Yes, she'd continued to think about that moment. Had it been an innocent gesture?

It wasn't something people did to Frankie just willy-nilly. People knew to keep their distance. For him to cross into her bubble, and for her to like it, and want more of it…

What was this woman doing here?

"I'm Sadie," the woman said. "I work at Luray Elementary

School. I was at the regional PTA conference and you were there, too. We met over drinks."

Frankie scoured her brain and shook her head. "You know, my brain is drowning in mojitos. But it's nice to meet you again."

"Right, well." Sadie glanced down at Frankie's hand. It was only then that Frankie realized that it had migrated to Ty's elbow, which she had in her grasp. "I'd better get going. Ty, it was good to meet you. Um…"

"Let me walk you out." Ty gently peeled off Frankie's hand. "Text you later, Frankie."

"Such a gentleman," Frankie mused as Ty walked away. "Always a nice guy."

Gabby laughed. "What is up with you and your vise grip on Dr. Ty?"

"It wasn't a vise grip."

"If it was on bare skin you would have left marks. And you just swooned."

Frankie scoffed. "I don't swoon."

"If you say so. C'mon, let's get some water into you." Gabby took her sister's hand and led her to the bar. Chip handed Gabby a bottled water without being asked.

The act made Frankie's heart ache.

"That's so damn cute."

"What?" They were headed back to their table.

"Chip just knew."

"Knew what?"

"You're so used to it, that you can't even tell." She groaned out of frustration, out of envy. And out of confusion, because she really didn't know what she wanted. What was clear, though, was that she was lonely. Especially tonight.

Gabby laughed. "What the hell was that? No more mojitos for you. Drink your water, Ate Frankie."

Frankie did what she was told, slightly refocused after

Gabby addressed her in the honorific of big sister, and gulped the rest of the bottle.

"I'll get you some more. Don't go anywhere, promise?"

"Promise." Because she was going to sit by her lonesome, as lonely people did.

Then, she took out her phone and clicked on the One Date app. A notification of a new match appeared. When she tapped on it, a guy's photo filled the screen.

A stranger's photo. A stranger who was not Ty.

She growled and set the phone face down on the table, then pressed the water bottle to her face.

She wasn't lonely enough for that.

Chapter Nine

Waiting next to the rumbling bus at the elementary school parking lot, Frankie stood with the other parent volunteers with a tea latte in her hand. They were huddled in a circle, the chill air still pervasive for the last Friday in March, and they shuffled from side to side to keep their bodies moving.

And though she was tired from her 5:00 a.m. wakeup so she could get her and Liam here on time, she was wired. Because Ty and Aria were still missing.

Vivian, on the other hand, was a chatterbox next to her. She must have had a shot of espresso before she left for the school. "So I'm looking at this summer camp for Ian for tennis, since that's what he loves, but it's got everything else, too… You know, swimming, hiking, et cetera. But I'm not sure about letting him go for a week." She lowered her voice, eyes scanning for her son in the crowd of kids milling about in the open space. "Plus, you know how he gets homesick. He doesn't even like going on sleepovers."

"Can't you choose a day camp instead?" Frankie asked, though her eyes darted everywhere, in search of Ty.

"That was my first choice, but he's obsessed with the coach in the sleepaway camp. As soon as he found out that that coach was going to be there, he all but begged to go."

"Hmm." She looked down at her phone, in case Ty had

texted, but there were no notifications. "Then it sounds like he might do better than you think."

Another parent chimed in with a suggestion, and another gave their opinion, and soon Frankie's mind wandered. She clicked on her and Ty's text thread. In it, he'd acknowledged that he knew what time to be at the field trip meet-up spot.

Since running into him at Mountain Rush and seeing him with his date, her curiosity had gone into overdrive. How often did he date? How did his last date go? He'd been private about it, so what did that mean?

"God, that camp is so expensive, too. And it's a week long. Shoot. Maybe it's me that's having separation anxiety," Vivian said. Then, after a beat, she asked, "Frankie?"

Frankie looked up from the screen and bared her teeth in a smile. "Yep."

"What do you think?"

"About what?" She glanced at the other parents, who seemed to be in agreement with whatever Vivian had proposed.

"That we should send all of our kids to the same camp. We can get a group rate, the kids'll know one other, and maybe they can even bunk together."

Frankie was momentarily stumped. She wasn't thinking as far as summer. Heck, would she survive the final fundraiser and fifth-grade graduation?

She swallowed the ball of nerves that had formed in her throat.

But in that group of parents, she couldn't not agree. "I think it's a great idea. I'll have to look into it, make sure we're not on vacation at that time."

"Great!" Vivian hopped once. "I'll keep everyone looped in. It should be fun."

"All righty, parent volunteers." Mrs. Caldwell, one of the fifth-grade teachers, stepped into the group formation. "We're about to take attendance and break the kids into groups. Can you all disperse a bit so the kids can get to know who their parent guide is?"

The parents agreed and Frankie walked in the same direction as the others.

"You seem distracted." Vivian clucked. "Does it have anything to do with the man who's been at the school toiling away to build bookcases, sometimes with shirts that are see-through?"

"What the—"

She raised a hand to cut her off. "I haven't witnessed it, but our dear friend Olivia has. And yet, all he does is talk about you."

Frankie looked off in the distance and feigned nonchalance. The more she avoided the bait, the better. "If you mean Ty then yes, I'm looking for him. He's volunteering for this field trip too, and he knew what time to get here."

"How do you know that?"

"He told me he was volunteering when Liam and I were over at his place, and we texted about the meet-up time last night," she said before realizing what she'd walked into.

Frankie internally groaned. Her honesty sometimes *did* get the best of her.

Viv shoved her gently and kept a hand on her forearm. "Did you say, texting at *night*? And over at *his place*?"

Frankie looked around at the other parents, who were all nosy in their own right. She lowered her voice. "It's no big deal. Liam and I went over to his place so our dogs could meet."

"*Sure*. The dogs."

"It's the truth."

"And?"

"And we talked."

Vivian peered at her. "Has anything happened?"

"No. Nothing." Though a part of her wished something had happened in the several small moments that could have meant more. The flirtation, their vulnerable conversations.

The problem was, she had once allowed another guy into her life, and he'd broken her heart.

"Just call him already," Viv said, looking at her watch. "Especially since we're supposed to leave in ten minutes."

The permission was enough. She dialed up Ty, and the phone rang just as a familiar SUV sped into the school parking lot. The doors flew open, and Ty and Aria jumped out.

"Speak of the devil," Vivian said.

By the time the two walked up with their luggage in tow, Mrs. Caldwell had gathered the kids together and told them the bus rules. As she did so, Ty turned in their luggage to the bus driver. The only other dad volunteer, Lance, sidled up to him.

When Ty's eyes met hers, he grinned.

Her heart flipped, the traitor.

The kids were divided into groups, and Frankie was assigned five, with Liam being one of them. They all made their introductions, and she handed each of them a Post-it with her phone number to place in their pockets. Then, after the kids loaded up, she made her way toward the back of the bus.

As she passed Ty's row, he tugged on her shirt. He gestured to the row in front of his. "Keep the new guy company?"

She noted that his tone wasn't his usual happy-go-lucky. She smiled. "I guess I can do that."

Frankie pulled her laptop from her bag and slipped the rest of her things under the seat in front of her.

"Don't tell me you brought work," he said.

Without looking at him, she logged in to her computer, and said, "Websites don't run themselves. Speaking of..."

"I know, I know. I owe you my website wish list."

The bus started and Mrs. Caldwell stood. "Now, everyone, please stay in your seats unless you have to go to the restroom."

A chorus of voices answered, "Yes, Mrs. Caldwell."

The bus made its way through the parking lot and then toward town, and after a few more minutes, the noise level simmered down. Frankie guessed that at least half the students and parents had fallen asleep.

"These next two days are going to be a vacation for me. I plan to do nothing else but take in the sights and make sure I haven't lost a kid. Not home improvement. Not work. Not bookshelves," Ty said from behind her.

She turned her head and spoke to the space in between the seats. "You almost didn't make it."

Though she could only see a slice of his face, she knew that he was smiling. "You noticed?"

"I didn't want Aria to miss the field trip."

"Ah, Aria, of course." His tone dipped. "It was a rough morning. I could barely get her off FaceTime with her mom."

She nodded, understanding the relief he had that his daughter and wife had a tight relationship, as well as the frustration that their appearance or disappearance could cause such havoc. "She must miss her."

"A lot. Sometimes, I'm not sure how to make it better, besides convincing Harper to move back."

"You never did mention what she did for work."

"She's a baker."

Then, silence. Ty didn't offer any more information, though Frankie's curiosity was at a ten. Not once had she heard him say a disparaging word about his ex. She leaned back in her seat, anticipating that he had more to say, and turned her face to look out the window.

"Sometimes, though," he continued, his voice softer. He'd leaned in so it was like a confessional, so only she could hear. "I think what Aria really wants is for us to get back together."

The mention took Frankie aback but she kept her eyes on the horizon. They had just passed downtown and were a few blocks from the entrance to the freeway. "Is that a possibility in the future?"

He half laughed. "No. Not at all. But sometimes, I wonder if it would be easier. If somehow there was a way that Harper and I could live amicably, and be friends, and raise Aria together."

"How long ago did you split up?"

"It's been about eighteen months."

"Wow." Something inside her withered. Eighteen months was recent, in her eyes. She and Reece had been apart for four years, and they still had issues.

At eighteen months, she'd still missed Reece.

It tracked what he was feeling. It tracked that he still had their family picture in his office. She couldn't blame him for it at all, but somehow, it placed whatever was growing between them in perspective.

They could only be friends.

"When does she come back from…work? You've been so vague." She laughed. The guy couldn't lie if he wanted to. "I can tell there's more."

He inhaled. "I'm sworn to secrecy. Harper signed an NDA."

"That serious?"

"Yes."

"And Aria knows?"

"Aria thinks she's working in a restaurant in London, and that it's an important job."

"Well, you don't have to say anything if you're not comfortable." She crossed her heart. "But I promise I won't say. You can trust me."

He nodded. "I do trust you."

She beamed. For all of her faults, Frankie considered herself to be a good person, and a good friend.

"Harper's a contestant in *Amateur Stars Baking Show*."

She thought she was hearing things, so she turned. She whispered between their seats. "The official one? The one where they go in that big tent? The one that's hosted by celebrity bakers?"

"That very one. It's been her dream to get on from the very first season, and finally, she's in. Though neither one of us thought about how stressful and isolating it would be for her, and how much Aria would miss her."

"Though you said it was her dream."

He nodded. "Enough to leave her kid behind for now."

Frankie felt empathy for their whole family. "I'm sorry, I take it back."

"Take what back?"

"That I didn't want to be compared to her. I see what you mean. She *is* passionate."

"I didn't want to stand in her way, even if I didn't agree with her choice. If Aria had come to me with the same dream, I would have done everything to support it."

"You're a good guy, Ty."

"Thanks, though sometimes I think that maybe I'm just a little too soft."

"Not soft. Kind."

"If you say so. I'm gonna take a nap. Too much has happened already and it's only seven in the morning."

"You do that." She laughed, turning back to her laptop. Though as she tinkered with the website code, she couldn't focus.

With each day she spent with Ty, Frankie continued to peel back the layers of his life. He continued to rise above all of her assumptions, disproving her first impression of him.

She'd been wrong, and because of her quick temper, she'd lost out in not only going on a second date, but also in the possibility of something even deeper and more meaningful.

* * *

Ty's win for the day: he didn't lose a kid. Though, he'd caught one trying to climb one of the cherry trees at the Tidal Basin. And he'd halted the start of a food fight between three of his assigned students before it turned into a full-on war while the class had a picnic on the National Mall.

But he'd started with five kids, and ended with five kids.

By the time they all entered the lobby of the Smithsonian National Museum of Natural History and were face-to-face with the famous T. rex skull, he was exhausted. And it was only three in the afternoon.

It had everything to do with the phone call he'd had in the morning with his ex, before he'd handed the phone over to Aria. Harper hadn't been in a good mood; she'd been rated one of the lowest contestants in the most recent challenge. Her feelings were valid—he would have been upset, too. But he and Aria had had to leave for the field trip, and Harper had kept Aria on the phone for too long.

He should have stepped in to end their conversation. Instead, he chose to wait, well after their house sitter arrived to take Bubba for a walk, and they'd almost missed the load time for the bus.

It wasn't a big deal in hindsight. No harm, no foul. But this happened all the time. Ty couldn't say no to Harper. He always allowed Harper to push the envelope, and it had been that way when they were married, too.

Harper wasn't a bad person, but Ty was a people pleaser.

Together, it made for a combination where he ended up frustrated. Which he was now. So much so that he was in a fog, his focus only on counting the five heads he was in charge of. As they wound through the first floor of the museum, passing the mammals and dinosaurs, and then the second floor, through the live butterfly pavilion, the scenes passed by in a kind of blur.

"You doing okay?" Lance, another fifth-grade parent, sidled up next to him. In his arms were a bundle of coats. As the only two dads on the field trip, they'd kept their groups close to one another during the day.

"Yeah. Just dragging." Ty kept his eyes trained to his assigned kids, now gawking over the mummies exhibit. He silently thanked whoever invented protective cases, especially with how close they were.

"Same here. This your first field trip?" Lance asked.

"Yep. How'd you know?"

"I could just tell. When you count your kids, you mouth out the numbers."

Ty cackled.

"That's okay. You'll get used to it. I stay at home with my four kids, so I'm automatically counting heads."

Ty had never met a stay-at-home dad. "Four kids. Wow."

"I know. And yes, I know how that happens." Looking up, he said, "Mason…no, sir, you may not climb that."

Up ahead, his son retracted his hands from the edge of a stand-alone display. He stuffed his hands in his pockets with a frown.

"That was close," Ty said.

"Mason's a sensory kind of kid. He loves textures, loves to look at things in different ways. Loves to get physical. He's curious and it's a great quality, but it makes for eagle eyes. Noelle, that's my wife, she's the same way."

"What does she do?"

"She works for the National Park Service. Wildlife management."

"Ah, cool."

"Yeah, I think so, too. We used to work together, but she loved the job more than I did, so it was best that I stay home until the kids were a little older. It was a challenge at first, with the switch in roles, but I'm good now. Change is hard, though."

"It's just me and Aria now, so don't I know it. We've been here months and I'm not close to being unpacked."

"I bet. Though at some point you're just gonna have to cut your losses and store the rest."

"You might be right."

"Hey, do you play poker?"

"I'm not really a cards kind of guy," Ty said.

"Well, I play with a few guys, just for fun. We try to meet up once every couple of months. No serious bets. But one of our guys just moved. You should come."

"Yeah?"

"We all have kids in the school. It'll be good company. Snacks. Beer. Or water, if you don't drink."

"I'll think about it. Thanks." Ty smiled, feeling himself perk up.

"I have your number on the class roster. When we get done tomorrow, I'll give you the info."

A tug on his arm drew his attention. Aria. "Dad, I need to use the bathroom."

Ty checked his watch. "Can you wait until we get to our break time?" They were in the middle of exhibits and the other students showed no signs of stopping.

She crossed her legs, wincing. "No. I need to go now."

"You should take her," Lance said, then said in a louder voice. "Groups three and four, give me your eyes, please." The children around them turned. "Mr. Ty's going to take Aria to the restroom. We're going to keep walking, but you all need to stay around me. Got it?"

A chorus of agreement came from the kids.

"Whoa, you're really good at that, Lance."

He shrugged. "I'm a veteran, what can I say? But you go on. We won't get too far ahead."

Aria took his hand and pulled him.

"You must really want to go," Ty said.

"So bad," she groaned.

The nearest restroom was temporarily closed for maintenance, so down to the first floor they went. Once there, Aria barged into the women's restroom. Ty leaned against a wall and pulled his phone out to check his notifications.

"Oooh, you know you're not supposed to be on your phone," a woman's voice said. A voice that these days calmed his insides.

He looked up to see Frankie and his heart leapt. He stood from the wall. "If they get a bathroom break, then I get a phone break." And because there wasn't anyone else in her group around, he said, "Is your group on bathroom break?"

"Nope. Is yours?"

"No, and we're actually on the third floor."

Her head tilted, mirroring his own curiosity. "Interesting."

"What do you think they're up to?" he mused.

Then, it came together: running into Frankie on her date. Frankie at his date with Sade. Ty gasped.

Her eyes widened as if reading his thoughts. "Holy mother of—"

"Matchmakers," he finished.

"That's why they kept disappearing that Sunday," she said.

"And why they insisted on getting the dogs together."

They both looked toward the bathroom hallway, which was still empty.

Frankie covered her mouth with a hand.

"What do we do?" Ty laughed, though quietly. "I'm both embarrassed but also impressed at their ingenuity."

"Same. To be honest, I'm stumped." She bit her bottom lip, and Ty tore his eyes away to keep from staring. "Maybe we shouldn't say anything. It's harmless, right?"

Harmless wasn't exactly what he would call it. More like ironic since he and Frankie did *try* to be together. "Right."

"Once they figure out that we're just friends, they'll give up."

Ouch. He felt that one in the ribs. "Exactly."

Worry splashed across her features. "Everything okay? Tough time with the kids?"

"No. Not that." Except he wasn't sure how to explain his unease. Of not only this mild rejection, but today's pervasive undercurrent of blah. "It's nothing."

"Sure?"

"Yeah. Anyway, no one likes a complainer."

She took his side and leaned back against the wall, too. "That depends if there's something real to complain about. Complaining for complaining's sake doesn't really have a purpose, but if you've got something to get off your chest, then you should."

He tried to triangulate the thing he was feeling. "I'm… bothered." He ran his hands though his hair. "I'm sorry. Sometimes dealing with Harper does this to me. I doubt myself. I question my motives. I wonder if I'm doing anything right."

"I know exactly what you're saying. When I talk to Reece… it could be an innocuous sentence and I'm left to mull it over for all of its hidden meanings. He could say that the sky's blue but I overthink why it's really more purple." She nudged her elbow against his. "I think our brains still like to grapple with the fact that what you thought was true wasn't. It's like you broke your own trust by completely misreading that whole relationship. But it gets better, you know? And then, hopefully, whenever you see and talk to her, it won't be such a mind game."

He took her words in and sank in relief that it wasn't just him who felt so destabilized. "So what do I do until then?"

"I don't know. I think that's the grief part of it all."

Grief.

He hadn't thought about it that way before. He associated grief with death and actual loss. With his patients who took their last breaths. With the owners—with family members, really—who held their pets in the last seconds of their lives. With the transition of having a pet, to not having one any longer.

Not this ever-complicated back-and-forth, of one second acknowledging that he no longer had the same relationship as he'd once had, and the next, having a lighthearted phone conversation.

"What it is, is damn confusing. How they're still in your life but not, and how I'll never be free of the past," he said.

"Do you want to be?"

He looked up at the ceiling, a crisscross of bars and lights. "No. That would make it tough for Aria, and I don't want that."

"Same here. About Liam, that is. The other day I wanted to throw Reece out by the scruff of his neck, but he's such a good dad to Liam." She blew out a breath. "If Liam grew up to be like his father, it would be a good thing."

"This sucks," he groaned, though admitting it felt like taking ten pounds off his shoulders.

"It does, but there'll be days when the thought of it won't sting."

Ty smiled, because he'd had those kinds of moments. Like that Sunday when they'd watched a movie together. When they'd had dessert in his kitchen. And she'd helped him with the lumber.

He bumped her shoulder with his. "This is just another thing you're good at."

"What?" She didn't lean away, even turning toward him.

"Being empathetic."

"Sure it's not me being overbearing?"

"No." He shook his head. "If anything, I think you're wise, and you know how to put that wisdom into words. And if that means telling the hard truth, then you do."

He was met with silence, though she leaned all the way in so their sides were touching. Her hands were clasped together, and he had the inclination to wrap an arm around her. To thank her. To show her that she was well beyond his first impressions at that first date.

And to perhaps see if a redo of that date was possible.

"Frankie," he began. "What do you think about…"

"Mom!" Liam came from around the corner with Aria. "We're ready."

Frankie left his side abruptly, and Ty stood to his full height.

"I guess it's time to go," Frankie said, avoiding his eyes.

But Ty didn't want to. He wanted to stay right there, with her.

Chapter Ten

Ty had opted for him and Aria to share a room with two double beds, while other students were grouped with their parents, or other kids, and the silence when he entered the room was heavenly. Before he unpacked, he threw himself on the bed and looked at the coffered ceiling.

What a day, and the field trip wasn't over yet. Tomorrow would be an early bus ride back to Peak, and then the rest of Sunday to prep before the week began.

Next to him, Aria yawned. "I'm gonna shower and change for bed. I'm so tired."

"Sounds good. I'll be right here, probably napping."

Except when he was finally alone, he couldn't relax. His mind had yet to cease its overthinking. This time, he was ruminating on the thought of being free, and what that meant.

And what part of him was still being held by someone else.

A knock on the door roused him from his thoughts, and he sat up. To the right, the window showcased the dark night and the bright lights of Dupont Circle.

No one should be coming to his door unless it was a fifth-grade parent issue.

He went to the door, ran his hand through his hair, and looked in the peephole, only to grin at who was on the other side.

"Damn, these kids are relentless," he said while opening the door. To Frankie. In a bacon-and-egg pajama set. "And what are you wearing?"

She looked down. "They're called jammies."

He shut his eyes for a beat. "Let me guess, you have a pajama set for every season."

Eyes widened. "Duh."

He cackled. This woman contained multitudes, and she continued to surprise him. "So Valentine's Day, Christmas…"

"Saint Patrick's Day, Easter. And the seasons. Food, as you can see. And dogs." She grinned.

"So if you had to put a number to your sets of pajamas, would you say a dozen?"

"Pshh, blew past that years ago."

"Okay, okay. Come in. I don't need to be embarrassed with a woman wearing bacon-and-egg pajamas at my door."

She entered, laughing. "You should be proud. It's your PTA president."

"Oh, are we going there now?" He was a giddy as a seventh grader with a crush, though he tried to contain himself.

But it was hard, because she smelled like soap and something sweet, like strawberries.

"So what do I owe this surprise visit, other than our children insisting on their matchmaking duties?"

She rolled her eyes. "So you didn't need toothpaste after all?" She presented a travel-size package.

"Nope." He raised an eyebrow. "But do you always carry a spare tube?"

"Yeah. Don't you?" She looked over his shoulder. "Aria in the shower?"

He nodded. "That's probably when she texted Liam. Where's he?"

"He's having a snack. You're only five rooms down from us." She shrugged and looked around. "If you don't need toothpaste, then…" She backed away.

He reached out for her hand with the toothpaste. "Wait."

Her skin was warm, and she didn't pull away. Slowly, her fingers linked with his.

He looked into her steady eyes, which held his gaze. Usually by now, she would have said something. Though they no longer fought, their banter acted like swords, a way to both communicate and protect themselves.

In the silence was…something. A stirring. And she was feeling it, too.

Then, the bathroom door opened. Warm steam escaped and it broke Ty and Frankie apart, leaving him the toothpaste. Frankie shuffled backward and seemed to right herself. "Aria, honey, how was your shower?"

Aria emerged from the steam, hair wet. She, too, wore pajamas. "Hi, Ms. Frankie. Yay. Are you here to bring the toothpaste?" Her smile was bright and mischievous.

Ty tried to contain his own smile, remembering how this was all a setup.

And because perhaps it was working.

"I just gave it to your dad." Frankie glanced up at him, and she grinned, too. "But I'd better go. Early morning tomorrow."

"Thank you," Aria said brightly.

Frankie stepped out into the hallway, lingering, until Ty discerned that Aria wasn't paying attention. He leaned against the doorway. "Thanks. Talk soon?"

She nodded. "We should. But, hey…"

"Hmm?"

"Your website wish list. You talked about wanting to be free. How about you start there?"

"Are you in my head?" He marveled at how they seemed to connect.

"I hope so." Then she walked away, leaving him speechless.

Frankie, when lacking sleep, was a cranky person. And that night, she'd tossed and turned on a bed that was too firm, with pillows that were too flat, in a room with a child who talked in his sleep. She'd forgotten how Liam did that, since he rarely jumped into bed with her. On the rare nights he had a nightmare and came to her bedroom, he oftentimes took her love seat.

She'd also been restless because of that brief interlude with Ty. They'd stepped over the threshold of friendship by a smidge. Though nothing was said or done except some hand-holding, that moment meant more. That they weren't just friends. That perhaps he had been feeling what she'd been all this time.

They would need to talk about it. She would need to explain that despite all this, that first dates might be all she was capable of. And that she suspected it was the same for him, too, with all they'd talked about yesterday.

Though not this morning, because she was cranky times two. Maybe times four. She could swear the Earl Grey tea did not have a microgram of caffeine in it.

"Did you have fun?" Frankie asked Liam, infusing enthusiasm in her voice. They were walking down the hallway from their room.

"Yep. The dinosaurs were the best." He was noshing on the last of his bagel. "Mom, I heard there's a spy museum here."

"In Washington, DC? Yep. Are you interested in going? We can come back another time."

"Okay. Dad and Bianca said that they might want to take me, too."

Frankie kept a straight face, despite feeling like she'd been sucker punched. "He said that?"

"Uh-huh. He said he would talk to you about it."

"Okay." That was the only thing she could think to say, as they approached the lobby. There, the fifth-grade class was lined up, a gaggle of children each dragging a backpack. Some had given up and sat on the ground, draping themselves over their things. Mrs. Caldwell commiserated with the hotel staff, and the parent volunteers guzzled coffee.

Then Ty walked in like a ray of sunshine, wearing a casual black T-shirt, blue jeans, and a big smile on his face.

He didn't see her at first, since he was checking in with Mrs. Caldwell. Then the bus driver entered and called for the class to load up. Ty looked up to scan the room.

When he met her eyes, they lit up, happy to see her.

Her exhaustion from people-ing too much? Her annoyance about this trip Reece was planning behind her back? Both were gone. She was light as air. She was a marshmallow in hot chocolate.

But she couldn't do anything about it but wave, in the midst of the bus-loading chaos. From behind her, someone grabbed her by the elbow and she turned to find Vivian.

"If there was a day to switch over to coffee, today would be the day." Vivian pulled her cap down over her face. "To think I had zero drinks yesterday. I have a bona fide field-trip hangover."

Frankie laughed. "It wasn't that bad."

"Says the A student," she chortled and stepped into the bus.

Ty had already loaded and had taken a seat in the middle on the left. As Frankie approached his row, he gestured for her to take the row behind him. But Vivian pushed her along and all but dragged her two rows down.

"Oh, okay." Disappointed, Frankie slumped into the chair.

Her conversation with Ty would have to wait.

The bus revved up and started down the road. A few minutes in, as Frankie was putting in her earbuds, Vivian said, "I've got something to tell you."

"For you to preface it without just saying it is a little ominous, but okay."

She lifted the bill of her cap. "It's not great. Or maybe it could be great. But not."

Frankie sat up. "That's not confusing at all."

"I'm sorry. It's just, don't shoot the messenger, okay?"

"When do I—?"

"All the time. You apologize after, but your first reaction is that you shoot." Vivian's smile was more like a grimace.

Frankie gestured for her to keep going.

"We had a couple of parents pull out of the PTA graduation-party committee."

"What?" Her voice was louder than Frankie had meant it to be. The kids in the row across the way gave them a side-eye. "Who?"

"The Dannons, and Vicky Ong."

"But…aren't Bill and Deidra heading up the games? And Vicky—she's in charge of the face painting."

Vivian winced. "*Was* in charge."

The party itinerary appeared in her head, with the names of her volunteers flip-flopping and then scrambling all at once. "Why did they back out?"

"They're all leaving on vacation early."

"But they said they would volunteer."

Vivian leveled her with a glare. "Seriously?"

"Ugh. I know. Obviously, I know they're allowed to go on vacation."

"Allowed?"

"You know what I mean, Viv." She leaned back. "What are we going to do? How are we going to get more volunteers?"

"We're going to have to ask around."

"That's the problem, we *have* asked. We've been asking since the beginning of the year." Frankie had repeatedly inserted a small tidbit in the weekly parent newsletter, and had posted on the school's social media. "Wouldn't you know that the year that it's our turn to shine is the year that folks don't want to volunteer?"

"Don't you mean it's our kids' turn to shine?"

"That's what I meant." Frankie pressed a finger against her throbbing temple. She massaged it, remembering the fifth-grade party she'd planned last year, when Liam was in the fourth grade. She'd assembled more volunteers than were needed; the money she'd raised had paid off the collective student-lunch debt.

A shame that there was student-lunch debt to begin with, but the PTA was unanimous in voting to eliminate it.

No, she wouldn't allow for less than a big blowout party, especially since it was Liam's year to celebrate. It was also her last hurrah for the school, and she wouldn't settle for anything but the best.

This was the same reason that Frankie was incapable of second dates. She didn't want to be in a position where she would be disappointed, replaced, or forgotten.

So if she had to do it all herself, she would.

Chapter Eleven

Sent you the website wish list.

Frankie typed a quick response. Received, thanks. Will work on it.

I also think that we should talk, about the field trip.

I'm busy until Friday next week.

LOL. Okay Friday then. I'll be at the school working.

I'll find you.

That Friday, Ty wiped the sweat off his brow and examined his handiwork. Then he remeasured the piece of plywood, grunting in satisfaction for one more step completed.

At least the work was going well. It dampened the sting of Frankie's flippant text and her absence since returning from the fifth-grade field trip last weekend.

He didn't know what was going on with her, but he wouldn't force their meeting. Life was complicated, and he knew it well. Could he have misread their handholding? If so, he couldn't take it back.

And there were more things pressing, such as building these

bookcases before graduation. After a few emails back and forth with Principal Murray, they'd settled on simple built-ins. While it would entail more work on Ty's end, the result will be a long-lasting and gorgeous product, and something he'll be proud to leave behind.

"Ready for me to take that down the hall?" Dante Sison said about the plywood Ty had just cut, appearing at the doorway of the classroom-turned-workplace. He was a firefighter, and a father of twins. He was one of the parents who'd volunteered to help him build the bookcases, and today was his day off.

"Yep. And if you could stick around, I'll need help spotting this to nail it to the wall."

With the project only halfway done, despite starting it weeks ago, Ty was grateful for any help he could get, even if the work gave him so much joy. Every time he walked into this room, the pressures of his day job eased. Building with his hands somehow gave him the space to be able to think, and at the same time, let go of the expectations thrust upon him.

Expectations such as his verbal agreement to extend his contract with Valley Pets, which sat like undigested food in his belly. With every day he'd gone into the clinic, he'd wished that it was the day his mind would change. That, he'd been wrong, that being a vet was enough.

Because it was, wasn't it? He had a home. He had food in his fridge. He helped innocent creatures daily, even if their owners ran the gamut of personalities.

"You've got it," Dante said, snapping Ty out of his thoughts. "At the risk of sounding like a broken record, I'm hella impressed that you can do this, man."

"Thanks. My mom was a painter, but did all kinds of art. She sometimes worked with wood, and I learned alongside her."

"My dad was in construction, and when I was a kid I ran away from anything to do with that as fast as I could. It's different now, though. Wish I could make things. I bought our house before my ex-wife and I had kids. It was our first home, too, so I was shortsighted in what I thought I needed. Two bedrooms just isn't enough these days, but if I knew a little bit about construction I could be more creative making our space work."

The thought of twins—of Aria times two—was enough to make Ty's heart palpitate. "You doing it as a single dad is pretty amazing, though."

"Thanks for saying that. Some days I can barely keep my eyes above water, especially with these odd shifts at the station. I've got my mom helping, but the boys are handfuls."

"Let me know if I can help you build something out. Or I can teach you, if you want," Ty offered, not sure if he was overstepping.

"Really?"

"Yeah."

"That's nice, man. Thanks."

The sound of footsteps brought them to silence and they both turned to the doorway, where Olivia, the school librarian, stood. "Hi, sorry to interrupt."

"Never," Dante answered before Ty could.

"Um, just an FYI that there's after-school testing starting in about an hour, so we might have to put a halt to the sawing and hammering. I hope that's okay."

"Okay with us," Dante said, even if it was Ty's question to answer.

Ty grinned as he darted his gaze between them. Something was brewing between these two.

"Great," Olivia said to Ty. "I'll see you later, I guess."

"Yep," Dante said.

Then there was silence.

After a few seconds, Ty cleared his throat. Dante snapped

to as if he'd been reanimated, color rushing to his cheeks. He made to lift the wood from the worktable. "Back at it."

But Ty wasn't ready. If anything, he was curious. So he kept his palm on the wood. "What was that about?"

"What was what?"

He nodded to the open door. "That."

"Who… Olivia?"

Ty nodded.

Dante rested a hand behind his neck. "I was that obvious?"

He measured a small distance between his thumb and his index finger. "Teeny. But it wasn't just you."

"Really?"

"Yeah."

Then, Dante winced. "Gah. It's not good, you know? Olivia's a baby."

"I don't understand."

"I'm probably ten years older than her. She's a child."

Ty burst out laughing. "That's funny. She's got to be at least thirty."

"I know. But I'm that old. And I've got kids. Dates, girlfriends—there's no time for that. Besides, my mother practically lives with me."

Ty raised a hand. "Whoa. That escalated quickly. Who's talking about living with anyone?"

"I know, I know." He pressed a hand against his heart. "See? I'm not built for this. I'm built to fight fires and rescue kittens from trees. Ride around in the truck with a Santa costume at Christmastime. I'm here to help people. I wrangle my kids and pick up my mom's prescriptions. I can't just be casually dating anyone. My brain goes right to that person coming to living with me and my mother and these kids who've added gray hairs to my damn beard."

Ty leaned against the workbench, surprised at the outburst, but thankful for it, too. It had to have been one of the sincerest conversations he'd had about love and relationships as a single dad.

"You're laughing at me on the inside, aren't you?" Dante said.

"Actually, no. Just…thanks."

"Thanks for what?"

"For opening up, I guess."

"For spilling my guts?"

"Yeah, that, too." He swiped an arm across his forehead while thinking on the last few days. "Things are…weird right now. Us moving, my relationship with Aria's mother. And then… Fr—" He halted, recalibrating. "Adjusting to someplace where everyone knows one another. And maybe trying to find a connection, too."

"Whiplash emotions."

"I need a neck brace." Ty laughed. "But all I want is to be settled."

"I wonder if there is such a thing, though. Maybe that's just some smoke influencers like to blow around."

"I don't know." Ty shook his head. "But listening to you, it feels good to know I'm not alone."

"So you're saying my life's a hot mess now, too?" Dante grinned.

"No—"

"I'm kidding." Dante approached him and settled a hand on his shoulder. "Listen, if you ever need anything, I'm here. Hopefully not because your house is on fire, but for anything else. We single dads have to take care of one another, you know?"

"Thanks." He looked away, emotions welling up in his chest. Clearing his throat, he picked up the piece of lumber and handed it to him.

"That my sign to get to work?" He took a few steps and

over his shoulder said, “Oh, if you play poker, me and a few guys are getting together.”

“No way. Lance—”

“Ah, he got to you first. Good. Which means you need to go. It’s next weekend.”

“Knock-knock,” someone said at the doorway. Ty looked up.

Frankie.

“Ruh-roh. It’s the boss,” Dante said in jest. “Run away!” He picked up the lumber and gingerly walked toward the door.

As he passed Frankie, she chided, “I hope you haven’t been distracting him.”

“No, ma’am,” he said, scurrying off.

Frankie entered the classroom, bringing her floral scent that Ty was instantly caught in. The instinct to bring her into his arms and bury his nose in her hair was indescribable.

But he kept himself where he was. Days had passed since returning from the field trip. From him almost asking her out on a bona fide date.

Looking back, maybe Aria’s interruption had been a good thing.

Because he obviously still needed to grieve. He needed to heal, and he didn’t want to ruin whatever this precarious thing he had going with Frankie.

Then, a to-go cup materialized in front of him.

“Coffee with milk,” she said.

“Thanks.” The cup was hot against his fingertips. He took a sip.

“Eh, just returning the favor.”

“Haven’t seen you in while.”

“I know, right? So much to do these days.” She avoided his eyes. “Sorry.”

He’d been right, something else was going on. “It’s fine.”

She ran her hand against the wood. “You’re moving along.”

"Nice and steady."

"Have you…" she gestured to his workspace, "taken a photo for your social media?"

"Didn't even think of it."

"Well set that coffee down, and I'll take a pic now."

"Aw, nah." His cheeks heated. "I'm a mess."

"You'll do as I say. C'mon." She slipped the phone out of her back pocket. "Make like you're about to saw something or whatever."

"Or whatever," he laughed, though he positioned his one hand on the handsaw and the other on the plywood.

"Okay, just hold right there." A series of clicks followed. "Great." She lowered the phone, grinning. "I'll keep the photos for when you finally set your socials up. When you finally do *something*." She eyed him.

"I know, I know. I've been occupied."

She raised her eyebrows.

"I'll get it set up soon. Promise."

With that, she smiled.

He grabbed his coffee and took a sip. "This hit the spot." He slumped down in one of the classroom chairs, relief spilling out of him. He glanced at his watch to keep himself from looking at her.

"I'm hitting the streets in a little while to fundraise donations. Wanna come with me?" She took the chair in front of him and turned. It reminded him of when he was in high school, and the cutest girl in class turned around and spoke to him.

He bit back a smile, especially since she'd all but ignored him since the field trip. "And walk away from my most favorite pastime? Why would I do that?"

"Because," she whined. "We need to get these requests out. Reece has Liam this week, so I finally have time. And you're here."

"Oh…so I'm a convenient friend now? Why don't you ask Dante?"

"He's the grumpiest of the firefighters. Whereas, people who meet you end up loving you, and won't be able to say no. And you said you'd help."

"Oh, so you *need* me?" he joked, though inside he thrilled with excitement, despite his best efforts.

"Yeah, okay? I *do* need you. And don't you have to take a break? Olivia said something about testing starting soon." She clasped her hands together and stuck out her bottom lip. "Please. Just an hour of your time."

"Okay, fine," he said.

In truth, he couldn't say no to Frankie even if he tried.

Nothing screamed "pick me" more than asking for donations, and that alone put Frankie ill at ease. Did she understand the importance of fundraising? One hundred percent. But she wished she could do it without asking point-blank for people to pull out their checkbooks.

She didn't have the countenance for it. One had to ask but not be pushy. Assertive but not aggressive. Convince but not force. Frankie often found herself tumbling over toward the other side where her strong personality won out.

Ty, on the other hand, had a smooth, amicable delivery. And his reputation as one of the town veterinarians made him a hero. People listened to him.

Like right now. Ty leaned over the linoleum countertop of Sweet Trip, a fudge shop. Cecilia Kerry, the owner, was giggling at some corny joke he'd delivered.

"Oh, you. You're so funny," Cecilia said. Her long hair was in an intricate French braid that trailed over her right shoulder, which she was now twirling.

Oh, goodness.

"According to my daughter, I'm not funny. I'm embarrassing." Ty was pulling out the stops, if Frankie was being honest. They'd been at it for a half hour now, going from business to business at the town square. Before they'd entered the first business, she'd given him brief instructions on how to solicit donations. *One: Introduce yourself as a PTA volunteer. Two: Give them the official letter and a small summary of what we're raising money for. Three: Tell them you'll come back to follow up.*

But the guy had run with it. He took the basic pitch and without a thought, simply asked people for help.

Wooing Cecilia wasn't a tough challenge for him. It was game over when he'd walked through her doors, since he was her chihuahua's vet.

A chihuahua that had a mean streak to it, from what Frankie had witnessed.

"I don't have any kids, but it's good to know that we've got someone so kind on the PTA," she said.

Ty slid the fundraising form across the counter. "Then I hope you'll consider donating to the fifth-grade graduation. A gift card, or a check. Anything, really. We want to give the kids and the parents the best event possible. And everything we don't use, we'll put into our school fund. For cxample, this year, we're building new shelves for the school library. I mean, *I'm* building shelves."

He said that last line with a heavy dose of flirt with a capital *F*, and Frankie didn't know whether she should clap or make puking noises.

"*You're* building the shelves?" she gasped, clutching her fake pearls.

"Yes, ma'am."

"Kind *and* strong." She gently touched Ty's forearm. "Don't you worry, we'll donate. I'll have a Visa gift card sent to the school by the end of the day."

"Thank you."

It took another few minutes and several more compliments before Frankie followed Ty out of the shop. Once they got about a half a block down, she said. "You are too much."

"Hey, did I seal the deal or did I seal the deal?"

"Okay fine. Yes, you sealed the deal."

"Deals," he reiterated. "*Four.* In less than an hour, I might add."

"Yes, okay, deals." She laughed. "Though, how do you do that?"

"Do what?"

"Sell. Flirt."

"I do not flirt."

"Yes, you do." She playfully tugged on his arm. "Don't tell that you weren't flirting with Cecilia back there."

"What you call flirting, I call connection."

"Huh." She thought about it, the word *connection.* In all of her first dates, it was what she looked for. Something to hang her hat on, something to jump back to, something to give her excitement. "I guess some of us are blessed to have that with everyone."

"Is it a blessing, though? You make it sound like some people can't have it. That it can't be a choice somehow."

The question halted her train of thought. Was it a choice? Wasn't connection supposed to be instantaneous and easy? Wasn't it supposed to be organic and sincere?

What did it mean that she was somebody who didn't have that connection with everyone?

"Wanna grab something to eat?" He looked at his watch. "I need some sustenance before I head back to the school and work. Phoebe's sitting with Aria for another couple of hours."

"Sure. How about some pizza?" She gestured at Crest Pizza across the street. Though the dining room was closed, their walk-up window had a line.

His stomach growled the answer and he clutched it. “That means yes.”

Once at the window, Frankie ordered a slice of Hawaiian pizza.

“Pineapple on pizza is a sacrilege,” Ty said. Leaning in, he pressed a hand against her phone, which she was going to use to pay for her slice. “I’ll get this.” Then to the server, he said, “I’ll take two slices with everything on them.”

She put away her phone. “I’ll get you next time.”

“Yep.” He reached beyond her and grabbed the tray from the server, along with two bottles of water.

The only free seats were in the town square, so they hoofed it back to the empty bench. By the time they sat down, Frankie’s stomach growled.

He laughed. “That was louder than mine. Then again, I’m not surprised.”

“Hey!” She tossed a napkin at him.

“Just telling the truth.” He opened his pizza box and lifted his pizza slice, but changed his mind as the toppings overflowed. Instead, he folded it in half.

“I didn’t take you for an everything-pizza kind of guy,” Frankie said, strategizing how she was going to take her first bite. Crest didn’t skimp on the toppings, and their individual slices were as big as a personal-size pizza.

“Why’s that?”

“An everything pizza is savory, spicy even.”

“I like a little spice.” He grinned while biting into the slice, and it sent a spiral of need through her.

“Well.” She cleared her throat to right her brain. “I like mine simple.”

He swallowed and wiped his chin with a napkin. “A Hawaiian pizza is far from simple. Pineapple with Canadian bacon is a taste that’s definitely acquired.”

She took a bite and breathed in the sweet of the pineapple

and the bacon's savory notes. A good slice of pizza was worth its weight in gold. As she chewed, she contemplated the comment, because she wasn't sure if he was only talking about pizza. After she swallowed, she said, "I guess I never thought about it that way. Then again, not everything needs to be easy."

"Nope, it's very much like you."

The pizza was halfway to her mouth and she giggled. "You're saying I'm an acquired taste?"

"It's not that, it's more like there are two sides of you."

Frankie was curious now. "Tell me what those two sides are then."

"There's the side that's a little…brash." A shy smile graced his face. "And then there's the side that's a total marshmallow."

"I *am* a little soft for Liam. And maybe for my family, too, at the end of the day."

He swallowed his food. "I think it says something, that you can only be vulnerable to the people that matter."

"But I'm brash, as you say."

"It's your armor. But once you get through it…" His voice softened, and she found herself leaning into him, to hear the rest of his words. He had set his pizza down, and his fingers fiddled with his napkin. There was more in the air, a stillness, a presence, and she held her breath. Her heartbeat filled her ears as she waited.

"I wish I was on the other side of that," he continued, his words a mere breath.

She looked up to meet his eyes, viewing their sincerity. His vulnerability, if she was being honest. From day one, on that date when she'd walked out, he was able to speak of his emotions calmly.

His honesty was a turn-on.

"But," he said, before she could answer him. "Sometimes it is tough to gauge you. You're expressive. You tell people how you feel. But at the same time, you keep so much to yourself. Like, what happened to you the last few days?"

She was taken aback at the questioning. It had been a while since a member of the opposite sex had asked her for accountability. First dates kept that from happening; Frankie didn't owe anyone an explanation.

"Stuff happened," she said, because she didn't want to unload PTA drama on Ty.

"Okay?" He gestured for more. "Does it have anything to do with me?"

"What?" She sat up. "No. It had nothing to do with you." She sighed, realizing her faux pas. Shaking her head, she said, "I didn't mean to ghost you. I was caught up with the PTA, with the graduation, and I let it rule me for a bit. You see, some folks had to back out from the planning committee, and I went into crisis mode. And when I'm in crisis mode, I'm focused. I should have communicated that better."

Relief passed through his features, and that alone allowed her feelings to rush back. She steeled herself against it so that she could say what she'd been harboring for some time. "What if I say okay, Ty? What if I want for us to get to the other side of my armor."

He didn't flinch; he didn't give away any evidence of surprise. "Then I would ask you on a second date and wouldn't take it for granted. And I would kiss you every chance I got. Like this very second."

Frankie inhaled, stunned at his honesty.

Tempted by it, too.

She was also aware that the square was crawling with people. That though they were somewhat shadowed by the square's cherry blossom trees, whatever happened here would be news to everyone by close of business. Them having lunch together would already be on everyone's lips, but anything more would set the town on fire.

She also hadn't shown any PDA with anyone since Reece.

But she couldn't resist this moment. She couldn't resist him. "Okay."

His eyes sharpened. "Okay?"

She grinned. "I've been wanting this, too."

"This, meaning?"

"Meaning, going on another date. And I don't know, maybe a kiss."

His face broke out into a smile that made her insides leap for joy. Then, he cupped the side of her face, pausing for beat, as if asking for permission. She leaned in to answer him, until their lips touched, chaste at first.

When he started to pull away, she angled toward him.

He rewarded her by deepening his kiss. With her eyes shut, she fell into the moment with abandon, trusting that he saw and appreciated every part of her.

When the kiss ended, she was breathless.

Opening her eyes, the rest of the world rushed back.

He leaned his forehead against hers. "Wow."

I know, right? was what she wanted to say. Never had she had a kiss as chaste as that but felt so deep in her core. But she was overcome with the thought that she couldn't mess this up. She couldn't make their next date their last one.

Chapter Twelve

"I don't think we should tell them right away." Ty pulled Frankie by the loop of her jeans and brought her to him. "I kind of like having this to ourselves for a while."

"I hate to keep it from them." Frankie inhaled the intimacy of the moment. And when he pressed his lips against the side of her neck, her eyes rolled back in ecstasy. "It's been tough enough keeping it a secret the last few days."

Their first kiss had released the dam of their emotions, and they'd acted on the attraction that they'd kept under wraps. And now, they couldn't contain themselves if they were in the vicinity of one another.

When they weren't nearby, they were texting, or on the phone. Frankie had Ty constantly at the forefront of her mind, despite her best efforts.

And though they hadn't yet had sex, she knew that it was just a matter of time. If anyone was to break first, it would be her.

As it was, the kids were outside playing with Bubba and Snowball—they were at Frankie's house to work on Ty's website, finally—and the only reason they weren't upstairs and in bed was because of them. Still, she slipped her fingers under his shirt and skimmed the skin just under his waistband, as she trailed kisses on his jawline. He hissed, hands trailing down to her bottom. "You're tempting me."

"I'm tempting myself. But I don't want the kids to find out about it from anyone else. We were lucky that no one saw us at the town square."

Frankie had kept her ears to the ground, too, in case someone had seen something. So far, so good.

"Damn small towns," he groaned. He captured her bottom lip with his, something he'd quickly learned that turned her on. She wrapped her arms around his neck. Gripping her by the waist, he lifted her on the kitchen countertop, and her libido surged to a level she had forgotten even existed. Standing in between her legs, her body temperature ratcheted up. Her instinct was to take off her clothes. To lock the doors and keep the whole world away. "People are so nosy."

"Makes me want to give them something to talk about," she said, allowing the thought to come through, feeling herself drawn to him more. Because a part of her did wish that she could just *be* and *do*.

"Naughty," he said, kissing her. "We should run away."

"Let's do it." She allowed her imagination to take over. "Just the two of us, with not another person around."

"On an island. No work, no kids, no dogs."

"Heaven." She reveled in his capable hands and deep kisses, while letting her mind run the gamut of their pretend vacation. She hadn't taken a vacation since Liam was born. Not a girl's weekend, not time off.

In the distance, a dog barked, and it popped the bubble of the moment. Then Aria laughed, which smothered the sizzle of her libido. She gently pushed Ty away. "Okay, we have to focus."

"You're right." Ty blew out a breath. His eyes were hazy, like he'd downed a couple of shots. It mirrored what she felt inside, which was a delicious confusion. "You look drunk."

"I was just thinking the same about you," she said, laughing. "You did this to me."

"I like that." She straightened his shirt, and with her right hand, cupped his jaw and gently wiped the side of his mouth with a thumb, which was smeared with some of her lip gloss. He turned slightly and kissed her hand, a gesture that sent her heart soaring.

The sweetest, she thought.

"What are you thinking about?" he asked.

She ran her fingers through his hair. There was some white interspersed in his hairline. She noted a mole at his temple and she kissed it. "It feels easy right now."

"You say that ominously."

"I don't mean it that way. I just mean that this is fun. Way more fun than our first date was."

"Yeah." He half laughed, his eyes glancing over her shoulder, out the window. "Looks like they're slowing down out there."

He picked her up by the waist and set her back on the ground. Frankie straightened her shirt, wet a paper towel, and pressed it against her face.

"I need a full-on shower," he said, kissing her on the lips.

"Shhhh…" She giggled. "So what are we going to do? Are we going to tell them?"

"You don't think they're going to be upset?"

She grabbed two Disney-character glasses from the cupboard and the orange juice from the refrigerator. "I think they're going to be thrilled they accomplished their mission."

"It's one thing to set your parents up, but it's another thing to actually realize that your parents are dating."

She nodded. "I hadn't thought of it that way."

"Can we…ease into this? Hang out more often, spend time together, but not give it a title."

She shifted her weight and crossed her arms. Unease crept in. Secrets weren't her thing. She'd rather know, rather be hurt by the truth than let down nicely.

And the mention of titles hit a nerve, so she backtracked. "Oh, I didn't mean that we should have a title. God, we've only been making out, what? Like three days."

"Frankie." He reached out and brought her close, and said, "You have been the only thing on my mind the last three days. Hell, ever since our first date. Not a day has gone by without me thinking about or talking about or seeing you. My hesitance isn't about us, or our status, or where we are. It's about our kids. Aria, especially. Aria and her mom are close. Aria and I are just starting to get closer. I don't want to put pressure on her to accept more than what she's ready for."

Frankie nodded, feeling the unease seep out of her. It was a heartfelt answer. It was honest. It was also a fair request. She shrugged. "I guess I'm the type to want to get things all official ASAP, you know?"

"Believe me, if there was a way I could lock you down, right now, right this second, with no consequence?" His expression turned mischievous.

The back door slapped open, followed by the sounds of running dogs and children, placing a distance between Frankie and Ty. Ty winked at Frankie, and she laughed.

"Oooh, orange juice," Liam said.

Frankie grabbed snacks from the pantry and passed them out.

Then, while leaning back against the counter, Ty said, "Kids, we hope you don't mind, but Ms. Frankie and I are going to be working together quite a bit."

"On your website, right, Dad?" Aria asked.

"Among other things." He glanced up at Frankie.

Frankie's insides melted. "Your dad needs a lot of help," she joked.

"I know. Dad doesn't do anything online," Aria agreed.

"I don't mind." Liam was inspecting one of the fruit snacks. Then he looked up. "How long are you staying today?"

"Oh, um, at least a couple of hours?" She looked at Ty for confirmation.

Ty nodded.

"So can I take Aria over to Tita Gabby's house to see Six?" Liam asked. "Now?"

"Yep, you can go," Frankie said. "If Mr. Ty's good with it."

"How far is it?" Ty asked.

"It's the next cabin down. You can see it from here." She gestured out the side window.

"Oh, sure." He smiled. "Let's keep both dogs here, though, so it's not too overwhelming for her."

The two kids jumped up, their chairs squeaking on the hardwood floor. "Okay, bye!"

"Please have your Tita text me to let me know when you get there!" Frankie yelled out the door.

Leaving them alone.

A tingle of need started in her core.

"I love that your family's so close." Then his lips quirked up. He walked to the front door, and clicked the bolt shut. "How far is your sister's cabin?"

"A short walk." She locked the back door. "And I have a security camera."

He took her by the hand, sending her heart rate into triple time. Then he paused, looking down at their interlaced hands, his thumb brushing against the top of hers, the action sending shivers through her. In his eyes was a question.

Do you want to?

Gosh, he was so sweet. She decided to put words to this next step. "Wanna come upstairs?"

"Only if you want to. Or we can go back to working on the website like we said we would."

She paused to think about what this would mean. Making out with another parent at the school, someone she would see in the future, for probably however long they lived in town, was one thing. But to have sex with them?

To be truly involved was another thing altogether.

And yet, she couldn't refuse this handsome man, who seemed to see through all of the walls she had erected. Someone who, since she had met him, had brought a little bit of light into her space.

"Eh, the website can wait another day," she said.

Then, she tugged him by the hand to pull him up the stairs, grabbing her phone on the way.

He raised an eyebrow.

"Gotta text Gabby so she'll keep them distracted with food. You never know with the kids."

Even at this moment, she was a mom first. Her fingers flew on the touchscreen, then she stuffed the phone in her back pocket.

At the top of the stairs, Frankie slowed. The air was warmer on the second floor, the décor cozier. While she'd kept downstairs neat and uncluttered, the walls bare, and the color palette neutral, up here, she displayed everything. Framed family photos covered the hallway walls. On a display case showcased all of Liam's little handmade projects. Her sheets didn't exactly match, and she had a million throw pillows she'd impulse-purchased over the years.

She didn't remember the last time she brought anyone up here.

She swallowed against her sudden nervousness.

From behind, Ty rested a hand on her waist, squeezing gently. "Frankie…we don't have to. If we're going too fast—"

"No, that's not it." She looked back and faced him; she saw that it wasn't him she was worried about. "I want this. But will you promise me one thing?"

"Yes."

"If anything changes between us. If at any point, you feel

different about me, you'll tell me. I need for us to be honest. Always."

He nodded, eyes wide in sincerity. "I promise."

"I believe you," she said. In that moment, she allowed a wall to come down. She reached out with both hands this time and pulled him backward toward her bedroom.

She let go and began to undress. She watched him as his jaw slipped up into a smile, as his expression changed from curiosity to need. Then she crawled onto the bed, pushing her throw pillows onto the floor, and beckoned him forward.

He peeled off his clothing, dropping them like breadcrumbs. Finally naked, he joined her on the bed, capturing her lips into a passionate kiss, the start of lovemaking that she knew would blow away any imagined magical vacation.

Ty had been living a dream the last week, since he and Frankie made love for the first time.

Lying on his side, Ty marveled at the woman lying next to him. He brushed Frankie's brown hair away from her cheeks, enamored at how peaceful she looked, when an hour ago she'd been animated, spirited, and downright feisty in bed.

She awoke, her eyes fluttering open.

"Hey," he said, taking every inch of her in. They were both on top of the covers, and the sun shone through the window, illuminating her curves. He followed the line of her body's profile: the rise of her shoulders and breasts, the dip of her waist, and curve of her hip.

"Hey." Her voice cracked minutely, and the vulnerability of it split his heart open a little more. This was a side of Frankie that very few people saw, as confident as she was in her outward persona, and he felt like the luckiest man to get to witness it.

Though it would only be a moment, since the sun was setting. "We probably need to get up."

Her lips turned downward. "I know."

"That was fun, though."

She bit her lip and her cheeks darkened. "It *was* fun. It has been fun."

In the last week, they'd been able to sneak in some alone-time when the kids were at school. They'd also seen each other often while clothed, too, with the bookcase and business projects overlapping. Tonight was a bonus getaway since both kids were at Vivian's house—Ian had invited them for a pizza dinner and a movie.

He and Frankie hadn't thought twice about coming back to his house.

Frankie climbed on top of him so their bodies were flush. She rested her chin against his chest. "Do you think Vivian knows?"

"I don't think so. Wouldn't she have said something?" Ty ran his fingers through her hair.

"You're right, she would."

"So you don't want to tell the town that I bedded the PTA president?" He rested his hands at the small of her back, and the heat of her body radiated through him. It felt right, and warm, and comforting.

"I've got a reputation to protect." She kissed him on the lips, and her hair fell over him, creating a curtain of darkness.

He moaned. "Little do they know that the hard-nosed, budget ball-busting…"

She giggled. "Ball-busting?"

"I said what I said." He pushed her hair back, trying to contain the emotions that had welled up inside him. "Look how fast I got everything done for my business? Website all but complete, social media account set up, LLC paperwork printed out. If you haven't been around to push me…"

"We push each other," she said. "The bookcases are almost finished."

"We make a great team," he responded, holding her gaze.

It was official. He really had it bad for this woman. The last week had solidified it. While he'd been unsure at first about telling Aria about this relationship, he thought that it was time. Aria had been more communicative, and she and Frankie got along well. The other day, he'd overheard Aria talk about Frankie to Harper on FaceTime—it was about the PTA, but it was something. It meant that Aria considered Frankie to be a part of her world.

Frankie looked away and shimmied down so she was nestled under his arm.

He tilted up her chin. "What's up?"

"I think that Reece and Bianca are getting serious."

The subject was unexpected. And the tone of her voice sounded like it held a bit of regret and disappointment. "Oh, wow. This isn't a good thing?" he asked.

"It's neither here nor there."

"So why does it sound like it's somewhere?"

"Because it's too soon, isn't it? He said they only started dating a few months ago."

The idea that she would care about Reece and Bianca's romantic timeline caused Ty to have doubts. Though, in the next second, he pushed them away. It was okay for people to feel complex emotions toward their exes. It wasn't as if he didn't have complicated feelings toward Harper.

"Ugh," she groaned. "She'll probably start coming to family things. To school things. Everything's going to change. It's already changing. He and Bianca are taking Liam out of town for spring break next week."

He wasn't sure where her head was at. He detected some jealousy in her tone. Then again, was it his place to probe? And wasn't she allowed to vent? "If it makes you feel better, it's not only you who's probably worried about these changes. Bianca knows she has big shoes to fill, especially with Liam."

"I didn't think of it that way." She looked up at him, relief playing across her features. "This is all a lot, for everyone."

"But, I bet I can find a way to help *you* relax..." He leaned in and whispered in her ear, recounting what they'd done just a few minutes before.

She giggled.

He drew her in closer and kissed her, to help dash his own inner worries, that Frankie was *too* concerned about Reece and Bianca's relationship. He wasn't worried about Frankie's faithfulness any more than he was concerned about her constant worry and attention to their relationship.

He knew how easy the past liked to rear its ugly head—it happened at the field trip, when he'd allowed Harper to get in his head.

In both of their cases, their exes would remain ever-present. To make their relationship work, to make it official and tell the kids and everyone else, it required that they each could position their exes in their proper places in their lives.

He shut his eyes tighter, to release himself from his fears. Frankie crawled above him once more, straddling him. Closer now, he felt comforted, like things would be okay. And at this moment, he wished this would never end.

Their phone alarms buzzed at the same time.

He groaned.

"No-o-o-o," she whined, as she somehow disentangled herself from him. They dressed quickly; like Cinderella, they were on borrowed time.

When Ty opened his bedroom door, Bubba was on the other side. He bent down to scratch him on the head, and doing so centered his thoughts.

He was overthinking again. He had a beautiful woman with him and his mind wasn't on the present.

Frankie was here, and that was what mattered.

She did a double take when she caught him staring. She

was in front of his dresser mirror taming back her hair. "What are you looking at?"

"You." He stood behind her, so they were both framed in the mirror. She swiped on lipstick. "And how hot you look when you get dressed."

She laughed and pulled his arms toward her so that they wrapped around her tightly. "No time to do anything about it now."

"Sadly, no. Also, I have poker tonight."

She turned and wrapped her arms around him. "You're going to have such a good time winning that *Monopoly* money. But hey, look at me."

He did as he was told.

"Your website is done, which frees me up a lot."

He remembered what she'd said about PTA issues cropping up. "Are you good with the PTA stuff? Do you need help with anything?"

She pressed her lips into a line for a moment. "I always need help, and you've already helped, and are helping still. But your LLC forms, have you filled them out?"

"Nope. But I swear, it's coming."

"Excuses, excuses… that's our next step, okay?"

He laughed. "See? If anyone can motivate folks, it's you."

Their phone alarms beeped once more.

"Time to go," she said. "Win big tonight, baby."

I already have, he said to himself, holding Frankie tight.

Chapter Thirteen

Ty exposed his hand, showing a royal flush.

The rest of the table erupted in groans.

"I can't believe that," Dante said, across from him. He wore dark sunglasses like a professional poker player and had a cigar perched between his fingers. "You killed it."

"Thank God we're not playing with real money," Lance said, setting his cards down. He took a swig of his beer. "I would have been the one killed. By my wife."

"Yeah, that sucked." Ryan Ortega tossed his cards in the middle of the table and readjusted his ball cap. Ryan was Ian's dad and Vivian's ex, whom he'd met earlier today at Ian's pizza night. "And I'm out. I'm beat."

They'd been at it for a couple of hours now. After Ty left Frankie, he'd picked up Aria, and Phoebe came over to babysit. And though he'd been hesitant at jumping into a poker group, seeing as he didn't play poker, and friend groups tended to be close, he felt comfortable and accepted.

It also helped that he kept winning.

"Beginner's luck." Ty grinned as he drew the *Monopoly* money from the middle of the table toward him. They were in Lance's two-car garage, next to an old Ford pickup. Hanging on the garage walls were power tools and posters of rock bands. The vibe was relaxed.

"Now, here's a question for everyone before we call it a

night," Ryan said. Ty had noticed that Ryan was the inquisitive type, and throughout the night, had asked theoretical questions, for discussion purposes. "What would you no longer do if you didn't have to?"

"Oooh, good question," Lance said. "That's easy, I wouldn't mop floors ever again. I'll do laundry and dishes forever. But mopping? I'd hire someone to help me with that."

"That's very practical." Ryan snickered.

"Dude, mopping a whole house full of hardwood floors is no joke."

"That's fair. Vacuuming is easier," Dante said, putting out his cigar. "Except when your kids decide to take a marker to it."

"How about you, Dante, what would you *not* do?" Lance asked.

"Oh, that's simple—I wouldn't have my mom take care of my kids. I'd rather get an au pair, or a nanny." He started to gather up the cards into a stack.

"But I love your mom. Her bibinka got me through Kyle's terrible threes," Lance said.

"I love my mom, too. She's the best. But this isn't exactly the retired life she dreamed of having. She never complains, but I can tell that the twins wear on her sometimes. She's seventy, and all…"

"So, a responsible choice from you." Ryan leaned back and crossed his arms. He jutted up his chin at Ty. "You?"

Ty didn't think twice. "I wouldn't be working as a veterinarian."

Though when the words left his mouth, and he registered the look of shock on the guys' faces, he regretted it. "I—"

"But, you just got here…"

"I know, and I love this job. But I love something else more."

Dante frowned. "You have a side job?"

"You've been helping me with it."

"No way."

"Way." Ty felt that he was in too deep now, so he dug into the reasons of why he wanted to start a business, but how he wasn't sure it was the right thing to do. "I would have to receive a very large windfall for me to leave this career, though. More than what's in that pile, that's for sure." He gestured to the fake money.

"Whenever you're ready, we're here to support you," Dante said.

"And if there's a place to take a risk like that, it's Peak," Ryan chimed in. "We appreciate mom-and-pop businesses around here, you know? Once folks see those bookcases, you won't even have to market yourself."

"I can tell you right now that I have a couple of things I need built for the house. I tried doing it myself." Lance gestured to his power tools. "You know how I use those things? Not safely."

The group broke out in laughter and the rest of the pressure on Ty's shoulders lifted. Earlier today, with Frankie asking him where he was in his business startup checklist, he'd felt stuck. Doubt had begun to creep in that he couldn't start a business after all—his time management since moving to Peak had been pushed to the limit.

But hearing the encouragement from these guys hit different.

"How about you?" Ty asked Ryan, to move the conversation along. "What would you not do?"

Ryan shoved his hands in his pockets. "I wouldn't just be a baby daddy."

"Shit, what does that mean?" Dante took off his shades.

Ty wasn't abreast of Ryan and Vivian's relationship, but he inferred from the other's expressions that this wasn't remotely accurate.

"I want to be a full-time dad. Not a part-time one. I would buy a compound big enough so me, Ian and Viv and her mom can stay on one piece of land. I would buy anything and everything Viv and Ian wanted so she could trust me again." After a few seconds of silence, he said, "I know that's far-fetched. See, Ty, not sure how much you know, but I've bounced in and out of town for work, though this time I'm here for the long term. I regret not being here when Ian was younger, and now I have a lot to make up to them both. I want to be the father Ian deserves."

"Wow. That's big," Lance said, standing, to grab another bottled water from the cooler. "How are things with you and Vivian?"

With a hint of sadness in his eyes, he said, "Things are actually going well between us. We've always coparented well, but it doesn't mean that she trusts me completely to stay. We're both walking on eggshells right now." He cleared his throat. "Though I'd appreciate it if you guys didn't say anything to anyone."

"Your secret is safe with me. Hell, I'd appreciate if you didn't say anything to my boss, either," Ty joked. But it wasn't just him who wanted a change, and he felt seen.

"I won't say a thing." Lance slashed a cross over his heart.

"Me, either," Dante said.

"Same," Ryan said.

"Me, too, for everyone," Ty added.

"Does that make us besties now?" Lance asked.

The group snorted.

"No, I think the most recent term is *gang*," Ryan said. "Gen Alpha lingo. You know you're a dad when you recognize the words, but don't actually know what they mean."

They continued cleaning up, and while gathering the *Monopoly* money, Ty's phone buzzed in his pocket. Looking at the caller ID, it wasn't Aria, but Dr. Peters.

He took the call. "Hi, Kyle."

"Ty." His voice was gruff. "I just got a call about some newborn puppies, but I'm sick. And so is Junior."

"Sick?"

"Virus, we think. Body aches and fever. I tried to get up just now and am pretty dizzy. I could call Dr. Velasquez from Peak Pets, but wanted to check if you were available, since it's your next-door neighbor. No pressure."

"No problem. I can get there. Just got done playing poker."

"Did you drink?"

"Just a lot of soda. Could you give me the exact address?"

"I'll text it to you. Thanks."

After they hung up, Ty bid the guys farewell and headed home to update the babysitter. Then he trudged to his neighbor on his left, whom he hadn't met officially, though they'd waved at each other now and again.

By the time he got to the house, Heath Chan, a man in his sixties, greeted him.

"Thank goodness you're here. I've never owned dogs, and I don't quite know how I'm supposed to handle this." Heath led the way to his back patio. Under the steps were five babies nursing against their mama, who was lying on her side.

"Looks like you've got yourself a family under your porch."

"I've never owned a pet except for beta fish that died, and a hermit crab that I forgot in my car overnight in the winter." He grimaced. "I'm no good at this."

"The good news is that they're safe for now. The weather's been mild, and the dogs appear to be healthy. We don't need to move them right this second, unless you want to. You can put out a water bowl, and I have dog food to lay out for the mama. Honestly, that mama's not going anywhere with her babies being so young. Tomorrow, you can call the animal shelter, and they'll give you the option of keeping them here or relocating them."

"Will it hurt to move them?"

"It will be confusing for them, same as it would be for us, but they'll settle back down. The shelter can assist in finding homes for the babies and mom. Our office has a ton of resources to help you as well. I'll make sure that one of our assistants calls you with all of that information."

He eyed them. "I—I think I'll keep them at least overnight. They look so peaceful. A couple of puppies are already asleep."

"I'm also right next door. If something happens overnight, feel free to knock."

"Thanks for coming over. It's good to meet you officially."

"Great to meet you, too." Ty looked at the dogs one last time, shook the man's hand, and headed back home. He felt the world shift a bit. Sweat built up behind his neck, and his face felt like it was on fire.

Once he entered the kitchen through the garage, he called out to Phoebe. "Hey, Phoebs, I'm home."

"Great." She slung her backpack over her shoulder. "I'll head out the front door. See you."

"Thanks, I'll Venmo you."

After turning on the faucet, he splashed his face with cold water.

He pressed his hand against his forehead, though it didn't give him much information except that his hand felt clammy against his skin.

Oh, no, was he sick, too?

Then, his phone rang, startling him.

Harper. He took it.

"Hello?"

"Oh, my god, Oh, my god!" Her voice screeched through the phone, and he turned down the volume.

"What's going on?" His voice felt unfamiliar and forced.

"I won. I won!" She repeated the same words at least twice

more, though they didn't quite settle into his bones. He opened the refrigerator and squinted against the dome light. But nothing looked appealing.

"You won what?"

"I won the competition. I won *Amateur Stars Baking Show*!"

"W-wow!" Still, it didn't sink in. "So you won the money?"

"Not just the money, but everything else. The prestige. Maybe a cookbook opportunity later on. Maybe even my own show. Lots of appearances, at the very least. The show's already scheduling them, after this wraps up."

"Congratulations." It was all he could say. "Does that mean that Aria stays with me?" It was the only thing he understood and landed on, since his insides were doing weird things.

"Yes. Is that okay with you? We can talk about it. I know that we only discussed our arrangement for the time I was on the show—"

"It's what I want, for Aria to stay with me." He couldn't imagine Aria leaving him, to have to do that horrible dance of switching homes again.

"Great. About Aria's graduation…"

"The twentieth of May," he said reflexively.

"I'll make sure the team knows. Is it okay that I come to stay with you?"

"Yes, of course." He pressed his fingers against the side of his nose. He hadn't cleaned up the additional dwelling out back. And things were currently going right in his world. Harper would make it all topsy-turvy.

Like he was feeling at the moment.

He migrated to the living room and sank into the sofa.

"Okay, talk later," he said.

Then, as he felt his face sink into the couch cushions, he closed his eyes.

* * *

Frankie buried her nose into the freshly cut flowers she bought at Peak's Sunday farmer's market. "Sublime," she said, paying Sharon, the owner of Winnebago, Peak's garden store.

"You're acting too happy." Next to her, Gabby strode along as they ducked out from underneath the tent, where the sun greeted them.

"I have no idea what you mean." She waved the thought away, caught up with the sounds around them. The weather was a perfect seventy-two degrees. The matcha that she'd made this morning hit the spot with an extra dose of caffeine.

They moseyed into Alison Agape's tent. Alison was a local painter, and her market set up always drew a crowd. She used her time at the market to paint something, and it was a bit of performance art. Her work reminded Frankie of Ty's mother's artwork, though Alison painted with oil and her favorite subjects were landscapes of the Shenandoah Valley.

She peeked behind the canvas for the price tag.

"Okay, now you're really acting weird," her sister said just loud enough for her to hear. "You hate art."

"I don't hate art." Frankie was thinking about where this could hang. In her front foyer? Above her bed? Or was that not allowed in feng shui?

She would have to think about it. So she picked up one of Alison's business cards instead, and tucked it into her purse.

"Correction, you have never owned a piece of art." They were walking again.

Frankie was tugged back by her purse. "Hmm?"

"Ate Frankie." Delight graced Gabby's features. "Do you *like* him? The vet?"

At the thought of the man, her insides shivered with glee.

"I knew it. I knew it!" her sister all but yelled. "I knew there was something going on with the both of you. You mention him a lot. And so does Liam. And I thought it was weird that you sent the kids to my house without instructions that I not feed them junk food. Oh…o-o-oh. So *that's* what you were doing."

"Shhh. Chill out."

"You're telling me to chill, when you're over here grinning like someone donated a thousand dollars to your precious PTA fund?" She laughed. "When what he was donating was—"

"Gabby!" Frankie gasped.

"Nope. You don't get to do that. You—" she lowered her voice "—are hooked."

Frankie's cheeks burned with the truth. They burned with the memory of *them*. They burned with the dizziness of lust that had consumed the both of them, it seemed.

She felt young and unstoppable and beautiful and wanted.

Still, she had to keep some kind of composure. "Not hooked. Just…content."

"Mmm-hmm," Gabby said, hooking an arm around hers. "Well, I like it. *Finally.*"

"Finally, what?"

"Finally, you don't look so serious all the time. Is this actually turning into something?"

They made their way to her car. This quick trip had become their routine the last few months, a time for the sisters to catch up. Since Gabby and Chip had become serious—and if she didn't get engaged soon, Frankie would be shocked—they'd made a concerted effort to have this hour together.

But now, it was time to head back to the B & B. Liam was with their mother, prepping to go with Reece for spring break, while the B & B staff coordinated Sunday brunch.

There was no rest for the weary in the business of customer service. Especially not on the weekends. Weekends were when the B & B did their best business, and every family member needed to be on board. Even Liam, if he didn't have an extracurricular activity.

Frankie stuffed the flowers into the hatchback of her car. The blooms acted like down bedding being stuffed into a dryer.

"We'll end up the way we're supposed to end up," Frankie said, because she didn't want to think too hard about her and Ty's status.

"But what do *you* want?"

"What I want is for you to stop being so nosy."

In truth, what Frankie wanted was to keep feeling this joy, which, by experience, she knew was precarious. It was first-date joy, except with them, they'd extended it to a blissful set of never-ending dates.

It's a secret, though.

Still, she wanted to hold all of these feelings to her chest.

A memory of Ty's arms around her popped up. At how she felt safe in them. At how she didn't feel like she needed to be any different than how she truly was in his presence. And how despite her sharing her insecurity about the PTA and Reece, he didn't show any judgment.

"Ahem?" Gabby woke her from her thoughts. She was at the passenger door, pulling on the handle.

Right. She closed the hatchback and entered the car. They both checked their phones.

A few texts in the family group chat, as usual. Though none from Ty.

Which was odd. He was the type to text her to just check in, and he hadn't sent his usual "good morning" text. His last had been from yesterday, when he was on his way to the poker game.

Had something happened?

A slew of what-ifs rushed into her head:

What if he got tired of her attitude?

What if he didn't want to hang out with her anymore?

What if he no longer liked her?

"Things okay?" Gabby was scrolling through her texts, which were innumerable, being that she was the B & B's wedding planner.

"Yeah, fine." Frankie admonished herself. She needed to temper her expectations. She and Ty didn't have a standing agreement that they needed to text every hour.

She started the car and made their way up the hill.

"So when will you bring him around? I know Mom's curious."

"Did you tell her?"

"I didn't have to. Liam told her that you guys have been hanging out."

"Well, we don't really have a label."

"That's a bunch of bull. Is that your decision, or his?"

"His at first, and I've come to agree. With both Reece and his ex and the kids. We don't want to say anything until we're sure."

"Sounds like you're playing games, and I thought you were done with those?" Gabby said pointedly.

Frankie knew Gabby was alluding to Frankie and Reece's tryst about a year ago. "That was a mistake, something we did and got out of our system."

"And after that you said that there would be no more games."

"Whatever." She huffed. "You and your memory. And, anyway, you already met Ty."

"Context matters." She grinned. "I guess what I'm asking is, is this going to a place where you'll bring him by mom's house as a boyfriend?"

Boyfriend. The word felt too young. Too innocent. Which Frankie wasn't. Though a part of her imagined what it would be like to bring Ty to meet her family, to have him sit down at the table with the chaos crew. Would he get along with her half-brother, Jared? How would he fit into their big, complex, loud group?

"It's a little too early for that. We're having fun right now. It's easy, just like I like it," Frankie said.

They'd risen to the crest of the hill to the B & B and turned into the parking lot, which was filled with people. They'd both gotten quiet—they would need to be "on" and ready as soon as they walked in. After stepping out onto the gravel parking lot, and gathering their purchases from the back, Frankie followed Gabby through the employee entrance and into the laundry room. The smell of detergent and fabric softener filled her lungs.

When they opened the door that led into the main corridor of the B & B, voices filled the space.

"Sounds like a celebration." Gabby smiled and led the way.

As they entered the light-filled dining room, banked with floor-to-ceiling windows that showcased the view of the back patio and the valley well beyond it, she was stunned, not by the view, but by a couple she hadn't expected would be there.

Reece, with Bianca by his side, meeting her mother Eva, Jared, and his wife and B & B manager, Matilda.

Reece's eyes met hers, and hesitation flashed in them. It woke her from her shock.

They were supposed to meet at her cabin a half hour from now. And *not* with Bianca.

Or this was what Frankie had assumed.

She schooled her features. "Hi."

"Bianca, this is Frankie. Frankie, this is Bianca."

Frankie stuck her hand out and shook Bianca's, attempting to radiate confidence and nonchalance. This wasn't a big deal, right? "Nice to meet you, officially, though I've seen you at the bakery."

"Oh my gosh, same." Bianca's blue eyes met hers, with sincerity. "Liam talks so much about you, and I see you around town and all. It's like I know you already."

"Oh, uh-huh." The whole situation had set Frankie off guard. It didn't help that Bianca looked impeccable with a milkmaid dress, and her no-makeup makeup.

"Since we were here to pick up Liam, I thought it was a good time to introduce her to Mom," Reece said.

Mom. As in *Frankie's* mom. Technically, Eva was Reece's former mother-in-law.

Frankie attempted to keep her sarcasm at bay. "Convenient."

"I always wanted to visit the B and B, and it doesn't disappoint. It's magnificent, Eva."

"That's very kind of you to say," Eva said. "That's what we hope everyone that walks in feels. That they're awed by it."

Why was her mother being so nice?

"Well, we'd better go. Our trip to DC starts now." Reece clapped, as if to move the moment along, and linked his hand with Bianca's.

Frankie tore her eyes away from the sight, and forced a smile on her face. "I'll grab Liam. Where is my little guy, anyway?"

"He's outside with Clark," Eva said of their groundskeeper, who was like a grandfather figure to Liam.

"Will you excuse me?" Frankie marched past everyone and only let her smile slip when she exited the back door. With that came clearer thoughts.

She couldn't believe that Reece had the audacity to bring Bianca by without telling her first. There had to be a rule against that. A warning text would have been the decent thing to do, so she had the time to gather her thoughts.

It was yet another way she hadn't been able to deal with Reece during their marriage. He didn't understand how important it was for her to be prepared.

Clark and Liam were easy to spot off in the distance. Liam was watering the tulips that had emerged in the last few days. The spray of the water created a rainbow.

"Son," she called out.

Liam turned to her and let go of the hose's trigger. "Hi, Mom!"

"Sweetie, your dad and Bianca are here."

"Oh, okay." He looked at Clark, who gave him a salute.

"Have fun on spring break, kiddo," Clark said.

"See you later, Mr. Seabird." He threw the hose onto the ground, and rushed past Frankie.

"Hold on. Where's my hug?" Her gut twisted at how quickly he wanted out of there, and away from her.

"Oh, right." Liam threw his arms around her waist.

"See you later this week."

"'Kay." Liam tried to let go, but Frankie kept ahold of his shoulder.

"Do you have your phone?" she asked him, trying to stall a bit. "Did you pack sunscreen? It's supposed to be hot this week."

"My phone's in my suitcase. With everything else."

"Okay, then. Be good."

"'Bye!"

Then she watched her son run back to his father.

Leaving her slightly bereft and confused.

Chapter Fourteen

As the sun set, Frankie couldn't take it anymore. It didn't help that her house was silent, except for the occasional footsteps of Snowball, and her ruminating thoughts from that afternoon. The fact that Reece had once more somehow destroyed her day truly didn't help at all.

The fact that Ty hadn't texted her back was the straw that broke her back.

She needed some noise. She needed some action. She needed to find out why she hadn't heard from Ty.

She texted Vivian an SOS: Talk me down before I make a mistake.

I'm calling you right now.

The phone rang two seconds later. Vivian spoke without preamble. "Do you need me to come over?"

"No. But thank you for offering before even finding out what happened."

"I'm your girl, you know that." From her side of the world, a car door shut. "Okay, I'm out in my driveway so no one can find me, hee hee."

Frankie laughed, and it was a reprieve from her swirling thoughts.

"Tell me everything."

Frankie shut her eyes for a beat and padded to the kitchen. After throwing the refrigerator door open, she scoured it for food while she explained what had been going on with Ty. The story came out like an avalanche, and Frankie found herself on her couch with a bowl of cereal mixed with chocolate chips.

"Wow. I did not expect that on a Sunday night. I feel like I should have a glass of wine or something," Vivian said. "Okay, so what exactly are you feeling?"

"I feel like I'm being ghosted. And wronged."

"Take a deep breath." Vivian paused. "Now."

Frankie did, though half-heartedly. Vivian was into the whole mind-body-connection thing and prefaced her heart-to-hearts with a cleansing breath.

Frankie just wanted straight talk.

"I guess that's good enough, even though I didn't hear you blow out a breath," Vivian said. "Any-hoo. Look, it's fair that you feel these things, but if you look at both situations objectively, it tells a different story. Ty could simply be busy. He could have lost his phone. And, well, Reece has always been this way. But *wronged* is such a strong word."

Frankie shook her head. Things were not right in her world, and it had everything to do with the two men in her life.

"Why not drive over to Ty's?"

"What? That… Is that something I can do without looking like a stalker?" After all, they weren't labeled as a couple yet.

"With the amount of times you both have ended up in bed and worked on your projects?"

"You're right."

"And when Reece gets back, you can give him a piece of your mind. It wouldn't be the first time, and you'll need to set new ground rules, anyway, now that there's another parent figure in the picture."

"Parent figure?"

Bianca, Liam's *parent*?

Frankie cradled her head.

"Forget what I said," Vivian said. "Just go. Take the dog, and pay Ty a visit."

"Dog. Visit." Frankie exhaled.

Vivian's voice became the voice of reason.

"Then text Vivian, okay?"

"Text Vivian." She heaved a breath, her emotions a smidge more regulated. "Thank you."

"Anytime. It's a rare moment that it's not you taking charge. You know I'm always here for you," Vivian said. "Okay, go."

After they hung up, Frankie scooped Snowball up, brought her to the car, and buckled her into the doggie car seat. Then she drove down the hill to Ty's house, only to halt just shy of turning into his driveway, the exterior lights shining a spotlight on his car. All of the lights in the home were on.

Then her brain righted itself.

What the hell was she doing here?

She and Ty didn't have anything concrete, nor did he owe her an explanation. They were friends. Friends with benefits. Friends who didn't need to check in on one another.

She pressed her hand against her heart and felt it pounding, knowing instantly where her anxiety was coming from.

This had everything to do with Reece. It wasn't Ty's fault. If anything, he was a saint. Forty-eight hours hadn't even passed. It was the weekend before spring break, and here she was trailing after him like a puppy.

This was exactly why she didn't take things to the next level. Because of this. This dependency, this anticipation. This expectation.

Behind her, Snowball was looking out the window and whimpering. She wanted out.

"No, honey, not today. I'm so sorry." She had to go. Now, before Ty looked out the window and saw her car.

She switched the gear to reverse, looking down for a beat. Then, as she backed up, she heard a thump against her car.

Frankie startled.

Aria was at her window.

Frankie rolled down the window, an excuse already at the tip of her tongue. "Sorry, I thought I…" she began, trying to find a good lie.

"Hi." Aria was breathless, and her expression told her something was wrong.

"Is everything okay, sweetheart?"

"My dad. He's sick," she said. "I texted Liam, but he didn't answer."

"Is he *sick* sick? Or just regular sick?" Frankie asked, skeptical. The brand of sick the men of her life were afflicted with—especially Reece—was the kind most women strapped on to their back and powered through their day with.

"*Sick* sick. He hasn't gotten up from bed all day except to go to the bathroom."

Frankie frowned and placed the car in Park, then set the emergency brake. "Should I check on him?"

Aria nodded vehemently.

Frankie scooped Snowball up from the back seat and followed Aria into the house, noting the open microwave door and the smell of food in the air. Bubba greeted her, bumping her leg with his nose and then trotting back down the hallway to where Ty's bedroom was.

Aside from that, it was quiet.

But she wasn't going into his bedroom without Aria's permission, even if she'd left that very room the other day.

"C'mon." Aria gestured her to the bedroom and opened the door.

Frankie set down Snowball, who pranced after Bubba.

When Frankie entered, what met her was a pathetic sight. Ty was under the covers, body curled into a bean, lying on his side. Beside him was a glass of water and a microwave dinner, warmed up by Aria, Frankie presumed.

Aria shook her dad by the shoulder. “Dad.”

“Mmm?” Ty didn’t open his eyes.

“Ms. Frankie’s here.” She stepped aside.

Frankie approached his bed as his eyes fluttered opened. His skin was dull, and there were dark circles under his eyes. She pressed a hand against his forehead, noting the heat. She hissed. “Oh, you’re burning up.”

He mumbled an answer, though it was incoherent.

“Did you have Motrin or Tylenol?”

He nodded. “In my bathroom cabinet. I don’t remember when I last took it, though.”

“Poor you.” She looked back at Aria, by way of permission. “I’ll need to go into the bathroom.”

“It’s over there.” She pointed to the door off to the side.

Frankie nodded and went to the bathroom. The faint smell of cologne lingered. From the cabinet, she retrieved the Tylenol.

Passing Aria, she said, “I saw that you made your dad dinner. That’s so nice, Aria. Have you eaten anything?”

She shook her head. “Not hungry.”

“I’ll make you something, okay?” Frankie smiled, then she went to his bedside, sitting down gently.

The dogs barked, and Aria said, “I’ll let them out.”

“Yes, and you can relax now, Aria, I’m here to help.”

Seconds later, Ty stirred. “What took you so long?”

“I’m here now.” Frankie welled with emotion. Ty was still so sweet, even when he didn’t feel well. She wanted to hug him senseless, to take away his illness. “Can you handle two Tylenols?”

“Yes.” Except he didn’t move.

Poor guy. She reached over and smoothed the wrinkles on his forehead, and a smile graced his face. Tenderness filled her for this man who not only wanted her, but also needed her, even in this temporary way. "C'mon, let me help you up." She leaned forward and lifted him by the shoulders, and his body followed suit. He shimmied just enough that she was able to prop a few more pillows under him. His eyes opened, and they were sad and tired.

"Ready?" She held out a palm, showcasing the caplets.

Slowly and methodically, he placed both pills in his mouth and sipped the water. "Do I look hot?"

"Not only do you look hot, baby, but you *are* hot. If I were to take a guess, I'd say a hundred and two."

"Damn. Lucky you," he said, breathless.

"Lucky me," she said, and as the words left her mouth, she found that she meant it.

She *was* lucky, because his was the kind of relationship in which she didn't feel like she had to change who she was. In his eyes, she was just as she needed to be.

"Was your day better than mine?" he asked.

"It was okay. Reece brought Bianca by."

"How was that?"

"Eh." She shrugged.

"'Eh' as in, you didn't care? Or 'eh' as in, it was painful."

"A little bit of both. I don't know what to make of it." Somehow, saying how she felt while Ty's eyes were shut was easier. "She's the complete opposite of me. Sweet. Gracious. Everyone loves her right away."

"Isn't that a good thing, that she seems to be a good person?"

"It is," she decided, swallowing the truth. "It makes me feel better that when I'm not around, Liam's in good hands."

"I think so, too." His Adam's apple bobbed. "It would be tough for me, but that's how I would try to think about it. If Harper were to find someone new, I would only hope that Aria and that person would get along, that she was safe with them."

"You're right," she said, nodding, even if heaviness still weighed in her chest, and a tinge of shame filled her. Much like assuming that Ty had been avoiding her, she was taking things wrong, as she was prone to do. As she'd been known to do.

"I'm going to get Aria settled, okay? I'll check on you in a little bit. I don't want to leave until your fever breaks."

"Mmm-hmm. Love you," he added, turning his head to the side. His breathing deepened, and he fell into a deep slumber.

Love.

Love?

She stilled, and whispered, "What did you say?"

But she was answered with snoring.

She left his side and closed the bedroom door behind her. While Aria was outside with the dogs, Frankie picked up around the kitchen, then loaded the dishwasher, still trying to process Ty's words.

It had to have been the fever. People said the funniest things while they were sick. Or maybe it was a reflexive answer. She couldn't count the number of times that she'd almost said, "Love you, 'bye" to Reece because she'd spent years doing so.

It was a mistake.

By the time Aria came back in with the dogs in better spirits, Frankie had made a grilled cheese sandwich and cut up apples.

"Ooooh." Aria hopped up on a bar stool and dug in, while Frankie poured her some lemonade from the refrigerator.

As she cleaned up, Frankie said, "You're such a special girl, do you know that? For not panicking while your dad's sick. And resourceful, knowing to bring him water and food."

"He kind of told me what he needed, but I had to figure it out, too. I can't turn on the stove yet, so I just got stuff from the freezer."

"You did everything right." Frankie washed her hands, and allowed the bubbles to gather in her palms. "I'm sorry that

Liam didn't get your messages. He's with his dad, and his phone's in his backpack."

"Then how did you know to come here?"

She cleared her throat and cobbled together an excuse. "PTA stuff, and I was in the neighborhood. I thought it would be easier to talk to him in person."

"I'm glad you did," Aria said.

"Well, I'll ask your dad later if you can have my phone number. You can call me for anything."

Her face lit up. "Okay. But you're not leaving yet, right?"

"No. I told your dad that I would stay until his fever breaks. Are you okay with that?"

"Uh-huh." Aria continued to chew. "Can you stay until tomorrow?"

"Oh, um..." She looked at his bedroom door. How would Ty feel about her staying the night? Would that be invading his privacy?

"Please? I really don't think he'll be better tonight. I want you here."

"Okay, Aria, I'll stay," Frankie said.

Aria had said the magic words.

Ty's slumber was filled with fits and starts, caused by alternately feeling like he was burning up from the inside to bone-chilling cold. His dreams were rife with faces and dogs barking, of the sound of wood being sawed. Of people laughing, and the bitter taste of medicine on his tongue. Then a dark nothingness.

And then, just as quickly as he'd descended into a feverish stupor, his eyes opened easily, without his body protesting. He awoke to his darkened bedroom. On his bedside table were two bottles of medication, a glass half-filled with water, and a thermometer.

He frowned, noticing a trace of headache against his temples and above his brow. His memory was in shambles, discombobulated. Hadn't he returned home from visiting the puppies just that morning? Who'd brought the medications?

Aria.

"Aria?" he called out as he pushed himself up to standing. Aria was fiercely independent, but he'd never taught her how to give meds; and how did she even know where they were?

"Hey, you." A figure graced the doorway, and stepping into the dim lamp light was Frankie. Her hair was down, and she wore a gentle smile. She was a sight to behold. "Aria's asleep right here on your couch."

Snippets of the night came back to him. Of opening his eyes and seeing Frankie, and the relief that had flooded through him. The cold compresses on his forehead. Her soothing voice.

"It's nighttime?"

She nodded. She pressed a finger against her lips, and then approached him. The bed dipped as she sat, and the warmth of her body was an instant relief. "She didn't want to leave you alone and insisted that I spend the night. I hope that's okay."

"It is. A hundred percent."

She smiled. "You have yourself a good girl. She made you a microwave meal. She fed Bubba. And she kept checking on you."

"So she likes me after all."

Her face softened. "She loves you, you know that."

And yet, it wasn't Aria's affection he was craving at the moment. It was that of the woman who was here.

"And you stayed."

She smiled.

"And Liam?"

"With his dad."

"Right. I remember now. Oh, my God, how about you? You're not feeling sick?"

"Nope. I'm invincible." She smiled. "I'm a mom. But do you remember anything else?"

He frowned and scoured his brain. "No. What did I miss?"

"Oh, um, nothing else. I just wondered if there was something I missed before I got here."

He reached out for her hand, which rested on the covers, though it couldn't convey how grateful he was. And how lucky he was, too. "Thank you."

"Don't thank me yet—you're not out of the woods."

"But you didn't have to come and stay." He thought about it. "Wait, how did you know I was sick? Did the kids coordinate this?"

"Um, well..." she hedged. "I actually came here on my own."

"Oh?"

"Yeah, I was wondering why you didn't text me back all day. I thought that something was up."

"You thought I was ignoring you?"

"Yeah." She didn't meet his eyes, and despite his exhaustion, he understood what she was trying to get at.

"You thought that I'd find a way to escape you in this small town?" he asked.

"It wouldn't be the first time," she said under her breath.

Ty gripped her hand as tightly as he could, though he didn't know what to say that would convey how he felt, so as not to scare her. What he'd learned from Frankie these last few weeks was that she needed to feel space around her. She needed to have choices, and he wanted her to feel as comfortable as possible. "I couldn't even if I tried. Everything in this town leads back to you."

She half laughed, and seeing her face lighten up made him feel a smidge better.

"Tell me everything I missed," he said.

She opened her mouth before shutting it. "Nothing, really.

We were watching you. Aria talked a lot about Harper. She really misses her."

The events from the day before returned to him, including his conversation with Harper. "Speaking of. Harper called yesterday. She won the show."

"What?" Frankie shouted, then slapped a hand over her mouth.

"There are a lot of moving parts, but she'll be here for graduation." He frowned, his head hurting again.

"That's great news. But now, it's time to rest." She bent down and kissed him on the forehead. Her lips were cool, and he shut his eyes to take it in. It was then he remembered something she'd said earlier, about Bianca.

She's the opposite of me. Sweet. Gracious. Everyone loves her right away.

"Wait," he said, swallowing as he sat back up.

"Mmm?"

"You mentioned earlier that you were the opposite of Bianca. And implied that because of that, you're unlovable. I think you're wrong."

"That's not what I meant." She looked away.

"Well, whatever you meant, you're wrong. Not only are you lovable, but there's no second-guessing how you feel or what your intentions are. When you care about someone, they feel it. *I* feel it." Ty swallowed against his rising emotions and brain fog. "Was that too much? I know that it's early between the two of us, but I already—"

Love you, was what he wanted to say.

He couldn't finish his sentence, because Frankie had leaned forward and hugged him. "It's not too much," she said into his ear.

With his limited strength, he wrapped his arm around her waist.

Then, just as abruptly, she sat up and turned away. "You

should get some rest. I'll be right outside, okay?" She walked to the door, and only turned when she was in the hallway. "Just holler if you need me."

"Okay," Ty said, relief overwhelming him, and with the safety of knowing that he was taken care of, that his daughter was safe, he quickly fell back to sleep.

Even if he didn't get to say what he wanted. It could wait.

Because he had everything he needed.

Chapter Fifteen

Ty woke up the next day and felt as if he'd gone ten rounds in an MMA match. He was simply making coffee, but the act of scooping coffee grounds into the basket was a feat. His muscle aches were gone, and when he checked his temperature after his shower, it was normal, but his strength was at zero.

Still, he was trying to be as silent as possible. Aria was asleep in his room with the dogs, and Frankie dozed on the living-room couch, a lump under two sets of fleece blankets.

He remembered waking up twice, having been fed more medicine, and encouraged to drink water.

The coffee smelled like heaven as it brewed, already a balm to the headache that he was pretty sure due to his lack of caffeine the last twenty-four hours as much as it was due to his illness. Still, he searched his cupboards for the lone box of tea he'd been gifted when he'd moved into the house. Finally, he found it, and boiled water in a tiny pot.

It was the least he could do.

"Hey, I should be doing that," a voice said from behind him.

He turned to find a disheveled Frankie in sweats. Her hair was in a braid, pulled over one shoulder, and she was walking over to him, concern in her eyes. "Come sit," she said, taking him gently by the arm and coaxing him to a countertop stool. "I'll make your coffee for you."

"I'm okay," Ty said.

"You might think so, but you're likely dehydrated, and you haven't eaten much in the last couple of days. Let's get you fed." She filled a glass of water for him. "I didn't expect you to be up this early."

"I couldn't sleep anymore," he said.

"I hope you're taking the day off." She opened the refrigerator and inspected the inside. "How do you feel about rice porridge?" She looked over her shoulder at him, the view stunning him for a beat. He had a vision of this, of them being together in the same kitchen for breakfast, perhaps a memory from another life.

"Rice porridge sounds perfect," he said, though he didn't quite know what it was. But he would eat anything she cooked.

At this point, he would do anything she asked of him.

I love you.

She grinned at his no-doubt stunned expression. "What?"

Could it really be love he was feeling? Or was this his sick brain talking? Patients loved their doctors, their caregivers. He'd been on the other side of that equation, where he'd received a great deal of affection from his patients' owners.

He needed to slow his roll. He couldn't gush over Frankie if she wasn't ready.

"I said yes, I took the day off. Even if I really want to work on the bookcases today."

"But the school's closed for spring break."

"I could pick up stain."

"Look who's headstrong now." She set a cup of coffee in front of him. "No work for you. Frankie's orders."

"Fine. To be honest, I'm still pretty beat. I just feel so guilty not doing anything."

"You're doing something. You're recovering. And, anyway, I got to thinking about how we can market your work." She continued on to talk about networking with local artists and media opportunities while grabbing the rice from his pantry, some garlic and onions from the refrigerator, and then firing up the stove.

Except he couldn't quite focus on her words, his brain fuzzy from lack of calories, and caffeine, and the woman in front of him. His imagination took flight again, and he was looking down from above, at their two children and two dogs making a glorious mess of the kitchen.

"Ty?"

He snapped back to awareness.

"What's up?" she asked.

Damn his sick brain. He said, "I like seeing you this way."

"What way?"

"In my kitchen."

She frowned at the implication, and he laughed.

"I knew that would get a reaction. But I'm not just talking about you in my kitchen. But you in my life," he said, the words flying out of him.

She stopped stirring the pot for a beat, and then resumed, though she didn't answer.

His confidence rose. Last night had unlocked something in him. Balancing their relationship with the kids and work and the dogs no longer seemed daunting or scary. While maybe he was a little rash, what he'd experienced overnight was the care he'd been looking for.

And she needed to know exactly where he stood.

Ty slipped off the chair and went to her. Her profile was serious, and the way she was stirring the garlic and onions, and then adding the rice and stirring that…it was as if she were on a mission that she couldn't be bothered from. He stopped a few steps away. He could still be contagious. "Can I come closer?"

She set the ladle down and turned to him, though she leaned against the stove as if it was providing her some support. She nodded.

"Thank you for staying last night."

"You're welcome. You would have done it for me, too."

"You're right, I would have. But…still, you did stay, and I appreciate it."

She smiled.

"These last few weeks…they've been good. More than good, actually. And I wonder if… I wonder if we should really do this."

He gaze dragged to the ground. "Do what?"

"You and me."

"Aren't we already doing you and me?"

"We are, but it's halfway, isn't it? We're not saying that we're anything. And I don't want there to be any question about what we are from anyone."

She hiked her hand on a hip. "I dunno. Are you ready for this? Are you ready to be in a relationship with me?"

He narrowed his eyes, confused. "What, are you some alien disguised as a gorgeous woman who could easily kick the ass of anyone I know?"

Her cheeks pinked. "Stop."

"I mean it. What's the downside here?"

"Well, let me remind you of what we'd discussed a couple of weeks ago—you'll have to meet my family, as my boyfriend." She counted out a finger. "Which means that it's open season for them to be in your business. And there's Liam and Aria. They'll have expectations, too, not just that we're spending time together."

"Two out of two, not worried."

"And then there's you and me."

He brought her closer. "This still okay? I don't want to pass on my germs."

"A sick person is most contagious before they come down with a fever, Doctor."

"See? Sassy *and* smart. It's why I can't imagine my days without you."

She grinned as if she couldn't help herself. He lifted his hand to her cheek. "That. That is the cutest."

She covered her face. "Stop, Ty."

"Why?"

"I don't know how you do that."

"Do what?"

"Say those things. When clearly I'm trying to deflect it."

He pulled her hands down. "And so self-aware." He dipped down to catch her eyes. "So what do you think? Will you be my girlfriend?"

She buried her face in his chest. Her voice was muffled. "Yes."

He laughed and tipped her chin up. "What's that?"

"I said yes. I'll be your girlfriend."

"That's what I thought I heard."

"Yes! Yes! Yes!" Aria yelled from the bedroom door. In pajamas, her hair stood out in places from the messy way she'd slept. Then, she lifted the phone in her hand. On the screen was Liam.

"Let's g-o-o-o-o!" Liam yelled.

Ty threw his head back in laughter, and he clutched a giggling Frankie against his chest.

Because this was just the beginning.

Spring break week meant a packed B & B, but Frankie, on cloud nine, moved through the motions of fielding guests at the front reception in a state of bliss the next day. There were zero vacancies all week, especially with Easter on Sunday. And though she was behind in her admin tasks after spending an extra night with Ty—on his couch for Aria's sake, and under the guise of him still being sick—all she felt was possibility and hope.

Her eyes were also on her watch, waiting for her lunch break. An hour-long mom-date at the square with Vivian. She needed time with her friend. She needed to process what had happened yesterday.

"You're in a good mood," her mother said. Eva carried a stack of menus and set them down on the pile next to the hostess table. Then she sidled up next to Frankie to check the list of reservations on the podium. "Looks like everyone's been served."

"Yep. Even the Jenkins." She eyed her mother knowingly.

The Jenkins had been late to every reservation during their stay, which caused some inconvenience for the kitchen. Still, the B & B was known for their great service, and they'd had to adjust.

"On the bright side, we have a couple of seconds to catch up." Eva nudged Frankie. "So what's this I've been hearing about the veterinarian?"

Frankie snickered. Her mother had the habit of calling anyone she dated by their occupation. "His name is Ty. I'm surprised it took you this long to ask."

"I've learned not to be invested until you say so."

After Frankie's father had died, and after her half brother came to town, the entire family treated crises with kid gloves. The less stress they had in their family, the better. Her reason for keeping everyone at an arm's length was not only for her protection, but also for Liam's, and for her family.

But, oh, Ty. The feelings that came up when he was around. The way he made her feel. It was as if she glowed from the inside out. Like she floated. Like everything around her was a dream.

"What if..." Frankie began, gazing around the room to make sure no one else was listening. "What if I told you that maybe I'm ready for you to be invested?"

Her mother's eyes rounded, and she turned to her daughter fully. Then she placed a hand on Frankie's elbow, grounding her to the moment, and the seriousness of the situation. "Frankie."

Her mother hugged her.

"Mom." She felt a little foolish. "I know this doesn't happen often, but you're being a little dramatic."

"You can say what you want." Eva stepped back. "But this is a big deal. Since when?"

"Yesterday."

"And how do you feel?"

"Good." She blew out a breath. "A little scared."

"Is it love?"

Frankie coughed. There went that *L* word again.

She had been tempted to say it to Ty this morning before she left to come to work. She'd waited for him to say it first. But he hadn't.

Perhaps he'd changed his mind. Or perhaps he hadn't meant it at all.

Her mother's eyes softened. "You know, when Cruz and I..."

Then, as if summoned, Eva's fiancé came in through the back door. He wore hiking gear and a small backpack.

"Of course, he walks in the moment you mention him." Frankie said this with pure affection. Cruz was perfect for her mother. They were also relationship goals. If love could happen to them, it could happen to anyone.

It's happening to you now, her conscience reminded her.

He kissed Eva on the cheek. He nodded to Frankie. "How's my little man doing?"

"They're in Old Town Alexandria today," Frankie said. "He's been sending me nonstop photos."

And that was another reason why she fell in love with Cruz. He loved Liam like his own grandson.

"Frankie has a new beau," her mother said.

"Whoa," Cruz said.

"It's Dr. Ty Golden," Eva supplied.

"The vet? Nice. So when are we meeting him?"

Eva's eyes lit. "Yes, when, Frankie?"

"I was wondering when you were going to ask that." Frankie braced herself.

"I met your whole family when your mother and I weren't even getting along," Cruz said. "I think your doctor's late to the game."

"See? That's why I haven't brought anyone home," Frankie said.

Cruz and Eva looked at one another, then back at Frankie. "I'm sure it didn't help that Reece brought his new girlfriend to meet everyone," Eva said.

Frankie blew out a breath. That moment felt so long ago, but it had only been a few days. Yet, now it sat heavy in her chest. "Yeah, that was a lot."

"I hope you know that as much as we're happy for Reece, you're my daughter, and Liam is my grandson."

"Oh, I know that, Mom. This isn't about alliances. I'm over Reece. I'm glad he's happy. It's the fact that he moved on. And way before me."

"I wouldn't say *way* before, right? Because you have Ty now."

"I guess." And yet, she and Ty were still at the starting gates, and while they'd upleveled, there was still more ahead.

"And it's not a competition," Eva said.

"I know it's not, and yet somehow, it matters."

Frankie hated that she couldn't just fall into a romance and ignore everything else that was going on. Real life had a way of reminding her that love was a marathon. That there would be ups and downs, despite her wishing or her attempting to control the outcome.

"You can have complicated feelings," Eva said. "And those

feelings might not go away. But it doesn't have to keep you from moving on."

Frankie nodded. Her mother was right, as usual. "But you have to promise not to scare him off."

"Aww, no. You can't say that." Her half brother, Jared, appeared from the kitchen. "You're the scariest person in the family. It's payback time."

"I am *not* scary," she quipped.

The three exploded in laughter, causing the guests in the dining room to turn their heads.

"Whatever. You know what? It's officially my lunch hour." Frankie walked away, turning one last time to give them a glare.

"Easter lunch," Eva called out. "Invite him."

Frankie knew that it was a nonnegotiable order, not a request, though she said, "Maybe."

Was she scary? She knew she was intimidating. She knew that she didn't suffer fools. But *scary*?

Frankie got in her car and made her way down the hill to the town square. Vivian was already there, sitting at a park bench, scrolling through her phone. Next to her was a picnic basket.

The sight of it made her smile. Vivian always had a keen sense of where Frankie's mind was at. Somehow, she just knew that Frankie needed to sit.

Vivian stood as Frankie walked up. "You're not going to believe it."

"I can't tell if it's good news or bad news."

"Good. And, well, some stuff that needs improvement." She dragged her to the bench and showed her their running list of donations. "Look at that."

Frankie gasped. "Wow. I did not expect this."

"Yep. We're getting closer to our goal to be able to put some money toward next year's events. And this was all because of you."

"Me and Ty," she told Vivian. "Those donors? Ty talked to those folks."

"He basically raised the money to pay himself for the bookshelves."

"Amazing. So, what needs improvement?" Frankie heaved a breath. She hadn't expected to talk business today, but there was no time like the present.

Vivian pulled up our volunteers list for the graduation party, and only half of the slots were filled. "What's up with the underclassmen parents?"

Frankie shook her head. "Don't they understand how important it is to volunteer? We don't want our fifth-grade parents to work at their own party."

"We've still got time." Vivian winced.

"It's a month away." Frustration clawed through her. "We have to find more volunteers."

But her mind migrated to beyond the fifth-grade graduation, to what would happen after. To what it all meant, and the changes forthcoming, and what changes had already occurred. With Ty.

A hand was waving in front of her. Vivian grinned. "Where'd you go?"

"I'm here. But, yeah, we'll figure it out. We have to have a game plan. Though not today. My brain is mush."

"I feel you. Ian was up half the night with a fever."

"God, that's really going around."

"Hopefully it won't be as bad as Ty's was. How is he today?"

"Much better—he's back at work. Who's with Ian now?"

"Ryan. I asked him to come over."

"So that you could spend the time with me? Thank you." She wrapped an arm around Vivian.

"To be honest, I also needed the break. Especially from Ryan."

"Uh-oh. Tell me about it."

Vivian grabbed things from the basket. "First, chicken salad on sourdough. Sparkling water."

"Delish." Frankie's stomach growled. "And apparently, right on time."

Vivian laughed and they dove into their sandwiches. After swallowing her first bite, Frankie gestured for Vivian to go on.

"Ryan and I have been spending a lot of time together."

"But you always do when he's in town." She took a sip of her sparkling water.

"And… I think I'm starting to feel things?"

Frankie coughed.

"I know, this isn't good. He's…a flight risk. Tell me to stop."

Frankie swallowed. "Stop?"

"You need to tell me, not ask me."

"What if I said that I thought this would happen? That you never did stop having feelings for him?"

"No. You're not supposed to say that to me. What am I supposed to do now?" Vivian pressed a palm against her forehead.

A laugh bubbled out of Frankie, and Vivian followed suit. "We're mothers, damn it. We're supposed to have our shit together," Frankie said.

"So tell me what to do."

"I can't, because I have no idea what I'm doing, too," Frankie said. "Ty asked me to be his girlfriend."

"What the—" Vivian pressed a napkin to her lips, then swallowed. She hugged Frankie. "I can't believe you didn't lead with that." A couple of kids ran past them with ice-cream cones.

"What we had to talk about was important."

"Matters of the PTA are infinitely less important than matters of the heart. And you've listened to me go on and on about Ryan in the past."

"I think the bottom line here is that we don't spend enough time together. If we did, we'd already know what was going on."

"We need more picnics," Vivian said.

"And maybe you need to get back out there. Maybe space from Ryan is the way to go."

"I'm not dealing with those apps. Watching you was enough to scare me off. Besides, you proved it with Ty. Finding someone in real life might be the better way to go. I mean, look at you now. With a *boyfriend*."

"You can stop now."

She cackled. "What I'm confused about is why you're not thrilled about it."

"What are you talking about? I'm thrilled."

"Really?" Vivian leveled her with a glare. "I can tell your happy, but there's something more there."

Frankie bit her lip. "I don't know. What if I find out something?"

"Have you found out something?"

"No."

"Have you heard of the saying that if you look hard enough for something wrong, you'll find it? Our brains are literally wired to look for the negative."

"And yet, that proves my point. That there *is* something to find." A gust of wind blew the napkins out of Frankie's hands. "Oh…crap."

"*This* is the reason why it took you so long to get past the first date."

"I'm allowed to be picky."

"You are, no doubt. You can do whatever you want. You can first-date until we're both seventy-five. But if you're really trying to give this relationship a chance, looking for something wrong won't really help it, will it? I think you need to enjoy the moment."

"Is that me, though?"

They both laughed.

Vivian ate the last bit of her sandwich. "Speaking of seventy-five. I've been thinking about how fast time is flying. Soon, the kids'll be older and there won't be playdates. They'll be making plans without us and seeing friends who we haven't vetted. Then they'll be driving and we won't know where they're going. Damn." She blew out a breath.

"I know." Frankie looked toward another picnic table, filled with three mothers and their children, still toddlers. "Those phones are already taking up so much of their time. And middle school feels big. The kids won't need our help as much anymore." Frankie wrinkled her nose.

"Nor will the school. Besides, Simone, the middle school PTA president, is in it to win it." She smiled. "But won't it be nice to not be in charge of everything?"

"I guess," Frankie said.

But the thought of not having control, of not being involved, sparked discomfort. Everything was changing, and with so much unknown, including how she and Ty would work out, she wasn't sure if she was ready for it.

Chapter Sixteen

Today was the day. He was going to meet Frankie's family, officially.

Ty and Frankie stood on her back porch. She'd handed him a shot glass of vodka moments before. She lifted her shot glass and he toasted his against hers.

"To meeting the parents," she said. "And praying that they don't embarrass me."

"To the parents," he echoed, and then to himself added, *that I come out unscathed.*

They were Frankie's family, after all. If they were half as straightforward as she was, then he'd needed the liquid courage to withstand the experience.

Droplets of clear liquid spilled over the side, a tiny consequence for what they were about to do.

"Here goes nothing," Frankie said, tipping the glass to her lips.

Ty did so, too, and the liquid burned as soon as it hit his tongue and throat. He imagined it bolstering his bravado. It undoubtedly killed off the last of the virus that lingered from his sickness last weekend.

"Mom! We have cucumbers!" Liam yelled from the garden gate. Behind him was Aria, who was carrying a basket.

Frankie sent him a thumbs-up, and gestured for them to come back to the house. As they neared, the sound of their conversation and laughter filtered in the air.

"They missed each other, I can tell," Ty mused.

"It's so nice to see."

But Frankie's tone was off, and she was worrying her lip.

She'd been tense all morning, and though he'd put on a good face while she lobbed "suggestions" on how to survive his first meeting with the family such as: *come with an empty stomach* and *if they fill your plate with food, do not under any circumstance refuse*, and *offer to do the dishes*, and more he couldn't remember at the moment, he knew she was just as nervous as he was.

Ty gently plucked the shot glass from her hand and set them both down. He settled his hands on her hips.

"It's going to be okay. We're gonna love each other, you'll see," Ty said cheerfully, though he'd had a stress dream last night. Objectively, meeting the parents was the next step in their relationship, and he knew what he felt for Frankie. But involving families raised the stakes.

"Oh my gosh, I *know* they're going to love you. They're going to love Aria, too. My mom has a whole Easter egg hunt planned for her and Liam." She wiggled out a smile. "I'm not worried about that at all. It's going to be great."

"But…"

"But, this isn't just an ordinary Easter lunch, you know?"

"I do know."

"Do you think that the kids understand what it all means?"

"I think they're up to speed. They were there when I popped the question, remember?" He smiled just thinking about it. "They were happy."

"But we haven't sat down and talked to them about it, together, and with this lunch, the kids are going to hear my family ask you a ton of questions. I hate that we have to make it a big deal, because it isn't, technically." She shook her head. "You must be thinking that you didn't sign up for this, that you shouldn't have to worry about meeting the parents so soon after dating. With any other person—"

"Any other person isn't you. And I quickly realized after moving into Peak that the rules are different here, too, that meeting the family is a given so early, with how small the town is. But we can talk to them now."

"I'd feel better."

"Okay, let's do it."

The kids had climbed the back porch. Aria lifted her basket. Tips of cucumbers stuck out from the top. "See how much we got."

"Looks like cucumber salad is on the menu for the next few days," Frankie said. Then she gave Ty the eyes, as if to say *you go first.*

Ty cleared his throat, suddenly parched, and gestured to the porch chairs. "Kids, could you sit down?"

"Okay," Liam said. Aria glanced at Liam and sat, too.

"Want a drink?"

Both kids shook their heads.

"Fruit snacks?" Frankie hustled into the kitchen, and one second later, carried out a couple of boxes she pulled from the pantry. "Yogurt-covered pretzels? Goldfish crackers?"

When she was answered with crickets, Ty jumped in. "So, Frankie and I… I mean, Ms. Frankie—"

"You see," Frankie interrupted. "We've gotten close as you know."

"Really well."

"Dad, we know you're boyfriend and girlfriend," Aria said.

"We were there," Liam said.

"But we wanted to make sure that you were both okay with that," Frankie said, jumping in.

"That you don't mind us spending more time together."

"And, like, meeting the rest of my family." Frankie winced. "Is that okay, Aria?"

"Yeah. It's no big deal," Aria said.

"And we spend time now." Liam shrugged. "We *wanted* to get you guys together. It's because of us that you guys are together, you know?"

"Really?" Ty said, feigning shock. "We would have never guessed."

"I can't believe it," Frankie said.

"Told you they had no clue, Aria." Liam jumped up. "Are we done? Can Aria and I play video games before we go to Lola's house?"

"Lola?" Ty asked.

"That means grandmother," Liam said.

Frankie grabbed the basket of vegetables. "We actually have to go now. But there'll be things to do there."

Their group made their way up the flagstone pathway to the farthest cabin in the row. It was on a hillside, with a path up an incline. The sun was high, the sky bright blue.

The view was spectacular, and that was from the front of the home.

The kids got well ahead of them and burst through the unlocked front door, and it shut behind them.

Just as Ty reached for the door handle, Frankie halted him. She turned him to face her fully. "Okay, whatever happens in there, I'm sorry." Her words came out in bursts.

"You know what I find sweet?" he said, holding her close to him with a hand on her back. "That for someone who usually doesn't care what anyone thinks, that this really matters to you."

"I love my family." Her face dipped down in a pensive smile. "And I always try to be the good *ate*. That means eldest daughter. You'll hear my siblings calling me that. And there are these tiny customs you're going to have to get used to, like—"

He stopped her chatter with a kiss, and to his relief, her lips softened against his. Heat rose between them; it was instantaneous, and it could have gotten away from him if he wasn't careful. As he eased off, he said, "It's going to be okay. Why are you so worried?"

She nodded. "It's been a while since I brought anyone home to meet my family."

"A while, meaning…"

"Since Reece."

"Ah." In the half second of her staring at him, he felt another niggle of fear. Meeting her family had to be done if he wanted to have some kind of a relationship with Frankie, even if it was one that was still in its beginning stages.

It was that, from the jump, he would be compared to Reece.

Still, he smiled, to lighten the mood. "Then aren't you glad it's me coming through those doors with you?"

She beamed. "I am. Because you…you're the best." Her chest rose and fell. "Ready?"

"Absolutely." *I think*, he concluded in his head.

Frankie stepped ahead of him and opened the door, presenting him as if he was the Easter Bunny himself.

Good thing he'd brought wine. So when Frankie said, "Everyone, this is Ty," he raised the bottle in the air.

Because saying something would have been useless with the ruckus he caused as he entered.

There were introductions. Her mother's fiancé, Cruz, her sister Gabby and her boyfriend, Chip, both whom he'd already met. Jared and his wife, Matilda. Then, at the end of the line was Evangeline Espiritu, the matriarch of the whole family.

She was an older version of Frankie, and for a beat Ty was mesmerized at that notion. Her eyes were exacting; they took Ty in, and he felt examined.

He stuck out a hand. "Mrs. Espiritu."

"Ty, call me Eva." She took his hand, but instead of shaking it, pulled him down and pressed her cheek against his. "Very nice to meet you."

"Likewise, and I'm here with my appetite," he said, his nerves taking over.

She laughed. "So you got the memo."

"Yes, ma'am. Read and memorized."

"Then this will be an even better lunch. Welcome."

She stepped aside, and there, her long dining-room table was lined with leaves. In the middle were small heaps of different kinds of dishes, the scents of which made his stomach growl. From his novice experience with Filipino food, he could make out rice, chicken, lumpia, and longanisa, which was a sweet sausage. All laid out on the table, sans plates, over leaves.

"Have you ever been to a kamayan?" Jared said, slipping on his apron. As if on cue, folks began to line up at the sink.

Ty shook his head.

"It's when everyone eats with their fingers. *Kamay* meaning hands. For our purposes today, we'll all be at our own place settings, you'll have your own rice, and you'll have a spoon and fork to take food from the dishes in the middle. It's a sign of camaraderie. It's like the most intimate family-style dinner."

"I don't know how to eat everything with my hands," Ty whispered. "I've seen it done, though."

He smiled. "Don't worry. We'll teach you. Go ahead and wash your hands, and I'll get the rest ready."

"Can I help?"

"Nope. You're the guest." He winked.

While waiting for his turn at the sink, he spied the bustling Espiritu women, and he noted how the three were so different. Frankie was a force, yes, but so were the others in their own way. Eva was quiet, though her expressions were serious. Gabby was always smiling, though she spoke up. Matilda sat back and seemed to moderate the conversation.

It was the kind of get-together he hadn't been a part of in a long time, not since his college undergrad days, where every weekend meant a dinner at someone's apartment. Vet school put a damper on all of that, and since then, he'd celebrated in small ways, with Harper, their tiny tight group of friends, or occasionally Harper's family when they'd been in town.

"I know what you're thinking, that it's going to be hard to get a word in." In front of him, Cruz lathered his hands. Up close, his features were rugged, almost unkempt, with a thick, five-o'clock shadow, and short hair that curled at the edges. He oozed of the outdoors. "But when these women take a liking to you, there's no question about it."

He stepped aside, so Ty took his turn. The water was warm when he turned on the faucet. "I've definitely been on the receiving end of when Frankie *didn't* like me."

As he wiped his hands on a paper towel, Cruz grinned. "I fear to even think about how that felt from Frankie. The first time I met her, she just leveled me with a glare." He shivered. "Freaks me out just thinking about it. But the mere fact you're here means that you must be an okay guy."

"I—I hope so." He wasn't sure what to do with that compliment. This all felt so overwhelming, so much more than he'd even built it up to be. And he'd thought he'd been silly before. But none of this felt silly. It all felt very serious.

"If you're not, then Eva'll suss you out soon enough."

After shutting off the water, Ty felt the chill almost immediately.

Then Cruz nudged him in his side. "Just kidding. Just be yourself."

Frankie's appetite was nil, though she continued to shove food into her mouth. It wasn't that the food wasn't delicious—it was. But the fact that her mother had decided on a kamayan for Easter lunch during Ty's first introduction—it was less about it being a test for him, than it being a test for her.

What were they, kids in high school? To subject him and

her to this extravagant show of a family dinner—it was her mother's not-so-subtle way of asking her if Ty was the one.

Frankie looked at Ty now, across the table. He was flanked by Gabby and Eva; Gabby was speaking. He was nodding, which was a good thing, she presumed. The kids were in and out of the dining room, engaged in a scavenger hunt her mother had devised for the afternoon.

Frankie hated that she couldn't be next to Ty, to guide him. To run interference. The most she could do was reach out with a foot to touch his.

Which she did now.

His eyes darted to hers and she raised her eyebrows, as if to ask *are you okay*?

They were getting good at communicating with their eyes, and they did it more often than not, what with having their kids around them all of the time.

The corner of his lips turned up as if to say *everything's fine*.

"You're especially quiet." Next to her, Jared nudged her with his elbow.

"Just enjoying this delicious food. You've outdone yourself."

"Thanks. I think my lechon could be better, but it'll do, I guess. But your guy seems to like it. He's taken seconds of everything."

"He arrived with an empty belly, like I told him to."

"So then what's up? Looks like he's getting along with Mom and Gabby. You'd think that you'd smile at least a little."

"This all seems, I don't know…extra."

"Ah, as if you aren't?"

She gave her half brother the side-eye while he chuckled silently.

"You've given every one of us trouble. This is all just payback." He grinned.

"I have never given you trouble. Or Matilda."

"Must I remind you of the time you scolded me in the garden?"

She thought back to that moment, shortly after Jared moved into the B and B. He had been hesitant staying, and she'd been so upset at him that she'd refused his offer to help in the garden. "What that was was a natural reaction, because I was starting to get attached to you, and I didn't want you to go."

"In that case, all this is a natural reaction to make sure we take care of the person who takes care of us."

Emotion balled in her throat at that, and she trained her gaze down to her food. At the effort that the family had gone through to source banana leaves, because it wasn't something you could just find in the local grocery store. "When did you get so corny?"

"Around the same time you got to be so stubborn." He grinned. "But I like him, too. I find him to be straightforward and patient. He's also good with our pets. And Liam talks a lot about Aria."

"He is, so far, everything I could ask for," she said sincerely. "But sometimes it all feels like too much, you know? Liam is graduating..."

"And Reece is getting serious with Bianca."

She sighed. "This has nothing to do with Reece."

"Yeah? You sure about that?"

She shook her head and gathered the rice into her fingers. She took a hearty bite, and allowed the flavor of the garlic to ease some of the tension that she'd been feeling all day. "One-hundred-percent. I'm happy that he's found someone. Bianca seems nice enough, and Liam likes her. And we've got nothing to prove. What happened between him and me was ages ago."

"I know things are over between the both of you, but..." He took a sip of his beer. "This kind of reminds me of Matilda," he said of his wife. His brown eyes tracked Matilda, who'd risen and was at the kitchen counter. She was slicing the Sans Rival for dessert.

Around the time those two got together, Matilda had been dealing with her ex-husband, who was also getting married.

Except. "My relationship with Reece is completely different than hers was with her ex. She *hated* her ex."

"Yeah, but the idea of an ex moving on, it still does something to you, doesn't it? Logic is one thing, but feelings and emotions are another."

God, did she know about that.

"I really like Ty," she admitted. And when she said it, she knew that her affection for him was more than that. "I like him more than I've ever liked anyone."

"That's pretty serious then." Jared took a sip of his water. "It makes sense that you're overwhelmed. Just don't let that get in the way of you showing him how you feel."

"I hear you're building bookshelves at the elementary-school library," Cruz said to Ty, which caught Frankie's attention.

"Yep. It's probably ninety-percent done," Ty said.

"Amazing. I've also built a thing or two." Cruz beamed.

"He's talking about the fence in my side and backyard," Eva said, gazing at Cruz.

"The one out there? I saw it on the way in," Ty said. "That's great."

"Ty's starting a woodworking business," Frankie announced.

"It's nothing." Ty looked away.

"No, it's not nothing. He's so talented. It's not launched yet but I built his website. You should see his gallery." She grinned.

Except when she looked at Ty, he avoided her gaze.

Cruz added more rice to his plate. "That fence project humbled me. Glad I had Chip to help me out. It was my first time building something that big. The best I did before that was a small bench."

Her mother's eyes rounded. "What? Are you serious?"

"I guess I didn't know back then how much I was in love with you. All I wanted to do was to impress you, and to give you what you wanted. Even if we weren't seeing eye-to-eye."

The two locked eyes for a beat, and Frankie's heart squeezed with happiness for her mother and Cruz, and with yearning. Yes, Frankie did want what her mother, her sister, and Jared had.

She wanted love.

Looking up at Ty, who was laughing at something Gabby had said, it dawned on Frankie.

That the love she wanted was here. In her mother's home. She didn't have to question, she didn't have to doubt.

"I want to make an announcement. Or *we* want to make an announcement. Can someone bring the kids in?" Eva said. Cruz stood to wash their hands.

Everyone's conversations halted. Chip called for the kids and they settled in the two empty chairs at the table.

What followed was a lingering silence until Eva and Cruz sat back down.

Frankie frowned. "Everything okay?"

"Yes. More than okay. We were going to make this announcement later on this week, but since we're here all together..." her mother said.

"Why not now?" Cruz said, finishing for her. His grin widened from ear to ear.

Gabby gasped, pressing her hand against her mouth. "Oh, my God, don't tell me you're pregnant."

Frankie took a sharp intake of breath. "What? Mom, aren't you in menopause? Is that even possible?"

"I know someone who got pregnant in their fifties," Matilda added. "And there's Janet Jackson."

"What's menopause?" Liam asked.

"It's a girl thing," Aria said matter-of-factly.

"No! No babies. That ship has sailed," Eva said, laughing.

"And that would be because of me, from my cancer treatments." Cruz raised his hand, then he looked at Eva tenderly. "And Eva's choice, at the end of the day."

"And I am happy, thrilled, blessed with all of you. But we're getting off topic," Eva said.

Frankie pressed her hand to her chest. "So you're *not* pregnant."

"No. But. Cruz and I…we eloped."

Frankie sat up. At the same time, conversation erupted from the table. "You're married? B-but your plans. Your Christmas wedding."

"Do you mean the plans that continued to be postponed?" Her mother smiled pointedly. "The plans that we couldn't seem to finalize? The point was for us to be together, yet we stalled and dragged out the planning because we were trying to make everything perfect."

"When everything was already perfect as it is," Cruz said. "So we made it official in Vegas. And now we can just plan a party."

"Vegas was weeks ago. And you're just saying so now?" Frankie asked.

"So are you Lolo Cruz now? Officially?" Liam asked, jumping out of his chair. He rounded the table and threw his arms around Cruz.

"Yeah, buddy. Officially your granddad, if that's what you want."

"I want!"

The table gushed at the sweet scene, and Frankie should have, too. But she was still caught up in the surprise, in the fact that she'd been kept in the dark for so long.

Her mother must have sensed her vibe, because she gave Frankie a grim smile. "We wanted everyone together so we could announce it at one time." Eva's voice had gone flat, and it was a warning Frankie knew well. It meant that Eva knew her temper was rising, and that perhaps she should take a breath.

But Frankie wasn't done. "We would have loved to have been there. Where are the pictures? Who officiated it?"

"We have photos to share, and we used the officiant of the chapel we chose."

Frankie pinched the bridge of her nose. It's like they'd reversed roles. Her mother was acting like a teenager.

"Wow. Congratulations." Ty broke the silence, though he looked at Frankie with a bewildered expression.

"Woohoo! I can't wait to plan your party!" Gabby cheered. What followed were a round of hugs, leaving Frankie as the last one to say something to her mother and Cruz.

She came around the table and hugged Eva. "I'm so happy for you both," she said while in her mom's embrace. She hugged Cruz, too, though all she could think of was that she wasn't in the know of her mother's plans. That Eva hadn't kept her in the loop.

Later on, as they were cleaning up, Frankie pulled Gabby to the side. "Are you shocked?"

"I was in the beginning." Her sister wiped her hands on a dish towel. "And then I thought…it makes sense. Those two, there's no time to lose, is there? They've made it through the toughest parts of their relationship already. Now, they just want to celebrate. I get it."

Frankie nodded for her sister's sake, but she still felt unnerved.

She just didn't like surprises.

Chapter Seventeen

That next Friday, Frankie was still bothered by Eva and Cruz's announcement, and while hiding in the stacks of the library before the start of the PTA meeting, rescheduled because of spring break, she was expressing her discontent to her now official boyfriend.

Except he didn't seem to be listening.

"Ty," she whispered. "Ty."

"Hmm?" His lips were on the underside of her neck as he peppered kisses on her skin. His hands had a firm grip on her waist. They'd escaped to this corner of the library, knowing they would be alone. Not only was it well after school, but it was also the farthest point away from the library doors.

"You don't think that they were acting like kids, getting married like that without telling any of us?"

"Why are we still talking about this?"

Though it had been days since their announcement, Frankie still had moments of outrage. "I just thought of it again."

He straightened and brushed her hair from her face. She shut her eyes at the contact. At his knowing that this would calm her. "They're not kids. They're grown adults. And they love one another."

"I know, but..." She looked down. She couldn't explain why this bothered her so much. "This was such an important occasion. And she waited so long to get remarried, and she did it without us."

"Do you know what will make you feel better?" He pulled her closer.

She knew what was coming. Ty was good at distraction. Still, she played along. "What?"

"This." He kissed her on the lips, with a knuckle under her chin. It was sweet and romantic, and it worked for now. When he eased back, she was left breathless.

"Yeah, I guess that made me feel a little bit better."

"Good." He smiled. "Now, what'll really help is if you talk to your mom about it."

She shook her head. "I've been so upset that I haven't really spoken to her."

He frowned. "But why? This isn't a bad thing."

"To you it doesn't seem like it, but to me it is. I hate that she kept it a secret."

"Maybe they weren't ready to share? I feel that way about certain things, too. Like starting my business." He added that last sentence in a whisper.

"What? But we've been working on it for weeks now. And you told the guys at poker."

He nodded. "It's not something I'm ready to announce to everyone, especially my boss."

The memory of Ty avoiding eye contact at Easter lunch flashed in her memory. The idea that she'd done something wrong brought up her defensiveness. "But it's nothing to be ashamed of. I'm so proud of you, Ty. You're so talented and—"

"I'm not ashamed of it. But if I'm not ready to say anything about it, then it's my prerogative." He raised his hands in a kind of surrender. "I only bring that up as an example, and to say that maybe your mom and Cruz felt that way, too."

"So you think I'm wrong to be angry."

"I didn't say that."

Voices came from the front of the library, and Frankie looked at her phone.

"Everyone's here," she said. She stepped away from Ty to gather herself and breathe through the frustration that had bubbled up at their conversation. In this upcoming meeting, she would need to be on it. It was time to motivate these parents to find volunteers for the graduation party.

She turned to walk away but was gently tugged back by Ty.

"Hey." His voice was soft.

"I've gotta do this meeting. I'm fine, okay?"

"Alright, um… I may need to go before the meeting ends because I'm on call."

"That's fine." She offered him a smile, and walked out to join the parents.

Straight to business she went, and after gathering and greeting everyone—there was a bigger group tonight—Frankie passed out outlines to the parents. The subcommittees gave their reports: the bookshelves status, yearbook status, and updates on fundraising. PTA officer candidates for next year were announced. Then it was Frankie's turn:

"Now, with a little more than three weeks until the fifth-grade graduation, it's time to set out duties. While this event is smaller, and not quite involving the whole community, it's still an important one."

She watched everyone scan the document, something she'd put together the other night, when she and Ty had been at her place, and the kids were doing their homework at the dining-room table.

And though they couldn't be intimate, they'd shared a lot of kisses that night, as they'd done in the stacks earlier.

Remorse filled Frankie. Her temper was getting the best of her, she knew. Ty was only trying to help.

She would need to make it up to him.

As if Ty knew she was thinking of him, he raised his eyes to her and winked.

She bit her lip.

"You guys need to stop with that. We can feel it from here," someone said. A laugh rippled through the crowd.

Since their relationship had become public, they hadn't heard the end of it from their friends and acquaintances. Comments came from the local grocer, the school crossing guard, even the school secretary.

It came with a thrill that people cared enough about her life to comment on it. That people did care about them both.

"Speaking of feelings." She had to wrangle her people to what was going on in front of them. "To be honest, I'm starting to feel the pressure of the fifth-grade graduation party. We need enough volunteers for the day to run every part of the event. We need people at the food table, at the photo booth, at the games. Specifically, parent volunteers who aren't fifth-grade parents, so that they have a chance to enjoy the event with their graduates."

She swallowed against the fact that she was talking about herself. That she was going to watch her baby graduate.

"Can I count on you all to reach out to your parent groups? Or if you haven't volunteered yet, will you volunteer now?" Frankie added.

She knew she was being pushy, but something had to be done.

A fourth-grade parent raised her hand. "I can sign up for the first shift of the photo booth."

"Fantastic. Thank you so much. I appreciate it."

Other parents raised their hands, though some reluctantly.

There was one hand left to call, and the person was in Frankie's periphery. When Frankie faced her, her vocal cords seized.

It was Bianca.

"Yes?" Frankie prompted, though her voice was too high. She tightened her grip on her paper outline to regain her composure, noting how the other parents had gone silent. Their eyes ping-ponged to her, then to Bianca, and back.

Frankie smiled big, with all of her teeth.

"Can we provide service hours? I have a few high-school students that work at the pastry shop that would probably be willing to volunteer for hours," Bianca said.

"Great idea," someone said.

It *was* a great idea, an idea Frankie hadn't thought of.

The fact that it was Bianca who'd thought of it annoyed her.

The moment was rife with tension, and Frankie shuffled the papers in front of her. "I'll have to see."

Then she looked away. "Vivian, can you update us on the budget so we can vote on it?"

Vivian stared at her for a long while before speaking. From her left, she could feel Ty's questioning glance.

Vivian covered the budget, which the group voted on.

"Great. Please keep an eye on your emails for the new library bookshelves unveiling, and for the yearbook dissemination. Meeting's adjourned."

Frankie started to shove her things into her bucket bag, glancing up occasionally to say goodbye. Home was where she wanted to be, away from everyone.

When Ty came up, she didn't meet his eyes. They would only reflect her awkwardness toward Bianca. "I don't want to talk about it," she said under her breath.

He nodded. "Text me when you get home."

"Yep," she said.

He stalled for a beat, and then walked away.

Frankie blew out a small breath, though as soon as she was packed up, she slung her purse over her shoulder.

A body blocked her way. Bianca.

Her hands were clasped in front of her, and her smile was

tentative. "Um. Just wondering if I could have a word with you, Frankie?"

Francesca was what she wanted to say, though she held her tongue. She'd been introduced to her as Frankie. "Yeah, sure."

"I hope you don't mind that I came. Reece mentioned the meeting and I thought it would be a great way for me to get involved, you know? Though, by the look on your face, you weren't expecting me."

"No."

"Of course." She laughed, though it died in her throat. "Listen, I know it was awkward for us to meet for the first time at your mom's place of business. But Reece insisted that it was fine. Though I wonder if it was really fine with you."

"It is what it is."

She nodded, swallowing, clearly showing her discomfort.

Frankie dragged her eyes away. Because this person was not a fly-by-night individual in Reece's life. And yet, she needed time to get used to this. To accept that another woman would be involved in her child's life was a feat that Frankie wasn't sure she could accomplish.

"If there's anything I can help with, let me know," Bianca said. "Any holes I can fill…we've got a full staff at the pastry shop, and I can be flexible…"

Her voice trailed off, leaving Frankie with her opportunity. To lay down her rules, to put up boundaries.

To accept Bianca.

But none of that felt right. Because this wasn't about Bianca. It was about herself. She couldn't even look at the woman, couldn't stand how gracious she was.

"Thanks, I'll get back to you," Frankie said.

Bianca's smile withered. "Okay. I'll stop and say goodbye to Liam at the cafeteria before I head out. I'll see you at the next meeting, or when you need me." And with a shy wave, she stepped away and walked out.

As soon as Bianca turned the corner, Frankie plopped into her chair. Then she let her head fall into her hands.

"Come on, little guy." Ty tried to coax a piglet from under a worktable in the corner of a storage shed, though it didn't budge. In his hand was syringe of antibiotic that he needed to administer, or else the animal's infection would worsen.

His watch lit up—it was almost 8:00 p.m, when his call time ended. It had been a slew of emergencies tonight: a poison check for a twelve-year-old English bulldog, a tabby who'd been vomiting all day. A limping boxer.

This was his last duty for the night.

"C'mon," he begged with a carrot stick.

This whole day had had this kind of a vibe, of him extracting, pleading, trying. If he looked back, it had been like this since Easter dinner.

Frankie was upset. She'd *been* upset. It was all for good reasons, but it seemed to bleed into their communication. Lately, despite him trying to help, she'd been impatient. Her constant reminders about his business bothered him, too.

And seeing how she'd treated Bianca in front of everyone had unnerved him.

It was the familiar sight of a woman who'd often been upset and demanding. Harper hadn't listened to him either. She'd often overstep or question him.

Harper, who, at the end of their relationship, made him feel useless and unworthy.

Finally, the piglet sniffed, its nose wiggling, and it took two steps forward.

Then, it retreated to the corner.

Ty growled, then sat back on his heels and took two deep breaths to calm himself.

He didn't want to be doing this right now.

Guilt set in—what was wrong with *this*? His job was noble.

It was fun, too, most of the time. It was financially lucrative. He wasn't in harm's way like other professions. And his patients were innocent and good, even if their humans, at times, were not.

And it wasn't as if it kept him from his woodworking business. He had his hands in wood almost every day, and he was slowly getting the business plan together.

Logically, he knew that it was simply a matter of time and patience before he'd feel comfortable enough to tell Dr. Peters. After all he couldn't be rash in leaving a stable job. He had to be a responsible parent. He had a child.

And he shouldn't have to explain to anyone, Frankie included, why his timeline was taking longer than he'd anticipated.

"Okay, I'm back." Al Verona, the piglet's owner, entered the shed, knocking Ty from his spiraling thoughts. He'd been attending to the piglet's sibling.

Al slid the door shut. "Sorry about that, Sunrise doesn't like being split up from Sunset."

"Where's Sunrise now?" Ty swiped his forearm against his forehead and looked at Al. He was wearing overalls, typical for someone with a small farm, but his hands were stained brown instead of crusted with dirt.

"Crying in the house." Al looked resigned. "I don't know how my kids convinced me to bring in piglets as pets. I'm out of my league. Give me chickens any day. I've gone half-gray with these two. And I'm worried about Sunset. What if we can't get this antibiotic in him?"

"We're not down that road yet." Ty smiled to reassure him. "Are you ready?"

"Ready as I'll ever be."

Ty stood. He braced his hands on the workbench. "On the count of three. One…two…three!"

He lifted the workbench and Sunset sprinted from underneath. Al lunged toward the piglet while Ty played zone defense to keep it from scurrying under another piece of furniture.

Finally, Al got two hands on Sunset and swiftly held her like a football, exposing the spot in the neck where Ty would have to administer the medication.

"Almost there," Ty said, attempting to right himself, then injecting Sunset, and only breathing easy when the entire plunger was administered.

Afterward, Al set Sunset down. He opened the shed door, and the piglet ran off, leaving Ty and Al behind and out of breath.

"Care for a beer?" Al asked.

"Nice of you, but I've got to drive back home."

"Soda, then?"

"I'm down for that." Ty pressed a hand behind his back. They looked at each other, realizing that Al was doing the exact same thing.

They both broke out into laughter.

They entered the house and Al grabbed an ice-cold cola from the refrigerator, popped the tab, and pushed it into Ty's hand.

He drank it gratefully. "This hits the spot."

"I still owe you a beer."

"You don't have to do that. It's my job."

"Yeah, but still." He hopped up on the countertop. "Heard that you're new in town. How do you like it here?"

Ty thought of Aria and how, recently, she looked forward to school; at Frankie, and that despite a rough few days, was the best thing that had since come into his life. "Love it."

"That's good to hear. Sometimes it's hard to break into a small town. People can get quite protective. Then again, you're with an Espiritu, so you might already be past all that."

Ty didn't bother to ask how he knew. "I have a daughter in the elementary school so the PTA keeps me busy, too."

"I heard about that PTA. They're all a bunch of single parents." He led the way through his living room, to walk Ty out. "They call the Peak PTA the single hearts club."

Ty cackled. "Wow."

Except as he continued to think about it, it sounded about right.

Ty noted the rustic furniture he passed. He touched the thick wood-slab dining-room table, which was meticulously crafted. "Did someone make all of this furniture?"

He beamed. "Great eye. I built them."

"No way. You mind if I take a closer look?"

"Don't mind at all."

Ty meandered to the living room, where he ran a hand over the lacquered tabletop. The grain of the wood shone through.

"Made that with birch." He pointed to the long table behind the sofa. "That one with oak. All with reclaimed wood."

"Gorgeous."

"Thanks. It's a satisfying process. When the wood comes to me, it's in rough shape." Al grabbed a card from the bookcase, which also looked handmade, and handed it to him. "I make furniture."

"I do some woodworking, too. I'm building the shelves for the elementary-school library."

"Ah, then you'll understand when I say this is a humbling profession. Lots of hard work noticed by very few people." His lips spread into a smile. "Have you checked in with Peak's artisan community? We've got meetings once a month."

"I heard mentions about it."

"You should come. There's another woodworker in town. Bea Francisco. She's into smaller projects. She and I get together and talk shop sometime, too. If you're interested…"

"Oh, I don't know."

"What? Why not?"

"It's sort of just a side thing." He looked down, not wanting to give attention to something that might never happen.

"You're building bookshelves for the elementary school, which is no small feat." Al examined him. "Do you have socials? A website?"

"A website that's not launched yet. And my social media's up but I haven't posted yet."

"It's a start. Before I did this full-time, I had another job, too. But once I realized this was what I wanted to do, things shaped up for me to make the jump. Not right away, but slowly. And you'll need support and resources when it's time."

"Yeah." He looked away.

"Have pictures? I'd love to see your work."

"Oh, nah." All of a sudden, Ty felt like an imposter. The things Al had in his home, now that he was really looking—they were impressive. He pressed a hand at the back of his head, felt the warmth of his blush.

"C'mon."

With the nudge, Ty relented, sighing and steeling himself from bashfulness. He clicked on to his favorite images, and peppered between photos of Aria were the projects he'd undertaken. A night table for Aria. Her desk. Innumerable wooden cutting boards. Old furniture he'd refurbished.

"Nice. Love this one." He zoomed onto a plant shelf he'd built for Harper so long ago.

"Thanks."

"There's a craft show in the fall on the Spirit of the Shenandoah B and B property, in fact. Their Fall Festival. Last year was the first year, and I was one of the lucky ones to get invited. It's not the kind of place you'd bring large furniture to sell, but smaller items like your wooden cutting boards would do well. Would you want to put stuff in my booth?"

"Really?"

“Yeah.”

“I’m not sure how much I can commit to.”

“I understand. You’ve got a whole career going on, and I get it. So how about this, you just get me what you can.”

“Wow. Do you want to split the booth cost?”

“We can do a commission structure, if you feel good about that. A straightforward contract.”

Ty sipped his soda, and blinked back his surprise, his gratefulness. Then he half laughed. “I can’t get over how nice everyone is here.” He thought of Frankie, at how easily she jumped into helping him. At how folks were generous with their free time with the PTA.

“If you can’t help your neighbor, then who else will?” He smirked, then added, “Besides, I wouldn’t have been able to corner Sunset on my own. That, I can’t ever repay. So are you in?”

“I’m in.”

Chapter Eighteen

"Surprise, the yearbooks are in," Ms. Ahmad said to Frankie when she entered the school foyer. "I was just about to call you."

"Perfect timing. I'm here to drop off Liam's lunch." She lifted the navy blue bag with a smile.

"I'll call his classroom to let his teacher know. You can go ahead and leave it in the pick-up zone."

Frankie set the lunch bag in a nearby cubby. How many times had she done this same thing over the last five years? And in the last week, how many times had she been in this office to check in before doing PTA stuff? Since the meeting—which was something she did not want to remember—she'd been at the school three times.

"The yearbooks are over here, Ms. Espiritu." Ms. Ahmad gestured toward the back of the office, near the paper supplies. "Unfortunately, we're getting another shipment of supplies, so they'll need to be relocated fairly quickly. And I'd love to help, but I'm swamped at the moment."

"Nope. Don't worry about it. You're a saint for having to deal with everything under the sun. I'll take it to the library. Is there a dolly somewhere?"

"Got you covered," said a voice behind her. On instinct, her belly fluttered, and Frankie turned. Sure enough, it was Ty. "I have one in my workroom."

"Hey, what are you doing here?" She bounded over and caught herself before throwing her arms around him, remembering at the last minute that they were at school.

Yes, they were public as a couple now, but she didn't need to rub it in.

But Ty leaned down and kissed her on the cheek. "My early afternoon appointments canceled, so I thought I'd get some hours in before the weekend."

Ty had been spending a great deal of time at the school as well, staining the bookshelves and cleaning up, all behind strategically hung curtains, to keep prying eyes from the final reveal. In the last week, she and Ty hadn't seen one another as often as she'd wished.

Still, she thrilled at how easy it was for him to show her affection.

"Aww, you two are so cute. Seriously, you're making me wish I was still in the honeymoon phase."

Ms. Ahmad had been working for the school at least a couple of decades, and if Frankie's memory served her right, she had been married for the same amount of time.

And though Frankie knew what Ms. Ahmad had meant in the "honeymoon" comment—that they were in the early and over-romantic stage in their relationship, and that she'd meant it as a compliment—it struck the tender part of Frankie's heart. That perhaps what she and Ty had wouldn't last.

Frankie attempted a grateful smile. "We'll get out of your way and get started."

"Ty, don't forget to sign my yearbook, too," Ms. Ahmad said.

"Yes, ma'am," he said, then picked up a box of books. To Frankie, he said, "Might as well grab a box now and dolly the rest."

"Good idea." Frankie picked up a box of books and led the way to the library. As they walked through the hallway, filled with the quiet echoes of teachers' and students' voices, she tried to breathe out the insecurity that had built up inside of her.

Finally, they made it to a secure corner of the library, where they could safely store the yearbooks.

"What's up?" Ty said, summoning Frankie out of her thoughts.

"Nothing's up," she said. What she was feeling was silly. And wrong.

"It's obviously something. You didn't say a word the whole time we walked here." He shimmied the box against the wall and retrieved the one in her arms.

"It's just…" She hesitated, not wanting to make the situation awkward. She followed Ty to his workroom, waving to Olivia and Christine behind the librarian's counter. "It's that honeymoon comment she made. Like things are going to change between us."

He opened the door to his workroom and went to the back, where his tools were stacked. What had been a room chock-full of lumber and a floor covered in sawdust was now clean and somewhat empty.

What a difference a week made.

The clang of the dolly brought her back to the present; Ty was pushing it toward the door. "Things do change," Ty said.

"Right, but what if it changes for the worse."

As the words left her mouth, she cringed. She sounded desperate. And Frankie was not that girl. She was confident. She knew her worth.

"Hey." Ty shut the workroom door and stepped up to her. Their torsos touched as he drew her into him with his hands on her waist. Then he lifted her chin with a knuckle. "What's really on your mind?"

She raised her gaze to meet his. Ty was so good at this—this drawing out of her thoughts. In the last week, after finding out that her mother was already married, she'd felt a little like she was on her back foot. She couldn't seem to explain how left out she felt.

At her silence, he said, "All relationships evolve. It just reaches another level, but it doesn't mean it's less meaningful or exciting."

"I know. It's not that…" She searched her brain for the right words. "I don't want things to hit me when I'm not ready for them."

His eyes clouded with worry. "You're worried about me hitting you with something you're not ready for?"

"I didn't say that. I just don't like surprises." She shook her head. "The dinner with my mom and her big news. Bianca coming to the PTA meeting without warning. It frustrates me. Sometimes it worries me, too."

He released a breath. "I know, I can tell. And I can feel it, too."

"What do you mean by that?"

Discomfort radiated from him, and she didn't like it. "I respect and accept how you feel about those situations, but you can't always have it your way. With Bianca…she was trying to help, and you iced her out at that meeting."

"You're just trying to be a devil's advocate. I didn't ice her out."

He smiled. "Maybe I am being a devil's advocate. But you can also try not to think the worst of people's intentions."

"I don't do that."

"Okay." He smiled. "Forget I said anything about it."

Shaking her head, Frankie wasn't ready to end the conversation. "I want to talk about it now."

He glanced at the closed doors. "We have yearbooks to pass out, and I've got staining to do, and we're counting down to graduation. Tension is high. But we're fine, okay?" He kissed her on the cheek.

She flushed with the start of frustration. "You're changing the subject."

"You bet I am. To something a little more pressing." He tugged her closer.

She looked down at their torsos, and despite her best effort, blushed at his flirtation. "Now, you're trying to distract me."

"See, I like this mode of conversation better," he said, dipping down and planting a kiss on her lips. "I have to say I love that we don't have to hide from everyone anymore."

"Why, so that you can kiss me whenever you want?"

"That." He hovered his lips over hers. "And that we don't have to sneak around on our dates, and *other things*."

At the thought of those other things, her body went to jelly. It was a perk, alright, to have everyone know who her date night was going to be with, and since their friends approved of their relationship, they were willing to watch their kids.

"When do we get to do the *other thing*?" She entwined her fingers behind the back of his neck.

"As soon as we're done here. Are you down?"

"Down, and around and through."

"Dang, girl, don't get me started."

"I mean it," she said, looking into his eyes. Her heart was full of a variety of emotions, but this, with Ty, she was sure of.

His expression softened, the mischief in it dashed. "I mean it, too."

Then he kissed her sweetly, intimately, with everything unsaid pressed between them.

The hallway filled with the sound of footsteps and they broke apart, though they kept their eyes locked.

"We'd better get the other books." He gestured for her to follow him.

Frankie would follow him everywhere.

The following Tuesday Ty stepped back from the newly black-oak stained shelves and nodded at his handiwork. It was a thing of beauty.

He could envision the spines of the books that would soon grace it.

He breathed in the heavy feeling in his chest. It was pride. Triumph. He'd invested two months of intense labor, and now it would be used by the students of this school for many years to come.

He hadn't felt this alive in a long time. To others, that might've not made much sense, that dealing with animals should've given him purpose, but not as much as this. Or not anymore.

He would need to pocket this feeling.

Olivia walked over and stood next to him. "Wow. That is beautiful. When you said you were going to build bookshelves, I thought of plain plywood held by brackets against the wall. But this." She raised her hands as if to present it. "These are custom built-ins. They're gorgeous."

"Thank you. I've touched things up, so there's some wet stain still. I'm going to keep the hanging sheets up to shield them from view and keep hands off of it, if that's okay."

"Sounds good to me. I can't wait for Principal Murray to see it. Has Frankie taken a look behind the curtain lately?"

"No, but I sent her a photo." When he'd texted her this morning, she was in a better mood. Besides dealing with the yearbook committee, she'd been busy following up regarding the PTA elections. Perhaps those things had taken her mind off of her mother's elopement and Bianca's appearance.

They would need to work on their communication, he knew. Their interaction at the library the other day had frustrated him. But for now, they were okay.

The phone in his pocket rang; a group video chat with Vince and Jeremiah. His body relaxed as he answered it; it had been a week since they'd had an actual conversation instead of their usual texting. "Hey, you two."

Olivia excused herself and backed away.

His friends' greetings overlapped one another. "Sorry I've been MIA. Been swamped," Jeremiah said.

"Nah, it's all good. It's been a while," Ty said.

"Too long," Vince agreed. "How's work out there?"

Ty looked up at the shelves. "It depends on what you mean by work."

Vince's face lit up. "No way. Did you finally do it? Did you open the business?"

"No, not yet. But I'm taking steps toward it. Look." He turned the camera around and heard his friends' praises.

"Wow. That's, like, art," Vince said.

"Respect, Ty. That's impressive," said Jeremiah.

He turned the camera around so that they were facing each other once more. "Thanks. The more I do this work, the more I know it's what I want to do in the long term."

"Have you talked to your boss yet?" Jeremiah asked.

"No."

Vince frowned. "What? You said you'd do it already."

He sighed. "I was thinking, I can do both at the same time, can't I? After all, I've got Aria's education to think of. I still have to put her through college."

"But you were going to make woodworking your primary job and maybe do some part-time vet work to make up the rest. It's all you talked about."

"I know, but…" Inside, he was starting to feel uncomfortable about it all. With Harper's probable travel, Ty would need to find a way to have enough money to send Aria to see her mother. And who knew if Harper would have the funds to help truly co-parent their daughter. Even with Al's encouragement, Ty was unsure he could make a real go at it. He didn't even have any inventory to start with. "Part-time work is great but it won't pay the bills. It definitely won't have benefits, and I'm just trying to do the right thing."

Jeremiah tsked. "You can't have cold feet. The main reason

you chose Peak was so you could have that work-life balance. So that you can do your passion at least part-time. What was the point of you moving all the way down there? You could have stayed here and done that."

"Okay, dads," he joked.

Jeremiah's eyes softened. "You told us to keep you accountable, and that's what we're doing. You did it for me."

Ty nodded. Jeremiah had gotten a little bit out of control with his partying last year, and that almost got him fired. Ty and Vince had had to stage an intervention that entailed a surprise meeting with the two of them and Jeremiah's boyfriend. It was a painful experience for all of them.

But this was different. "I'm not in trouble."

"You don't have to feel like you're in trouble for you to be. Or even call it trouble for it to be a life-changing fork in the road. And that's where you are, my friend. The only things keeping your spirit up right now is Aria and your girlfriend. And though we know Frankie means a lot to you, you'll be a better man if you're satisfied with what you're doing." Then, Vince smirked. "Besides, you owe me a dining-room table."

Ty snorted. "I *owe* you a table?"

"Yep, you said that once I have a dining room, that you'd make me an actual table, and well..." Vince stalled.

"You're moving out." Ty had promised Vince that he would build him a four-person dining-room table once he finally moved into a place he deserved. Though Vince was a successful real estate agent, he kept a tight grip over his money, and lived in the tiniest apartment. His furnishings were worn down; he lived on bare bones. One night, he'd admitted to Ty and Jeremiah that he was afraid of going broke, even if he had enough savings to reward himself.

"Yep. Gave my notice," Vince said.

"I'm happy for you, man."

"Thanks. When I signed the new lease, it made me realize—why did I wait so long?" He eyed Ty.

"I'm going to ignore you trying to change the subject."

Vince's office door opened behind him, and a guy nodded to him. "Whoops, I gotta head out. Need to see my next client. Catch you both later."

"See ya," Jeremiah said.

"Yeah, talk soon." Ty hung up, taking in his friends' words, proud of what he himself had accomplished, and a little mollified at what he'd admitted. Ty was never the kind to go back on his word. When he'd expressed something, he meant it. Go to vet school, check. Marry, check, have kid, check.

But he'd also experienced what it was like to have plans change, starting with his marriage. And now, with Harper's career plans up in the air, he had to recalibrate. Growing up with parents who loved him but didn't put stock into financial stability had a negative effect on him, and he didn't want that for Aria. Until he could find the balance, he would need to stay put where he was.

Ty gathered his tools and set them on one side of the library. He grabbed a broom and swept up the dust that had kicked up from his work. All the while, he listened to the kids in the hallway, the teachers talking, the occasional overhead announcement.

While loading up his car, his phone rang again. "Hello."

"Where are you?"

He looked at the screen, confirmed what he'd suspected. Harper. "At the school. Why?"

"What are you doing there? Why aren't you at work?"

Confused at the line of questioning, he asked, "What?"

"I'm at Valley Pets, where you're not."

"What are you doing there?"

"Why else, silly? To surprise you and Aria."

Chapter Nineteen

Though it had only been about five months since Ty had last seen Harper, it felt like a lifetime. And now, while driving her to his home, it was as if she was a stranger.

Or maybe it was him who had changed.

She wore a floral dress, and she had a face full of make-up. A year ago, he would have secretly fawned over her. Harper was a beautiful woman.

Now, he felt nothing.

Nothing but a slight annoyance at her surprise arrival, that was.

"So you were at the elementary school during the school day? When has that ever happened?"

He frowned. "What's that supposed to mean?"

"C'mon, you were never really interested in school stuff."

She wasn't lying but it arrowed into him. Harper had a way of reminding him of the things that he hadn't done well enough.

"I'm doing a project for the PTA," he said.

"The PTA? Who would have thought." Her eyes widened. "Wait. Aria mentioned something about this, about you building bookshelves. What, they didn't have anyone else that could put them together?"

He steadied his breath. "I built them from scratch."

"Oh, wow." She leaned back in the seat. "I sure hope they're paying you."

"It's not just about the money." He didn't like her tone—he didn't know what she meant by it. Harper wasn't a big believer in his woodworking. She didn't understand why a person would make something from scratch when there was plenty of furniture to buy. A bit ironic coming from a baker.

But he moved the conversation along; he didn't want to rehash. "I would have appreciated a heads-up that you were coming."

"Can't a mom surprise her child?" She glanced at him, her pink-stained lips pressed into a line.

"You could have surprised her, but kept me in the loop."

"I didn't think you'd mind. I promise I won't spread out too much. I know you hate that."

"That's not it."

"I can book a hotel."

Inside, he grumbled. Aria expected her mother to stay in the guesthouse out back. Except that he didn't have it ready yet. The space needed a mattress, new bedding, and a professional cleaning. "No, that won't be necessary. You don't have a car. But you'll be set up in the guest room until I get the guesthouse ready. How long are you staying?"

"I've got my first gig scheduled a couple of days after graduation, so I'll need to leave the night of."

"That's fast." Ty inwardly winced. "Aria's going to be disappointed."

"It's why I decided to come a little earlier. Spend some time with my girl before I have to take off again."

He turned into his driveway and parked. He got out and opened the trunk, took Harper's suitcase out, and rolled it to the front door. Sensing that she wasn't following, he looked back. Harper gaped from the sidewalk. "How cute."

"We like it," he said.

He knew his tone was off, but Harper's appearance had bolstered his defensiveness.

He needed to chill. After all, he and Harper had a collaborative co-parenting relationship. Their divorce was amicable. Harper was a good person.

So, he added, "Aria liked it best out of all the places we saw. The backyard won her over. You'll like it, too."

She smiled then, and he felt himself relax. It was going to be fine. Having Harper here wouldn't be any different than it had been in the past, where they'd live apart but had a key to his place. It would only be for a couple of weeks.

And Aria was going to be thrilled when she got home from school.

But Frankie…wasn't going to like this. With how she'd been the last few days, he didn't know how he was going to break it to her that Harper was here, and in his house.

He opened the door and let Harper in. They were greeted by Bubba.

"Hey, sweet thing." Harper got down on one knee and snuggled with Bubba, who licked her face. "Yes, I missed you, too. I promise we're going to play a lot. After I get a tour, okay?"

She hopped back up and proceeded to meander through the front rooms, seemingly appraising it. And because she always did have an opinion on everything, Ty said, "Out with it. I know you're dying to give me your design thoughts."

"No, Ty. I—I love it. You did good." She ran her hand against the couch. "This is new. You always did want an L-shaped couch. Not my style but it looks comfy in here."

"That almost sounded sincere."

"I'm telling the truth." She half laughed. "I guess I assumed that this place would look like our last place."

The place you left? was what he wanted to ask.

He scanned his living room, his foyer, and his dining room

with new eyes, and he realized that in fact, it looked totally unlike their last home.

And it was because this time, he'd purchased things that he and Aria loved. This home wasn't half stripped by someone who'd wanted a different life.

She was at the refrigerator now, and she'd plucked the cherry-blossom magnet from it. "We never did make it to DC together. Was this field trip fun?"

"Yes. It was pretty incredible," he said truthfully, with Frankie on his mind. But he sought to move her along. "Let's show you the backyard and guesthouse."

"Oh, great." Her face lit up as she followed him, and he led her outside.

"Wow, this is huge! With a playground set and a half basketball court. This is heaven for our girl."

Our girl.

Yes, Aria was their girl. They were both her parents, and he must try to be more welcoming.

"It's hard to get her inside most days," he offered.

"I don't blame her."

Bubba came around from behind them, darting out to the side yard and then galloping to the guesthouse.

"All right buddy, I'm coming," Harper said.

Ty followed too, and unlocked the guest house.

"Now this, I love," she said, sighing when she entered the space.

"The previous owner kept this unit as an Airbnb, so I asked for everything to convey. But as you can see, it's not all ready just yet, and I'll need to have it cleaned. It should be done by the end of the week."

"Good thinking. And everything works?"

"Yep, it's a sparse kitchen, but you can make your own breakfast here as needed. And, I'll give you the code to get into the house."

Harper was full of compliments on the walk back to the house. Once inside, she fell onto the couch and sighed. "It's so good to be home."

Ty was struck by her words. Was this her home? He'd moved out here to start anew, but with the way she'd already stretched out on his couch, it felt as if things were rolling back to how it used to be.

The sound of squeaking brakes took his attention: the school bus. A minute later, Aria came through the side gate, to greet Bubba. When she caught sight of Ty at the back door she waved. "Hi, Dad!"

He was knocked aside by Harper, who yelled, "Surprise!"

"Mom?" Aria said, her smile brightening in recognition.

Then her daughter started running. Harper bent down and accepted Aria's tackle, and they both wound up on the ground.

This reunion should have caused him joy, but he was filled with foreboding. That he and Harper's usually peaceful co-parenting might not be so peaceful this time around.

The next day, Frankie and Vivian left the Party Store Warehouse, satisfied with their day's work. All of the festival games for the fifth-grade graduation party had been picked out and reserved. The shopping cart Frankie was pushing contained all of the décor, festival prizes, and face paint.

"I can't believe how much that dunk tank is to rent." Vivian wore her prescription glasses and peered at the mile-long receipt. "It cost twice as much to rent as compared to last year."

"Everything's up. Mom's thinking of getting chickens for the B and B." Frankie struggled against the cart as they walked to the parking lot. "What is up with this wheel?"

Vivian pulled from the front. "I don't blame her. I was tempted to pick up fertilized eggs from Jameson's the other day. But I remembered Ian has camp this summer."

"Why does that matter?"

"Because I'm volunteering and won't be around to take care of them."

"What?"

She glanced back. "I didn't mention it? Liam should go, too. That way, we can volunteer together."

"To be honest, I haven't given summer a thought. But they take volunteers at camp?" Now, Frankie's mind was whirring. Growing up, she and Gabby had gone to overnight camp with other military kids. She thought of that time as a period of growth—she'd enjoyed the freedom. "That's a twenty-four-hour-a-day volunteer gig. Are you up for that?"

"I'm going to have to be. You know Ian, he's super shy, and it's hard enough for him to get out there. And with Sean going to camp too—"

Sean was Ian's friend-turned-bully. Frankie frowned. "Is Sean still messing with him?"

"We thought it was nipped in the bud when Principal Murray brought Sean's parents in. And on the surface, it seems to be okay between them. But I think there's still an issue there. Anyhoo, you should keep me company. Unless…" She waggled her eyebrows.

"What?"

"Maybe I'm speaking too soon? Are you planning to get away with your man this summer?"

That, too, Frankie hadn't thought of, though the sound of it made her blush. "That's twenty-four-hours-a-day, too."

"You bad, bad girl."

Frankie laughed and allowed herself to revel in the knowledge that finally, she had someone to celebrate with. Someone to be with. Someone to have fun with. And didn't she deserve it? Like everyone else around her, didn't she deserve the hope of something long-term? Or—gasp!—something forever?

"You're smiling over there," Vivian said.

She sighed. "I am."

They'd made it to their cars; the trunk of Vivian's SUV lifted. "I, for one, am so happy for you," Vivian said. "In fact, I'm rooting for you so much that I hope I don't see you all summer long." She bit her lip. "I take that back, I would miss you too much. You don't think Ty'll mind sharing you one week out of this summer, will he?"

"Are you kidding? Sisters before misters." She raised her hand for a high five and they linked fingers. "But I'll check if Liam's interested in going. Aria, too."

Vivian beamed. "Great."

After they loaded Vivian's car of the cart's contents, and returned the cart, Frankie said, "T-minus two weeks to graduation."

"I know. T-minus two weeks before the last hurrah, the grandest grad party thrown in the history of Peak Elementary."

"Woo-hoo!"

Vivian opened her car door. "I forgot to ask, did you follow up with Bianca about helping with the grad party?"

Frankie stiffened and shook her head.

"What?" Vivian frowned. "Why? She wants to help, and she has connections. And she's right about the volunteer hours."

"I know, I know. I'll get to it," she said in a quieter tone.

Vivian tsk'd. "C'mon, you're not like this, Frankie."

"Like what?"

"Petty. You might have a hot temper, but petty's not a good look. Bianca hasn't done a single wrong thing to you or to Liam."

In the last few days, she'd tried to not overthink things. Not to be disappointed with her mom, not to be bothered by Bianca. And she was starting to process her feelings; she was starting to accept that surprise and change was inevitable and could be for the better.

Starting.

But perhaps Vivian was right, as was Ty.

Sometimes she *was* a little stubborn.

"Okay. I'll contact her. Promise," Frankie said.

"That's better." Vivian smiled. "So what are you up to tonight?"

"Liam is at Reece's for the night. And Aria might have a sleepover with one of her friends, I think."

"So your mind was already in the gutter."

She winked at her friend, then said, "How about you?"

"Ryan's picking Ian up from his guitar lesson as we speak. I get a night to myself, too. So if you find yourself alone…"

"I'll call you," she said, though she hoped that wouldn't be the case.

After saying goodbye, Frankie slipped into her car, smiling to herself, with the thought that despite all of the changes in her life, there were things to look forward to on the other side of it. That beyond the PTA, beyond volunteering, beyond this drama with Reece was her own joy, her own person.

Frankie started up her car, then checked her texts to make sure that Liam was safe and sound at Reece's. Then she switched over to her text thread with Ty and zoomed in on the photo of the shelves he took the other day, a photo she had liked, hearted, and followed up with even more emojis.

What he had created was truly impressive, his effort priceless, and certainly worth more than he'd charged the PTA.

Frankie started to type out a message to Ty, to touch base with his plans. They'd both been swamped with Ty on call and her at the B & B.

Then, she paused. She was free the rest of the night. They were a couple now. So why not just show up at his place like he'd always asked her to do?

She placed her car in Drive and headed north to Ty's house, heart in her throat. This spontaneity felt intimate. As her car's tires rumbled across the town square, her excitement kicked up.

Frankie rounded the corner; Ty's car was parked in the

driveway. She parked behind it, and when she stepped out, she was greeted by the smell of charcoal, of food being grilled. With very few homes on this block, it was likely coming from his place.

Perhaps it was a surprise for her? He had been talking about grilling for her the next time they had dinner at home.

She strode up to the door and knocked.

When the door opened with a whoosh, she was taken aback at the person who answered. It was a woman Frankie couldn't place.

"Hi. Can I help you?" The woman had a wide smile. She was taller than Frankie by a couple of inches, and about her age. She was also pretty, with wavy dark hair. The scent that Frankie had detected outside was coming from inside the house.

The woman was also wearing an apron—Ty's.

"Oh, um, I'm Frankie."

The woman's eyebrows dipped in confusion.

Frankie felt like she was in an alternate universe. She tried again. "Is Ty or Aria here?"

She straightened. "Oh, they're outside with Bubba." The door widened. "I can get them."

Frankie nodded, though was tempted to step past the woman. Was this a new babysitter? Or someone from Valley Pets that happened to have stopped by? And perhaps there was a kitchen emergency that required for them to put on *her boyfriend's* apron? "That would be nice."

"Okay." She raised a finger. "Give me a sec."

Then, the woman closed the door. On her.

Frankie was left standing there, stunned.

What the heck was going on?

A second later, the door opened to reveal Ty. He was freshly showered, hair damp, and he smelled of soap.

He was in the shower while that woman wearing his robe was in his house?

"Frankie. Hey." His voice was tinged with surprise, and not the pleasant kind.

And he had yet to let her in.

"Hey. I thought I'd stop by instead of texting. I was free tonight and wondered if you had plans."

But he wasn't listening to her. His gaze continued to slide over to the right, where she assumed the woman was. From where Aria called out, saying, "Mom! I want to show you something."

Frankie let out a breath, piecing together who she was. "That's Harper."

"Yes."

But with this initial relief came confusion. Why didn't Ty tell her of Harper's plans?

Frankie waited for more. An explanation. An invitation into his home. An introduction, even. Instead, she was met with Ty's blank expression.

"I'd better go. You're obviously busy. Family time and all," Frankie said.

All she wanted to do was go. She felt like an intruder.

She stepped back.

"No, wait." Ty crossed the threshold and closed the door behind him. "Harper's here early, for Aria's graduation. She's done with that show, and because she has to be back overseas the day after graduation, she thought it was best that she come now. And she's staying with us."

"You don't need to explain." Frankie was taking it in, feeling the anger and the hurt boil inside of her. She was definitely not processing nor accepting what was happening. She laughed.

"What's so funny?"

"That I'm just hearing about it now. We both have phones.

You could have called me. Or at least texted. And then I show up here, and she doesn't know who I am? You didn't tell her about me, Ty?" Her voice was rising.

"I'm sorry. The timing is off, I know. She got here yesterday afternoon, and it's been a whirlwind. Between work and cleaning up the guest house, I haven't had a chance—"

"And yet, that's not an excuse. You had all day."

"I know. And I'm sorry."

She shook her head. "Saying sorry doesn't make this better."

"Nothing's better if you're upset."

"What do you mean by that?"

"That even if I feel bad, and even if I'm sorry, which I am, it doesn't matter. You're going to overreact and be mad at me for the next two weeks. Sometimes, people mess up, Frankie. And I messed up."

Frankie recoiled as if she'd been shot right in the heart. That this man, whom she'd finally bared herself to, had done exactly what she feared he would do. She let down her walls, and he'd blindsided her.

"I'd rather be somebody who's known to react about something as big as this than someone who excuses problematic behavior and lies," she said.

"I didn't lie."

"Omission is just as harmful. Though, I should have known, with the way you avoid hard things. You minimize situations when things are slightly uncomfortable. Just like your woodworking business."

Ty reddened. "You're not gonna go there."

"I am. I believe in you, Ty. I believe in what you want to do. But you're running away from something you told me was important to you. You hate being uncomfortable and that's what you've done the last day. You didn't want to tell me that Harper was here, when I would have been fine with it."

It was his turn to laugh now. "I don't know about that, Frankie. Because you can't handle change that's not made by your own hands. If something isn't orchestrated by you, you shut them out. So yeah, I made a mistake. It was the wrong call not to text you right away. But you've been bothered since Easter, since Reece started dating Bianca."

"I don't care about those two."

"And yet, you let whatever hangup you still have about Reece color how you treat someone when they were simply trying to help. So again. I am sorry. But the fact that you're categorizing me as problematic over one mistake? I'd rather err on giving people the benefit of the doubt rather than icing them out, which you are an expert at."

Frankie gathered her anger and tucked it behind her diaphragm. It threatened to choke her; it caused tears to well up behind her eyes. She couldn't breathe. "I'm going to make this easy for you. I don't need to be judged so harshly for who I am, nor do I need to stick around with someone who can't be a hundred percent transparent with me. It's all I asked for, Ty. I'm going. For items concerning the bookshelves, you can talk to Vivian."

Frankie turned and got into her car, and somehow, through a haze of anger, drove back to her cabin on the Spirit of the Shenandoah property.

Chapter Twenty

Frankie hammered the nails of the Plinko board, and with every slam, felt the vibration in her wrists. But she welcomed it—it distracted her from the pervasive ache in her heart.

It had been a week since her fight with Ty. A week where she'd tried to fill it with busy work and projects but failed at feeling an iota better.

"Sweetie, soon that Plinko board's gonna be flat and useless," Vivian said, appearing in her periphery. Gently, Vivian took the hammer from her. "Do you want to talk about it?"

"No, I'm tired of hearing myself speak." Frankie sat back on her butt and viewed the cafeteria, which was on its way to being transformed into a carnival. With a few days to graduation, a handful of volunteers milled about to knock out the to-do list she had laid out for the day. Slow but sure, they'd taken out school-owned festival games to rehab and they'd moved tables around to make room for festival storage.

Normally, a day like this would be a dopamine hit. But she couldn't ignore what was a poor show of volunteers and the marked absence of the person who'd been by her side since February.

"And yet, you haven't really said anything about your fight, except that Ty was jerk and that you should have known all along." Vivian frowned.

"Details, shmetails." She rolled her eyes. "Does it matter

what he did? The bottom line is that he lied. You should have seen that guilty look on his face."

"Okay. That's it. It's time." Vivian looked up at Olivia, who carried a basket of acrylic paints to the parent touching up cakewalks signs, and gestured her over.

"Time for what?" Frankie asked.

"You need a drink."

"No, I don't. We have too much to do."

"The work will be here when we return. And the incoming PTA president is here—he can handle it." Vivian jutted her chin toward current third-grade parent Manuel Arguello, who won last week's elections.

"I agree. And you haven't given yourself a break all week." Olivia called out to the room, "Hey, all, is it cool if the three of us take off?"

"Yes!" The answer was unanimous.

"See?" Olivia said.

"But who's going to supervise," Frankie asked.

"They're adults." Vivian slipped her arm around Frankie. "And they need a break from your micromanaging."

Without a choice, Frankie ambled out of the school and turned toward the parking lot, only for the other two to head toward the town square.

"Wait, aren't we going to Mountain Rush?" Frankie asked.

"What? No. We're not day drinking. You need a sugary drink. Let's get milkshakes," Olivia said.

Frankie groaned. "Milkshakes?"

Vivian waved her over. "Ugh, we've had enough of sad Frankie. We want Frankie and her spicy energy."

It took coaxing, but the three reached Swirl Haven, where Vivian ordered and Frankie was led to one of the nearby picnic benches.

It was the bench where she and Ty had held hands, where they'd had their first kiss. And though she tried to summon her logical nature that reminded her that this bench was simply a piece of furniture, upon sitting, she was hit with grief.

How had it gone wrong so fast?

The milkshake appeared under her nose seconds later and Frankie sipped it. As soon as the sugar hit her tongue, Frankie exhaled.

"See? You were hangry," Vivian said.

"And heartsick," Olivia said. "We all noticed, though no one wanted to say anything about it."

"Everyone heard, huh?"

She frowned. "Pretty much. Are you okay?"

"No," Frankie said definitively. "Our argument. It was bad."

Snippets of it flashed through her head, and she tried to swat them away. What she hadn't been able to erase was knowing that it wasn't just him who'd said horrible things. She hadn't held back either.

Though, I should have known, with the way you avoid hard things.

She inwardly winced at her accusation.

"We can help if you let us in," Vivian said.

"I don't even want to say," Frankie said.

"Does it have anything to do with his ex?" Olivia asked. "Someone mentioned that she showed up at his work unannounced. That she's staying with him."

Frankie nodded.

"But I hear they're superplatonic. Truly co-parents."

As they should be.

As she was with Reece.

Frankie said, "We didn't fight because she arrived. We fought because he didn't tell me right away. She'd been in town overnight and didn't call or text about it. You know how often we text, and not a word."

"That's unacceptable," Vivian agreed.

Olivia nodded.

"Things were building up between us, and I'd been…upset about other things, and he was trying to sweep things under the rug. And, we had words. Words that might be true, but hurt just the same. It showed how different we are, though." She half laughed. "I should have known. We fought like we did on our first date. I didn't like the way he chose to minimize issues, and he thought I blew things way out of proportion."

Vivian raised an eyebrow. "You make it seem like you were expecting it."

"Maybe I should have done a better job expecting." She retorted. "I wouldn't be in this drama right now."

But that means you wouldn't have been together.

Frankie shoved that thought away. This was a clear-cut situation. Ty had lied to spare her feelings, and it was a lie nonetheless.

"I've seen him around town. He's as bad off as you are," Olivia said. "I brought Katja for her cat-wellness checkup the other day, and you could tell he was dying to ask how you are."

"Did he?"

"No, because he's a professional. Much like how he volunteered to shelve the books on the bookcases, even if he didn't have to, even at the risk of running into you."

Frankie groaned. "They look good, don't they?"

They both nodded.

"He's so talented," Frankie admitted, smiling. "He makes a great vet, but he is so creative…once he finally decides to move forward, you'll get to see the gallery photos. They're gorgeous."

"He went above and beyond with the bookshelves," Olivia said. "But I don't know…he was inspired building it, and I do believe it was largely due to you. This is all just sad."

"Are you planning on talking to him anytime soon? We have the bookshelf reveal in a couple of days," Vivian said.

Frankie sighed. "There's no way around it. The PTA. Our kids..."

While she'd been able to avoid him this last week, it would only be a matter of time before they ran into one another. How was she going to be able to see him and not remember all of the times they'd shared with and without their kids? She rested her elbows on her thighs and then cradled her head. "I hate that Liam and Aria are rolled up into this. As it is, Liam hasn't mentioned Aria once, and I know it's because he doesn't want to hurt my feelings."

The tears that she'd kept at bay since her fight with Ty rushed through now, and along with it, regret that she'd let him in so quickly. That she'd broken all her rules with him. She'd decided to date someone in town. She'd decided on a second date, period. "Ugh. This hurts. I haven't hurt like this since..." She couldn't finish the sentence, knowing right then what she felt for him.

Love.

Though she'd never verbalized it, she'd felt it. It was the undercurrent to all of their interactions and their conversations.

Arms encircled her, along with the murmurs of support from her friends.

"Can the two of you talk this out?" Vivian asked. Frankie looked at her, flummoxed. "I know, I know. You don't need my advice. Only the two of you know how your relationship is going to fare, but this seems like a thoughtless mistake. One of you needs to open the door for the other to come through."

Frankie shook her head. "It might have started as a mistake, but we said things. Things that we can't take back. We're just not for each other. We're just too different."

"Oh, sweetie," she started, but thank goodness, nothing

more. Because Frankie couldn't take any more advice or cheerleading.

What she needed was to get back on her feet, not only for herself, but also for Liam, who deserved to have the best graduation.

Speaking of.

Frankie looked back at the school, to where she knew her tired but loyal volunteers stood by.

For the sake of the school, for her son, she would consider opening the door of her pride.

"Do you have Bianca's phone number by chance?" Frankie asked her friends. "It's time to ask for some help."

That Monday, in front of his full-length mirror, Ty held up two ties against his light blue shirt, though neither looked good to him.

As if it mattered. If he had a choice, he would've opted for black on black, to reflect his mood. Alas, it wasn't the best color combination for today's PTA event that would introduce the new PTA officers for the upcoming year, and present the bookshelves to the school.

It hadn't been Ty's choice to have a presentation, but because today was a teacher workday—it was a warm winter and the district didn't use any of their allocated snow days—he was going to be forced into the limelight.

He blew out a breath of apprehension. Olivia had mentioned that their school community had been invited to the event.

Which meant that Frankie would be there.

"I think the gray paisley's the better of the two."

Ty turned to the bedroom door, to see Harper, arms crossed, leaning on its frame. She was wearing a sundress, hair up in a ponytail. Without waiting for his answer, she approached him and gestured for him to hand her the tie.

She made quick work of flipping up his collar and threading the tie through. Like old times.

Her eyebrows wiggled as she focused. “I’m sorry about the other week. I didn’t mean to get in between the two of you.”

They hadn’t spoken about Frankie. Harper had known him well enough not to bring her up until he was ready. And it hadn’t been difficult to avoid the subject because she was settled in the guest house.

“It’s not your fault. It’s mine,” he said.

“Why didn’t you tell me about her? And why didn’t you tell her that I was here?” The tie flipped back as she worked it into a knot.

“Honestly, I don’t know.”

Her brown eyes met his; her hands stilled. “That’s a cop-out answer if I ever heard one.”

The dig was a sock to the gut, but Ty schooled his features. “Are you almost done?”

After a quick tug, she smoothed the ends down. “There you go. Prim and wrinkle-free, just the way you like it.”

He frowned, exhaling. “Guess you’re *not* done.”

“No. I’m not.” She crossed her arms. “I feel a kind of solidarity with this Francesca Espiritu.”

“Solidarity?”

“Yep. Solidarity in frustration with the way you sometimes handle things. You—” her fingers did a version of jazz hands “—like to brush things off. You just want to make things okay.”

“You’re not wrong there. Why wouldn’t I want to make things better?”

“Exactly. It’s even your job! You cure animals. Talk about a hero—this is what you are. You don’t like mess. When things feel like they’re pushing your envelope, you take a step back.”

“That’s not fair. There’s nothing wrong with remaining calm, with reevaluating.”

Her eyes softened. "You're right. It's *not* fair. You have changed, because when we met and married, you had a stick up your butt."

He snickered, taken aback.

"Not even joking. And no, there's nothing wrong with remaining calm and reevaluating and being a hero and cleaning up messes but guess what? You're not dealing with things when you do so. You're not having to face things." She swallowed. "You and I, we've grown over the years, I'd like to think. I hope I'm less judgmental and critical. And you…you really have stepped up and made something here in Peak. You are stronger than you've ever been. Whatever we lost when we were married, we both gained back. But I think that deep down inside, you know why you didn't text her right away to let her know that I was here. There was a reason why you didn't tell me about her, and that I should have expected to meet her. You made a choice, Ty. You did this to yourself."

Ty shook his head. "I think you've been spending too much time reading self-help books."

"That's not the insult you think it is."

Ty grabbed his sport coat draped on his bed, a signal that they should be on their way soon. As he passed her, she said, "You're pushing her away, you know. Just like the business you were going to start as soon as you got here. For what reason, I don't know, but you can work on that while building something good and true to you. Because look at what you've built thus far. A relationship with me. A relationship with your daughter. This beautiful home. So keep going, Ty."

His ex's words landed brick by brick into his subconscious as he walked out of his bedroom, and his body felt heavy with the truth. Was she right? Had he deliberately pushed Frankie away?

Aria was seated on the couch, texting when Ty entered the living room.

"Ready to go?" he said.

She stuffed her phone into her back pocket. "Yep." Her voice was flat.

Inside, he wilted. He hated how their relationship had regressed. He'd had a bare bones conversation with Aria about Frankie, simply telling her that they'd broken up, but she'd been cold then. Her disappointment had been written all over her face after she'd witnessed his and Frankie's fight through the front windows.

And with Harper's accusation fresh in his mind, that he didn't like to face his problems, he sat on the ottoman across from her.

Aria's posture was indignant.

"Talk to me," he said.

"About what?"

A twinge of hesitation reared up. What if her affect had nothing to do with him? He cleared his throat. "About anything you want."

"Are you getting back together?"

He inhaled, taken aback by her bravado. "I don't know. We both got really angry."

"But you can say sorry."

"It's not as easy as that."

"It is. Grown-ups tell us kids that all the time. You know what you did wrong, so you should apologize."

If felt as if the tables were turned; she was the parent, and he was the stubborn kid who didn't want to own up to his side of an argument. He pressed his lips together and nodded.

He and Frankie's conversation returned to him now, at the words they arrowed to one another. His chest ached with how they'd raised their voices.

His stomach hurt because Frankie'd been right about many things.

"I don't get it. You love her. She loves you," Aria said.

He shut his eyes against this greatest regret.

Truth be told, he knew he loved her when she took care of him overnight. He felt it during the quiet moments hanging out with the kids. He mourned it now, because he'd failed to tell her. Would it have made a difference in how their relationship had evolved?

"I see the way you look at her. And the way she looks at you," Aria continued, and her eyes darted down to her lap. "You look at her like you used to look at Mom."

He turned to Harper, who stood off to the side. She was sporting a sad smile.

He cleared his throat, because he didn't see this coming, this frontal assault of the truth.

Maybe he had been scared. Maybe he still was.

But he wasn't sure where to go from here. Clarity was not his friend at the moment. "I don't know if an apology can fix it, Aria. Sometimes…sometimes it is what it is. Sometimes, people say or do things that even with an apology things don't go back to the way they were."

"So you're not gonna try?"

His neck warmed with discomfort. As a dad, he'd been humbled time and again by his daughter; she pushed him to the limit. But he'd taken it in stride because he couldn't afford not to be the best father he could be.

But with everyone and everything else? He'd been willing to retreat, to change his mind.

You're running away from something you told me was important to you.

He sucked in a breath as her words belatedly struck him.

Frankie was important to him, just as his woodworking business was. And he was choosing to retreat.

"I do want things to get better, but what if I can't fix it?" Admitting this to his daughter rendered him unsteady. It brought him back to when he was a kid when he pushed down his disappointment when he didn't have enough lunch money. When he smiled through friends' birthday parties despite wishing his parents threw one for him. To ignoring his inner voice while at veterinary school, that maybe, he'd chosen the wrong career. "Or what if I make it worse?"

Aria shrugged. "I'll still love you, Dad." Then, she threw her arms around him.

I'll still love you.

Four simple words.

But it meant everything.

It meant unconditional, even if he made a mistake, even if he continued to make mistakes.

"I love you, too." He sniffed away the start of tears, because time was of the essence. And because, armed with those four words, he could do what his daughter challenged him to do. To try. "We'd better go. We've got people to see."

They arrived at the library, and to Ty's surprise, the area was full. A hum of noise was present, though it quieted down as he made his way to where the principal was standing, in front of the protective sheets that shielded the new bookshelves.

Principal Murray was dressed in a polo with the school's name on his breast pocket. He shook Ty's hand. "Welcome. Get a load of this crowd. We've even got folks from the local TV station." He gestured to a group with cameras to the side, and then to another group huddling to the rear.

"Wow. I didn't expect this."

"When word gets around about a good deed, we celebrate it." He clapped him on the back, the impact almost launching Ty across the room. "By that, I mean Frankie reached out to put some eyes on this event."

"She did?"

"She wanted everyone to see how the library was transformed, seeing that the last time we spruced things up was a decade ago. She's really proud of what you've done."

He bit the inside of his cheek at the rush of emotions. That despite their fight and their lack of communication, she'd still supported him.

Ty scanned the room for her, spotting her among the group of their PTA parents. While she avoided his eyes, the others waved and gave him a thumbs-up. Also among them, he noticed, were Bianca and Reece.

"Ty!" someone said. On the other side of the room were a few of his work colleagues at the clinic, including Dr. Peters, who nodded at him.

He raised a shaky hand to greet them, before being called to an open chair next to Aria.

"Alright everyone, we can get this started," Principal Murray said. He lifted his arms. "We're so pleased all of you can be here today, giving up your lunch hour, but we have a couple of things to announce. First, we'd like to introduce next year's PTA board." He announced the names of each officer, and they rose to the front of the room, where they received a round of applause.

"As you all know, continued improvements to the school take time and money, and not everything can be accomplished immediately. That's where our PTA comes in. So, thank you, officers, for volunteering in a leadership capacity for this upcoming year." He nodded, excusing the board, who sat back down.

He rolled his shoulders back. "Now, PTAs can get a bad rap, but our PTA here at Peak Elementary is something special. They've donated their time to fundraising, to throwing appreciation parties, to managing our yearbook. They volunteer so that our teachers can focus on what they do best, and that is to teach. And our library has gone through the wringer, after decades of use, of kids calling this a sanctuary, slowly, our bookshelves have taken a beating. Over the President's Day holiday weekend, our nonfiction shelves fell. Shelves that spanned the largest wall in the library. This is where the PTA and Ty Golden came in. He's new to our town, not even six months here, and he's already made something for us, something our kids can talk about and use for many years to come. Ty, will you do the honors?"

Ty's face burned with embarrassment, but at Principal Murray's cue, he pulled down the sheets, displaying the new bookshelves.

The library erupted in applause.

Ty didn't know what to do with the joy he was feeling, the pride he had. That he'd used his hands to build something that made a difference. That he'd been capable of it. That they appreciated it.

But he knew that it wasn't all just him.

"You have the floor, Ty," Principal Murray said.

"Oh," he said, in surprise, heat rising to his cheeks. He hadn't prepared a speech.

Ty glanced at his daughter in the second row and remembered her encouragement. *I'll still love you, Dad.*

"Thank you for coming," he started. "This project was challenging but rewarding. And it wouldn't have been possible without the other volunteers who helped with this project." Ty named the parents who assisted him over the couple of months. He continued, "But the engine of our PTA is Frankie Espiritu, who, in the short time I have known her, has inspired me and so many others to give our best to this school community." He turned to where Frankie was standing.

Her expression was stoic, but he didn't avert his gaze.

"She raises the bar, for someone's effort, and honesty. And at times it was hard to live up to. Some might call her brand of encouragement 'tough love.' But it's love nonetheless. And

I hope—" He swallowed against his fear. "That this isn't the end of our work together. Of us."

He cut his eyes to the silence that met him, to Aria's grin. "I hope you enjoy the bookshelves."

Aria clapped, and the rest of the room followed. Ty glance up to Frankie, and she was clapping, too.

Chapter Twenty-One

By the time Ty pulled himself away from the local TV reporter, where he gave a short interview, Frankie was gone.

Dr. Peters, however, had stayed until the very end. At the school's front foyer, Kyle extended a hand. "Ty. Well done, son."

His grip was strong. "Thank you," Ty said.

"You mentioned that you knew how to build things, but I didn't quite understand. We're lucky to have such a talented person in our practice."

"That's actually what I wanted to talk to you about, sir." Ty swallowed the bubbles of anxiety that tumbled around his belly. Because halfheartedly trying had only gotten him so far. He had to follow through. He had to prove to himself that he could do this for himself, that he deserved it. That he could trust himself and his instincts.

"What's on your mind, Ty? You usually aren't tongue-tied."

Ty cleared his throat; it was like the fear had gotten a vise grip on it. "You see, about the woodworking. I really like doing it."

Gah, he knew he sounded like a little kid.

"I'm glad." Dr. Peters smiled.

But you're not done.

"But." He moved the moment forward, gathering all of

the strength he could muster in his vocal cords. “I'd like to do it more.”

“I can see why.” Dr. Peters meandered toward the school's front doors and opened it. He retrieved his car key fob from his pocket as he stepped out into the parking lot.

Ty was at his heels; he was running out of time.

“And I'd like, if I may.” His voice was rising again. No, he wouldn't act like this wasn't important to him. “I'd like to revisit our conversation, about my contract extension.”

Dr. Peters frowned. “You want to leave the practice?”

“No, but I'd like to negotiate that after my initial year, that my position switch to part time, with benefits.” He forced himself to hold still, to not give any quarter.

They'd made it to Dr. Peters's car. He stuffed his hands in his pockets. He examined Ty, the wrinkles in his forehead folding in on themselves. He heaved a breath. “Not exactly what I was hoping for when we took you on.”

“No, and I'm sorry about that. I don't want to leave the practice, but I'd like the time to work with my hands. It's what I hoped I'd be able to do moving to Peak, though I had my initial doubts. I'm sure of it now.”

Seconds passed. Voices of people leaving the school filtered through the air, but Ty didn't allow himself to be distracted. Dr. Peters could very well let Ty go today. He could lose his job, and now with a mortgage, with Aria…

I'll still love you, Dad.

I believe in you, Ty.

“Okay,” Dr. Peters said.

Ty inhaled, sharply, that one word a shock. “Okay?”

“Yes, I'll consider it. Mind you, I'll need for you to finish out your initial year at full time. That will give me the opportunity to explore options with other physicians to hire. I imagine you'll need that transition time, too. Let's get a meeting in the books in the next couple of weeks. If this is what you really want."

He couldn't believe what he was hearing. "It is what I want."

"Alright. We'll figure it out. We certainly don't want to lose you." He offered his hand again. "See you in the clinic."

"Yes. Thank you." Speechless, though grateful, Ty stepped aside as Dr. Peters entered his vehicle, backed out from his spot, and drove away.

"Everything okay?" Coming his way was Harper. "You're, like, frozen."

He nodded. "Yep. I think it's going to be." Looking off to the side, Aria and Liam stood close together. She leaned in to speak to him.

Relief coursed through him, that they were still friends. They were good together; they balanced each other out.

Harper turned. "They look like they're conspiring, don't they?" She half laughed. "Aria confessed that they parent-trapped you and Frankie, which is wild. Seriously though, maybe you should have them do it again. It's obvious that you both still have it bad for one another."

He grinned at his ex-wife.

Now that he had put everything on the line, there was nothing else to lose.

Under the guise of pre-celebrating the fifth-grade graduation tomorrow, Frankie hopped up on a bar stool at Mountain Rush, with Vivian on her left and Olivia to her right.

Chip set a glass of wine in front of her, and she took a long sip.

"Those were really pretty shelves, weren't they?" It was all she could say about the presentation the other day.

She'd left as soon as Ty had finished up his speech. It had been a heartfelt thing for him to thank her, but at the mention of tough love, that he hoped wouldn't be the end of them, she'd been overcome.

Since then, she'd buried herself in work. In *any* kind of work that came up.

"Gorgeous craftsmanship." Vivian took a sip of her drink. "And the things he said. All so sweet."

"So sweet," said Olivia. "He looked at you the entire time he spoke."

"You could tell he meant everything he said," Vivian said. "He looked for you at the end, too."

"I couldn't do it. I couldn't stay." She took another sip of her drink.

"Why not?"

"Because."

She couldn't put words to her hesitance. These last few days without him illuminated how much he had filled the empty spaces in her life.

Her phone buzzed on the bar countertop, interrupting her train of thought. A text from Reece: Where are you? Liam needs his phone.

Shoot. Frankie opened up her purse. She'd dropped Liam off at Reece's before coming to Mountain Rush. Sure enough, Liam's phone was in it.

Frankie replied: I'm at Mountain Rush.

Reece responded: Around the corner. Be there in two min.

She grabbed Liam's phone, and told her friends that she would return, then walked out into the bright sun. Reece's SUV was in the parking lot, and as she approached it, Reece came out and met her halfway.

She looked over his shoulder. "Where's Liam?"

"Mom came over to drop off some food and offered to hang out for a bit."

She nodded, handing him his phone. "Here you go."

"You okay?"

"Yep." Her voice wavered. "Girls and I are just having a drink before the excitement tomorrow."

"Ah, okay. Well." He stepped backward, raising the phone. "Thanks." He started to walk away, but spun around. "By the way, I just wanted to say I'm happy for you and the animal doctor."

She snorted, never mind the fact that he was wrong about their status, but for how he couldn't call Ty by his first name. "Thanks."

"And thanks for including Bianca with the PTA stuff. It was important to her."

Frankie shook her head. "I was rude to her at first, and I was wrong to be that way. Hopefully she'll forgive me."

"She doesn't see it that way at all." He stuffed a hand in his pocket. "Look, I know that you and I, for as much as we try to get along for Liam, have this tension." He half laughed. "And I get that I sometimes stoke it. That I say things that are maybe out of pocket. But at the end of the day, the best of who Liam is comes from you. His best qualities are because you are his mother."

A ball of emotion rose up in Frankie's throat, though she tried to laugh through it. "You always did say that I was too much."

"Yeah, I said that, didn't I?" He shook his head. "I say stupid things. A lot of it I regret. But it doesn't take away from the fact that I want you to be happy. You deserve it. Anyway, I'd better get back. See you tomorrow."

She nodded and headed back inside. She entered Mountain Rush, and when she knew she was back in the safety of her friends, she broke down in tears.

After she dried them, she knew what she needed to do.

Chapter Twenty-Two

The alarm came too quickly, and Frankie blinked against the bright light. She was parched, and her head was pounding, and it took her half a second too long to realize that it wasn't the alarm that had woken her up, but her phone ringing.

She jumped out of bed, startling Snowball, whom she'd brought into her room last night. It was nine in the morning.

Liam.

He'd stayed the night at Reece's, though graduates didn't have to attend school before the ceremony. Frankie scrambled for her phone, pressing the answer button. "Sweetheart?"

"Mom. You have to come to the school right away."

"What? Why? Graduation isn't until one." She pressed her fingers against her temple.

She'd had too much wine with her friends, as they'd created an intricate plan to get Ty alone so Frankie could make a grand gesture, but at the moment, she couldn't recall what it was.

"Something happened with the games," Liam said.

"What do you mean?"

"Someone stole the games for the party."

"What? Oh, my gosh!" Her mind jolted awake. She leapt out of bed. But something didn't make sense. "Wait, how do you know?"

"Um...someone posted it on Snap." His voice was regretful.

"Liam. How do you have Snapchat? I never gave you permission." She turned on her shower. She was sure she looked a mess. "You must be legally thirteen to download the app. And even then, no, sir, you're not allowed on it until you can drive. We're going to talk about this later. I need to get ready and head to the school."

"Yes, Mom. Can I come, too?"

"You know what? That's a better idea so we can talk about the safety of these apps. I'll text you when I'm on my way."

There was no time to lose, so Frankie entered the lukewarm water. Snippets of yesterday flashed through her mind as she washed away the grime of Mountain Rush karaoke and the shock of her ex-husband's apology. An apology that she hadn't realized she'd needed to hear, because her doubts had been fueled by the past stories she told herself.

His apology didn't solve everything between her and Reece, though. And it didn't solve all her insecurities, but it validated her experience. Instead of stoking doubt, it stoked her self-confidence and her self-worth.

And just in time for another crisis. She had to stay focused.

She was out of the house in twenty minutes, still looping her wet hair up into a bun as she ducked into her car. She texted Liam that she was on her way and pointed the car south, to Reece's place. Liam was standing in the open door with Reece. He bounded to her.

Reece waved at her from the house. "See you at graduation!"

It was the kind of jazz-hand wave that was just weird enough to make Frankie frown.

"Mom, let's go!" Liam said, waking her from her thoughts.

He didn't have to tell her twice. She drove straight to the school, where there were few cars present.

But when she entered the school, things were…calm. Quiet, since grades kindergarten to fourth grade were in session. Ms.

Ahmad was on the phone. One of the custodians, Mr. Frasier, smiled at her while pushing a cart of supplies.

After signing in, she went straight to the cafeteria, to find the games exactly where the PTA had set them the day before.

She halted in her tracks. "What the—"

From the back of the room, Ty came out from the wings. "Hi. Did you get a call, too? Liam told me about the games, but they look like they're all fine." She turned around to see that Liam hadn't followed her in. From behind Ty, Aria appeared, and she shuffled past Frankie and out the other cafeteria door.

"Wait. What's happening?"

He stepped closer and waited, his eyes tracking Aria as she left the room. Then his eyes met hers. "They were planning a way for us to get together, and I pretended not to know. Because I wanted to see you. I hoped like hell that you would be here."

Frankie's heart was pounding; they were alone. She tried to ignore how good he looked, and how much she had missed him. And yet, every cell in her body gravitated toward him.

She allowed the walls that had been haphazardly rebuilt the last few days to fall, brick by brick. "I definitely fell for it. Those kids."

"They're really determined."

"I guess I don't blame them. What the heart wants..." Her voice cracked.

Something stirred in his eyes, and it allowed hope to flare in her heart. Did he feel the same for her? Had she been too rash?

"I know what my heart wants." He was only two paces in front of her, and Frankie's belly was doing somersaults.

"I do, too. But it's hard for me to say I'm sorry," she said after searching for the next thing to say.

"Then let me do it," he said, his voice pleading. He took her hands into his, and the touch of his skin brought her much-needed relief. "Because this was all my fault. You asked only one thing from me, and that was to be honest. And I let you down. I didn't text you when Harper arrived because I was scared. When things get stressful, when I'm pushed to my limit, I run away. I realize now that I've been doing it my whole life, where I kind of retreat into myself. I did it with my business. Despite me wanting to establish it, the idea of branching out, of changing, of failing, scared me. Instead of being upfront with you about Harper, or with Dr. Peters about my business, I minimized what was the right thing to do. And I did it with you. I was scared that I finally found someone that I love and I was afraid I wouldn't be enough for them. I was afraid to take the risk and I made excuses just so I *wouldn't* take it."

Frankie was dizzy with all the words, and most especially… "Love?"

His blue eyes never lost contact with hers. "Love. Because I love you. I love you for exactly who you are. I love you for seeing me for exactly who I am."

She smiled, emotion threatening to overwhelm her. "I love you, too, Ty."

"You do?"

"I do, and that's why I was scared, too. When I saw Harper—"

"There's nothing going on—"

She held up a hand. She wanted to express herself solidly. "I never thought that there was anything going on. But I was looking for anything wrong about you from the very start. I was looking for all of your flaws. I was looking for a reason for you not to like me. It's been my go-to coping, to find fault, and I don't want to be that way anymore. I don't want to push you away. I said some awful things that I wish I could take back. I'm so sorry."

"I'm so sorry, too. But I want to be here. Please give me another chance." Ty brought her hands to his lips, and the kiss toppled over every single brick in her heart. Because it was never about grand gestures for Frankie. It was him showing up for his family, for his work, for her. It was them, working toward the same goal.

"Ty, I don't want to fight anymore. Not like this."

"We'll work on it. I will be here."

"I will be here, too," she said back in a whisper, crossing the foot of space between them. She got on her tiptoes and kissed him.

"I love you, Frankie," Ty said.

"I love you, too."

She leaned in for another kiss, only to be bowled over from the side. Aria and Liam hugged them around the waists, and through the start of happy tears, Frankie joined Ty in laughter.

Later, as they all made their way to their cars, with Ty holding Frankie's hand, he said, "I know a great way to celebrate, after the graduation party, of course."

"I'm game, what is it?"

"We should do a repeat first date. Same restaurant, but we arrive and leave together."

"Our second first date?" Frankie grinned.

With a gleam in his eyes, he said, "Our second and last first date."

Epilogue

One year later

Frankie stuck forks into slices of ube cake set upon dessert plates. “These are ready,” she called out to her helpers.

“Got it.” Aria took a plate in each hand, and Liam followed suit. They shuttled the slices toward those guests who were empty-handed.

From the two-tier cake baked by her brother Jared for Ty’s grand opening event, only a quarter of the smallest tier was left. Ty and Aria’s backyard was packed with more attendees than she had anticipated, and everyone came hungry for a sweet treat.

They were also enthusiastic. A steady rotation of people meandered into Ty’s guesthouse, now his studio showroom, to view and reserve his most recent projects. Some posed for a photo in front of a wooden signage that read The Rustic Grain. Folks bore wide smiles; they chatted and cheered. Ty’s friends from Philly were talking it up at the basketball half-court with the PTA crew, a sight that made Frankie’s heart skip a beat. That their friendship circles had intertwined.

Frankie too, was smiling. She’d been smiling for a better part of the year, since she and Ty decided to give their relationship another go.

“This is the best cake I have ever eaten, hands down.” From

behind, Harper, Ty's ex-wife swept over to Frankie's side, her slice almost gone. "Do you think that Jared will give me the recipe? It would be a great thing to introduce into Baker's TV," she said of her new hosting gig.

"He doesn't gatekeep. You should ask him."

She scraped the last of the cake off her plate. "Better yet, what if I ask him to come on as a guest?" Her eyes widened at the idea, and she slipped her phone out of her dress pocket. She spoke into it. "Pitch Chef Sotheby for an appearance."

"Well, he actually has some local TV experience in his background. He'd be great at it. He's around here somewhere if you can find him."

"Will do. Thank you. You Espiritus are a talented bunch. All you need is a doctor and a lawyer in your family lineup and you're all set. And maybe a vet." She winked.

Frankie laughed. When Ty had said that Harper was passionate, he was not exaggerating.

And Frankie respected Harper's passion, her energy, her optimism, and her baking skills. Watching her show had become an Espiritu family activity.

"Though, Frankie, it's not just the cake that's good. This party is perfect, and I know you planned all of it. How did you get him to agree?" Harper asked.

Him, meaning Ty.

Frankie's eyes landed on her boyfriend—it still made her giddy calling him that—who was standing with Reece. By the way her ex-husband was talking with his hands, the subject was either cars or furniture. It turned out that power tools had the ability to bring exes together.

And like Reece, Ty didn't like the spotlight.

"I just told him that it would be a good idea," Frankie said.

"That's it?" Harper set a hand on her hip.

"Yep," Frankie fibbed. Harper didn't need to know that

she'd also plied the request with lovemaking and a promise to adopt a dog together, for when she and Liam moved in.

Though that was all still a secret.

"Huh, I guess I shouldn't be surprised. It would behoove of him to listen because you've got a great mind for business. But above all that, you know what you're talking about."

She turned to Harper then and was met with a sincere expression. "Thanks. I really appreciate that."

"Look, I know that in the last year I haven't been around as often as I should be." She set her plate on the table.

"Aw, Harper, I don't judge."

"I know you don't. But I have to get this off my chest. This day is about Ty, sure, but I want to make sure you know how I appreciate you." She smiled. "You're a good person, Frankie. To Ty, and to my Aria. I trust my girl with you, and I know how lucky that is, for the three of us."

"Aria is amazing." Frankie's voice cracked, her emotions threatening to break through. "She's so independent and thoughtful. Headstrong."

They both laughed.

"She's so loving, too. Just like her mama," Frankie added. She grasped Harper's hand and squeezed. Warmed with the start of tears, she added, "Thank you for saying that. I love being a part of your family."

"That's good. Because I love being a part of yours." Harper pressed a knuckle against the side of her eyes.

"Mom!" called Aria from the swings. "I wanna show you something!"

"That's my cue." Harper let go and padded backward. "Go get your man, he's waiting."

Frankie turned toward Ty. He was alone and was headed in her direction. She met him halfway, into his open arms. He enveloped her into a tight hug, in a hold she knew she could count on night after night.

"Love you," he whispered into her ear.

"Love you so much."

He searched her eyes. "You all right?"

"Yeah," she said, feeling content for the first time in a long, long time. "Everything is perfect."

* * * * *

Look for Vivian and Ryan's story,
the next installment in The Single Hearts Club
USA TODAY *bestselling author*
Tif Marcelo's new miniseries for
Harlequin Special Edition

Coming soon!